CROAK

GINA DAMICO

Houghton Mifflin Harcourt

Boston New York

Graphia and the Graphia logo are trademarks of
Houghton Mifflin Harcourt Publishing Company.

www.hmhco.com

Text set in Garamond Premier Pro

Library of Congress Cataloging-in-Publication Data
Damico, Gina.
Croak / by Gina Damico.
p. cm.
Summary: A delinquent sixteen-year-old girl is sent to live with her uncle for the summer,
only to learn that he is a Grim Reaper who wants to teach her the family business.
ISBN: 978-0-547-60832-7
[1. Death — Fiction. 2. Future life — Fiction.] I. Title.
PZ7.D1838CR 2012
[Fic] — dc23
2011017125

Manufactured in the United States of America
DOC 10 9 8

4500491441

For Mom, Dad, and Lisa.
In exchange for years upon years of supporting my
nincompoopery, I offer you this simple, heartfelt dedication.

Call it even?

ACKNOWLEDGMENTS

Let's kick off this shindig with a *Titanic*-size thank-you to my rocktastic agent, Tina Wexler. Simply put, none of this would exist without you and your steadfast kickassery. You've breathed life into my work, loved my characters as if they were family, and read more emails, drafts, and misguided tangents than I can shake a scythe at. Thank you so, so much for seeing a spark and sticking it out with me.

To my editor Julie Tibbott, who finds the humor in board games, gentlemanly named roosters, and death-related puns and is therefore a rare, treasured find. Thank you for your encouragement, collaboration, and adoption of my merry band of misfits. Thanks also to Michael Neff and the New York Pitch Conference for giving me the kick in the pants I so dearly needed.

To my parents, for their unflagging love in all its forms (encouragement, money, eye-rolling). Mom, thank you for reading to me from day one—it made all the difference. Dad, thank you for keeping bookstores in business.

To my sister, Lisa, whose refusal to be killed by the Lego I fed her when she was a baby made me rather angry at the time but now pleases me greatly, as I can't imagine life without her.

To my big, awesome Italian family for always sending good thoughts and good eggplant parm my way. And to the in-law clan, for coming with a pre-established YA fan club.

To every single member of the Committee for Creative Enactments at Boston College between 2001 and 2005: You are the reason I started writing. Hands down. I adore you more than any drunken Baggo words can say, and I thank you dearly. Profigliano!

To Brittany "Hotpants" Wilcox, for the countless Red Lobster dinners, and Allison "Nickname Unprintable" D'Orazio, for agreeing with me in thinking — nay, knowing — that sad trombones are the funniest things on earth.

To the Onondaga County Public Library for publishing my very first work when I was five years old, a story about dead rabbits that, in retrospect, makes a hell of a lot more sense now. Also, huge thanks to all libraries and librarians everywhere. Keep at it.

Other invaluable contributors include Azadeh Ariatabar Brown and her bitchin' website skills, TVGasm, and everyone at all the jobs I've ever had, even that crappy temp one. Thanks also to milk, Australia, whoever invented the DVR, *The Simpsons,* Kurt Vonnegut, Jack Bauer, Toby the wee computer, and, finally, Utz Cheese Balls, for being both delicious *and* packaged in massive, heart-disease-inducing buckets.

To Big Fat Lenny Cat: your unconditional enthusiasm for anything having to do with me is so appreciated, even if you are roughly the same weight and shape of a bowling ball. To Carl, the other cat: you're okay too.

To my husband, Will, whose adamant insistence that I not get a real job and instead pursue these writing shenanigans is the very reason this is an actual book and not some forgotten, scribbled notes on the back of a crossword puzzle. Thank you for not hurling me out of the house every time I've asked you to read the newest revision. Sooo much.

And finally, to you, dear reader, for picking up this book! There's no way you could have known that it was rigged with explosives, but since it would be disastrous to put it down now, enjoy!

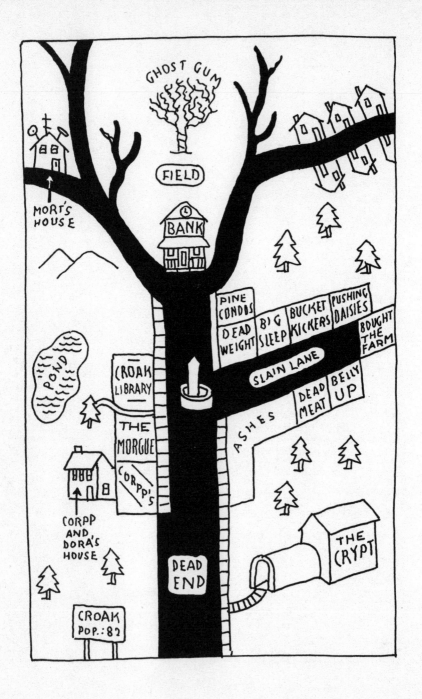

Lex wondered, for a fleeting moment, what her principal's head might look like if it were stabbed atop a giant wooden spear.

"I can't imagine why you're smiling, young lady," Mr. Truitt said from behind his desk, "but I can assure you that there is nothing funny about this situation. How many of your classmates must end up in the emergency room before you get it through that head of yours that fighting on school property is strictly forbidden?"

Lex yawned and pulled the hood of her black sweatshirt even farther over her face.

"Stop that." Her mother pushed it back to reveal a messy head of long black hair. "You're being rude."

"I'm in an awkward position here," the principal continued, running a hand through his greasy comb-over. "I don't *want* to expel Lex. I know you two are good parents; Cordy is practically a model student!" He paused and eyed Lex for a moment to let this sink in, hoping to maybe guilt the wicked girl into obedience. Her face, however, remained stony.

"But when it comes to Lex, I don't see any other choice in the matter," he went on, frowning. "I'm sorry, but the list of scars that my students have sustained at the hand of your daughter grows longer each week. Poor Logan Hochspring's arm will forever carry an imprint of her dental records!"

"You *bit* him?" Lex's father said.

"He called me a wannabe vampire," she said. "What was I supposed to do?"

"Oh, I don't know — maybe *not* bite him?"

Lex zoned out as her parents once again launched into the traditional practice of begging Mr. Truitt for just one more chance. She had heard it so many times by now that she could even mouth the words in certain places, with a little "She's just troubled, you see" sprinkled with a dollop of "It's probably just a phase" and closing, of course, with the ever-popular "It'll be different this time, you have our word." Lex stuck a slender finger into her mouth and fished around until she found a small blond hair. She pulled it out of her teeth with a quick snap, the memory of Logan Hochspring's startled cries of pain ringing through her ears.

"Very well," Mr. Truitt finally said, standing up. "One more chance. With only a week left in the school year, I can hardly justify an expulsion." He shook her parents' hands with a meaty paw, then regarded Lex with a smile. "Perhaps a summer away will do you some good."

Lex hissed.

As she was yanked out to the parking lot, however, the principal's cryptic farewell began to trouble her. And something about the way he had smiled — the way doctors beam at children right before jabbing them with tetanus shots — felt very ominous.

"What did he mean, a summer away?" she asked.

"I *knew* you weren't listening," said her mother. "We'll talk about it over dinner."

"Can't wait," Lex said as her father shoved her into the back seat, taking note of the adorable way he attempted to engage the child safety lock without her noticing.

||||||

Lexington Bartleby, age sixteen, had spent the last two years transforming her squeaky-clean, straight-A life into that of a hooligan. A delinquent. A naughty little rapscallion, as it were.

To the untrained eye, it appeared as though Lex had simply grown bored. She had begun acting out in every way that a frustrated bundle of pubescence possibly could: she stole things, she swore like a drunken pirate, and she punched people. A lot of people. Nerds, jocks, cheerleaders, goths, gays, straights, blacks, whites, that kid in the wheelchair — no one was safe. Her peers had to admire her for that, at least — Tyrannosaurus Lex, as they called her, was an equal opportunity predator.

But something about this transformation didn't quite add up. Her outbursts were triggered by the smallest of annoyances, bubbling up from nowhere, no matter how hard she tried to resist them. And worse still, they seemed to grow stronger as time went on. By the end of Lex's junior year, every swear word was reverberating at a deafening volume, and each human punching bag lost at least one of his or her permanent bicuspids.

Parents, teachers, and classmates were stymied by the atrocious behavior of the menace in the black hoodie. These crime sprees simply did not fit with the bright, affable Lex everyone had known and loved for fourteen years prior. Even her twin sister, Concord, who knew her better than anyone, could not come up with a way to unravel this massive conspiracy. Lex was furious at *something,* and no one could figure out what.

But the truth was, Lex didn't know either. It was as if her psyche had been infected with an insidious pathogen, like the viruses in all those zombie movies that turn otherwise decent human beings into bloodthirsty, unkempt maniacs who are powerless to stop themselves from unleashing their wrath upon the woefully underprepared masses. She just felt angry, all the time, at absolutely nothing. And whenever she tried to pinpoint the reason why, no matter how hard she tried, she was never able to come up with a single, solitary explanation.

The Bartleby house was a modest abode, squeezed and cramped onto a crowded neighborhood street in Queens, New York. One got the impression that the city planners, when making room for the slender pile of wood that the Bartlebys would one day call home, simply shoved the adjacent houses to either side, dumped a truckload of floorboards and piping and electrical wires into the empty space, and let nature take its course.

The dining room was at the rear of the house, overlooking a small backyard that contained the following items: a rusty swing set, a faded plastic turtle sandbox, a charcoal grill still crusty with the forgotten remains of last summer's cookouts, and a once-beloved tree house now inhabited by a family of raccoons.

Lex looked out the sliding glass door at the remnants of her childhood and wondered if the tree house's new tenants were rabid. Maybe she could train them as her minions.

"Lex," said Mrs. Bartleby, rousing her daughter from her maniacal fantasies, "your father and I are going to talk at you. And you are going to sit here and listen. Any questions?"

"Yes," said Lex. "Are restraints really necessary this time?"

"You bet." Her mother sharply tightened the tangled mess of jump ropes around Lex's midsection, all the while struggling not to let her heartache show. Mrs. Bartleby, despite all current appearances to the contrary, loved her children more than anything in the world. Each double knot she made in the rope mirrored the increasingly gnarled lumps tugging deep within her gut.

"Isn't this child abuse?" Cordy piped up from across the table, eyeing her writhing twin. "She's not going to bite *us*."

"She might, once we start talking. Note the absence of cutlery as well. There's a darn good reason I made tacos tonight."

Lex wriggled some more, but soon found that the ropes were tighter than usual. "This is insane!" she yelled, tearing at the knots. "Seriously, what the f — "

"Lexington!" Her mother pointed across the room to a large pickle jar filled to the brim with dollar bills. "I don't think I need to remind you that you're already forty-two dollars in debt. You can't afford to swear any more, my dear child." Mrs. Bartleby loathed swearing, but was in fact beginning to secretly enjoy the small stash her daughter's foul mouth had produced. She was thinking of using the proceeds to purchase a desktop Civil War cannon replica for her fifth grade classroom, as the only thing Mrs. Bartleby loved more than her children was American history and the spectacular weaponry it had produced.

"Can we get on with this?" Mr. Bartleby said. "The game starts in twenty minutes."

"You and that infernal team, honestly — " she started, but then closed her mouth after receiving a harsh glare from her husband, who often asserted that anyone crazy enough to name her daughters after the first battles of the American Revolution waived all rights to accuse anyone else of being too obsessed with anything.

Mr. Bartleby took a deep breath and gazed across the table at his small but loving family. Storm clouds were beginning to gather in the murky sky outside, artfully adding the right amount of gloom to the situation.

"Okay, Lex," he began, "here's the deal. You're our daughter, and we love you very much." He briefly glanced at his tired wife, as if to receive verification of this fact. "But enough is enough. I don't know what's gotten into you over the past couple of years, but I don't like what I've seen, and I definitely don't like where it's heading." He scratched at his goatee, trying to think of how to say what he had to say next. His shiny bald head, shaved smooth every morning, gleamed in the dull glow of the dining room light.

He looked helplessly at his daughter with kind, sad eyes. "We think — your mother and I think — that it would be best for you to go away for a little while."

Lex's eyes widened. Cordy dropped her taco.

"Go where?" Lex said, doubling her unknotting efforts. "You're kicking me out of the house?"

Her mother shook her head. "No, honey, of course not. We'd never put you out on the street."

"Then what?"

Mr. Bartleby looked at his wife, then at his non-tethered daughter, then up, at nothing. Anything to avoid the squirmy, hurt visage of his troubled baby girl. "You're going to go stay up north with Uncle Mort for the summer," he told the ceiling.

Lex, who a second ago had been fully prepared to explode

into a vicious rage and had even started planning some sort of dramatic dive through the plate glass window, chair and all, was for once shocked into speechlessness.

Mrs. Bartleby put her hand on Lex's shoulder. "I know it's a rather odd decision, but we think that a few months of fresh air could do you some good. You can get in touch with nature, lend a hand on Uncle Mort's farm, maybe even learn something! You could milk a cow!"

Cordy let out a snort. "She'd probably punch the cow."

"We've been thinking this over for a while now, and we really believe it is the best thing for everyone at the moment," said Mr. Bartleby. "It'll only be for the summer, sweetie."

Lex couldn't believe what she was hearing. They were really doing it. They were kicking her out.

But they were her *parents!* Putting up with all of her crap was their official job — they couldn't just wriggle out of it! She tried to swallow the lump forming in her throat. How could they do this to her? How could they not see past all the recklessness and beatings and remember the real daughter they had raised? She was still in there somewhere, deep down. Wasn't she?

Almost as an answer to that very question, the inescapable anger arose once again. With one last tug at the knots, Lex stood up, slammed the untangled jump rope onto the table, and, well aware of how bratty it sounded, spat out the only thing her reeling temper could think of.

"I hate you!"

Her father sighed as she thundered upstairs. "I know."

Lex flopped onto her bed and stared at the ceiling. She wished, as almost all kids wish at one point or another, that she could turn into a pterodactyl and fly away and never come back.

Cordy cautiously made her way into the room that she and her sister had shared for the entirety of their sixteen years together. It should be noted, however, that the mere word "room" could in no way convey the sheer dimensions of it all; it seemed, in fact, to bend the very fabric of space. A normal bedroom could not possibly contain this much *stuff*.

Clothing littered every available surface. Schoolwork converged in a pile in the middle of the floor. Walls were no longer visible behind a plethora of posters, tapestries, and artwork. Cordy, who from the age of five had dreamed only of designing roller coasters for a living, kept a trunk full of engineering projects under the window; while Lex, who despite years of flawless report cards had yet to be struck by a single career aspiration, stored a graveyard of abandoned hobbies under her bed. Bowing wooden shelves held scores of books, candles, McDonald's Happy Meal toys, movies, snow globes, awards, and stale, forgotten pieces of candy. It was a veritable museum of useless crap.

But all of these treasures paled in comparison to the photographs.

Pictures of Lex and Cordy blanketed the room like oversize confetti, not an inch of blank space left exposed. An inseparable childhood, all summed up in an endless series of four-by-six-inch prints: several taken in the hospital nursery shortly after their birth, a few of their first steps, two featuring their matching pink backpacks on the first day of school, one taken on Halloween when they were eight and had dressed as salt and pepper shakers, and another taken five seconds later, as the cumbersome headpiece had toppled Lex to the floor. Birthday parties, backyard antics, school plays, soccer games — no event escaped diligent documentation.

And although the more recent photos implied the evolution of two separate, distinct species, the Bartleby girls were undeniably twins, through and through. The shared room was merely an extension of their shared lives, and Lex found her hands trembling as Cordy sat down on her bed. She couldn't remember the last time they had been separated, because it had never happened.

"Hey," Cordy said softly, "are you okay?"

Lex sat up and looked at the person with whom she had shared a womb, studying the contours of the face that was so very similar to her own. Though the girls were not identical twins, many features were still mirrored in perfect biological harmony: the small nose, the light olive complexion, and, of course, the large, almost black eyes that both sisters considered to be their best feature.

Unanimously agreed upon as their worst feature, on the other hand, was the dark, pathetic excuse for hair atop their heads: Lex's a long, thick, wavy mop, and Cordy's an irreparable mess of frizz and curls. Neither took any interest in this hopeless situation, which led to more fights with their mother than anyone would dare to count.

"What do you think about all of this?" Lex asked.

Cordy picked up a nearby rubber band and absent-mindedly tangled it through her fingers. "I don't know. It sucks."

"Yeah," said Lex. Cordy wasn't looking at her. "It's just not fair," she went on. "I mean, I know I've been a total sh— " She cut herself off, wondering if her mother could possibly be listening right outside the room, ready with the swear jar. "I've been a brat. But — "

"But *why* have you been a brat? Why are you acting like this?" Cordy narrowed her eyes. "You used to be a hall monitor."

"Yeah, those were truly magical days. Nothing like the tyrannical power to give detentions to freshmen."

"But now you give them concussions!" Cordy jumped to her feet, her face flushing red with anger. "I just don't understand why you have to be this way! Do you realize how many times I've defended you, told people that this isn't the real you, only to have it shoved right back in my face whenever you get suspended for breaking someone's nose? Can't you just stop?" she said, desperation straining her voice.

"I've tried!" Lex looked down. "You know I've tried."

Cordy slumped. "Then go," she said, her voice cracking. "I don't want you to, but if Uncle Mort is the only thing that'll keep you from decimating the school population, if that's what it takes to bring back the old you, go."

She crossed the room and sat down on her own bed. Lex watched, forlorn, unable to argue with her sister's logic — until something occurred to her. She gave Cordy a funny look. "Huh."

"What?" Cordy asked irritably.

"It's kind of weird, isn't it?"

"What's weird?"

"That they picked Uncle *Mort*."

"So? What's wrong with Uncle Mort?"

"Cordy, come on. We haven't seen him in years. Can you even remember the last time he visited?"

Cordy scrunched up her face. "Sort of. We were six, right? He brought those things, whatever they are." She pointed to a pair of spherical glass trinkets on a nearby shelf. They featured a whirl of small lights inside, and smelled faintly of alcohol.

"Exactly. Other than the random crap he sends for birthdays, we barely know the guy. Half the time it's like Dad forgets he even *has* a little brother. So why him?" She crept to the edge of the bed. "Why not Aunt Veronica, in Oregon? Or Uncle Mike? Or Mom's cousin Dom — he's a corrections officer!" She lowered her voice. "For all we know, Uncle Mort could be some dumbass hillbilly who lives off roadkill and drinks his own urine. How is spending two months in some disgusting shack in upstate rural hell going to turn me into an obedient young woman?"

Cordy furrowed her brow. "Mom and Dad must have their reasons. They wouldn't just ship you off to a mass murderer. Maybe they want you to get to know him better. Maybe he's a cool guy?"

"That doesn't make any sense."

"Well, you don't make any sense either."

Lex looked wearily at her twin, whom she had never once punched, smacked, bitten, or even noogied. "I'm sorry, Cordy," she said. "I mean, I'm sorry that you're a part of this. I can handle leaving the city, but leaving you . . ."

Cordy lay down and hugged her tattered plush octopus, Captain Wiggles. Lex looked at her sister's watering eyes and sighed. How upset could they really get over this? They'd probably just be separated next year anyway, if they went to different colleges (if Lex managed to scrounge up the teacher recommendations to even get *into* college). They couldn't stay kids forever.

Afraid that much more introspection would lead to a frustrated crying jag, Lex sniffed back her own tears and fell into her pillow. "I just can't believe I'm really going," she said finally, in what she hoped was a mature-sounding voice.

Cordy nodded. "It's going to be so weird."

Lex glanced at the bookshelf. There, nestled snugly between a softball trophy and a photo of the two girls grinning with finger paint smeared all over their faces, their arms wrapped tightly around each other's shoulders, sat Uncle Mort's strange glass contraptions, wobbling ever so slightly.

She raised a single eyebrow. "No kidding."

2

Lex stared out the window of the Greyhound bus at the raging, apocalyptic storm. Ferocious winds whipped through the blackened sky, massive drops of rain pelted the glass, and every so often a lightning bolt would illuminate the entirety of the coach, repeatedly terrifying the man sitting behind her whose cocaine habit had become obvious to anyone within a five-seat radius.

Clearly, the weather was not the only foul element of this trip.

Lex was quite unhappily sitting next to a homebound college student. She was able to discern this by the sweatshirt he was wearing, which boasted a trio of Greek letters, and by his shirt collar underneath, which was unabashedly popped and sticking straight up. He resembled a preppy Count Chocula. And, as with most preppy Count Choculas, he had no idea how ridiculous he looked.

Deducing that any interaction with her fellow bus travelers would likely lead to some form of manslaughter, Lex had done everything in her power to avoid getting stuck with a seatmate. She had poured all the contents of her bag onto the empty seat beside her. She spread out her body and pretended to be asleep. And when the driver ordered her to give up the seat, she threw a shoe at his face.

All in vain, she thought bitterly as she glared at the kid, who had put on his best "I'm a douchebag" face and tried to strike up a conversation the second he sat down.

"Hey there, cutie," he said. "What's your name?"

Lex rolled her eyes and turned toward the window. "Kill me."

"Kimmy? I'm Steve," he went on, undeterred. "So, are you in school? I go to NYU. Where do you go?"

Lex gave him the same look a cheetah makes just before devouring a gazelle. "Listen, I really appreciate your efforts to make my trip infinitely more torturous than it already is, but do you think that you could maybe just shut the hell up for the rest of the ride, lest I rip off those hideous sunglasses and start beating you over the head with them?"

Steve looked as though he had just swallowed a socket wrench. "Sor-*ry*," he said. "Just trying to be friendly."

"Cram it, Steve."

Lex's mood was fouler than usual. Not only she was getting shipped off to Uncle Dementia's Land of Psychosis, but she had also received the mother of all gloomy farewells when her family deposited her at the bus station. Mom had cried. Dad's chin quivered. And Cordy wrapped her in a sullen embrace, digging her nails into Lex's back as she whispered, "Get it all out of your system. Bring back the old Lex, or so help me God, I'll tell everyone you went to musical theater camp."

The two sisters had locked eyes once more as Lex took her seat by the window and the bus started to pull away. Lex broke the stare first, glaring sourly at the seat in front of her. If Cordy couldn't see that this separation was equally excruciating on both ends, well, then, she deserved to be miserable.

Lex tried to return to her book, but even good old Edgar Allan couldn't improve the dreadful situation into which she was being dragged at sixty-five miles an hour. Scowling at the total injustice of her life, she slammed the book shut and had just started scanning the vicinity for something to punch when a flash of red and blue lights caught her eye.

She squinted through the rain as the bus slowed to a crawl. A tractor-trailer had jackknifed across the highway, taking three cars with it. Everything was jumbled together on the grassy median in a tortured, twisted mass of metal. It was hard to tell where one vehicle ended and another began.

Both sides of the highway came to a standstill. Ambulance sirens screamed through the dull thudding of the rain as more emergency vehicles tore onto the scene. Lex surveyed the wreck with nothing more than a fleeting interest and a grim expression — until something bizarre appeared.

A white, blinding flash of light.

Startled, Lex peered through the rain. It was so brief — like the flash of a camera — that she couldn't even be sure she had seen it at all. Or if she had, it must have been lightning — except hadn't the light come from *inside* one of the cars? But that made no sense. The vehicle was crumpled beyond recognition, there were no signs of life.

Another flash, this time definitely emanating from within a rolled-over SUV. Lex looked at the paramedics, some of whom were shining flashlights into the cars — but none of their lights matched the brilliance, or the brevity, of the powerful blazes she had just seen.

Momentarily forgetting her policy of isolationism from the dreaded Bus People, Lex whipped her gaze around the coach, expecting the passengers to be gawking at the lights as well, but it seemed as if no one had even noticed. Some scanned the wreckage; a few grumbled about traffic. Lex huffed impatiently. Were these people blind?

She jabbed Steve, who was listening to music and attempting to sleep. "Ow! What?"

"Watch."

He removed his headphones. "Oh, *now* you want to talk?"

"Grow up, Steve. This is purely out of necessity." She leaned back in her seat so he could see out the window. "Look — there's another one!" she yelled as the peculiar electricity sparked once more. "What is that?"

Steve squinted. "Um, a car accident, I think?"

Lex resisted the urge to grab his popped collar and send his head on a whimsical voyage through the glass. "*No,* I mean *that.*" She pointed at the SUV. "The weird flash that just came from that car!"

"You mean lightning?"

"*NO,* the — that!" she cried at another burst of light. "Right there!" She pounded her finger on the windowpane for emphasis, but Steve's face remained quizzical.

A chill ran through Lex's body. "Can't you see them?"

"I don't see anything but a massive car wreck and probably a lot of casualties." Steve frowned in disapproval. "You shouldn't rubberneck like that, it's kind of an awful thing to do."

Lex was about to dispense a salty retort, but she lost her chance as the bus sprang to life and they were jerked back in their seats. "No no no," she whispered, twisting around as the bus picked up speed. "I'm not done yet." But the bus driver pressed on, pumping the accelerator until the grisly scene was nothing more than a blur of lights fading into the distance.

Steve, disgusted, put his headphones back on. Lex swallowed and looked at her watch. An hour more until they reached Albany, then another two to Uncle Mort's stop.

She reclined the seat and closed her eyes. Surely it had been some sort of meteorological phenomenon. Or maybe a bit of the lingering cocaine in the air had found its way into her system. Either way, hallucinations were not something she needed to add to her list of problems right now. There was too much other crap to deal with.

Including a snoring Steve, who was coming closer and closer to getting *The Complete Works of Edgar Allan Poe* shoved right down his throat.

Three hours later Lex finally stepped off the bus.

And into a gigantic puddle of water.

Luckily, by that point, hardly any passengers remained to witness her misfortune. Steve had gotten off in Albany, along with the cocaine guy and anyone else with enough sense not to continue farther upstate. She mumbled a thanks to the driver, who, obviously still bitter over the whole shoe-throwing incident, quickly closed the door behind her and mouthed, "Good luck."

As Lex assessed her surroundings, she began to see why luck had suddenly become so essential. She was standing in a muddy trench on the side of the road, a road that stretched for about fifty feet in both directions before being swallowed up by trees. And the trees — Lex had never imagined that a forest could be so thick. It seemed as if they were actually fighting one another for floor space, an inextricable web of broad trunks and tangled, sprawling limbs.

She took out her phone. No reception. "Awesome."

At least the rain had stopped. Lex shouldered her bag, pulled her hood up to block out the dismal gray sky, and scanned the road for any hints of human civilization. As her feet squelched in her soggy sneakers, she desperately hoped that the luggage her mother had packed and shipped ahead to her uncle's house would contain at least one pair of extra shoes.

Of course it would. Knowing her mom, she had probably packed five, along with several handwritten notes proclaiming her unconditional love. A pang of guilt poked at Lex's chest.

Whatever, she thought, putting it out of her mind. *It was their foolish idea for me to come here, not mine.*

Yet as she adjusted her bulging backpack and thought of Cordy — probably at work by now, scooping ice cream down at the local Baskin-Robbins, enjoying an endless supply of free chocolate chip cookie dough — Lex came to the conclusion that this whole insidious, rage-filled zombie thing, whatever it was, had been colossally unfair. Why her? And why smack-dab in the middle of high school, when it's hard enough as it is to act like a normal, well-adjusted earthling?

She sighed and looked at her watch. Uncle Mort was supposed to have picked her up five minutes ago. Restless, she began walking down the muddy road, not even sure if she was going in the right direction. A bear would arrive to eat her soon, no doubt. She certainly hoped Mr. Truitt would be happy upon learning that her bloodied corpse had been found in a muck-filled ditch.

A loud rumbling in the distance paused her steps. Lex spun around. Something was coming.

She resumed walking. Nothing could scare her now. She'd welcome a hint of danger, in fact. A deadly grizzly attack would certainly be preferable to a summer of cow wrangling.

The noise grew louder, echoing off the damp trunks of the forest. It was only a few yards behind her now. Lex crammed her hands over her ears and finally broke into a run, but it was no use. The roar drew closer and closer —

And stopped.

Lex lowered her hands, turned around, and nearly shat her pants.

Sitting atop a black and purple–streaked motorcycle was, in a startling number of details, the exact type of villain depicted in the *Never Talk to Strangers!* picture book that had been drilled into Lex as a child: a man six feet tall, in his late thirties, lean but strong, roguishly attractive, and sporting the rather nondescript ensemble of a smudged white T-shirt, a pair of jeans, and heavy black combat boots. Peeking out from underneath his sleeves were samplings of what was undoubtedly an impressive array of tattoos, and a red, craggy scar ran from his right earlobe to the corner of whatever sort of eye hid behind his sunglasses. Clearly, this was a man who would waste no time in snapping the neck of anyone who happened to piss him off.

Yet this was only the beginning of what had unnerved Lex.

A distinct change in the air had settled over her skin the moment the engine stopped. The atmosphere itself started to crackle with a bizarre, nameless electricity. As she searched the man's figure for an explanation, more and more peculiarities began to pop out. The pale, slender fingers wrapped around the handlebars looked like those of a skeleton, yet his face was tanned and featured at least two days' worth of stubble. Circling his wrist was a dark gray iron band about an inch wide, the surface of which seemed to turn to static every few seconds or so, as if it were a television screen with bad reception. And topping it all off was the chaotic mess of hair on his head. Blacker even than Lex's, and streaked with purple just like the bike, it stuck out in windblown, tousled spikes, as if he had stuck his finger into a charged socket only seconds before.

He cracked his knuckles. "Hop on."

Lex remained very still. "Um, my ride should be here soon."

"Aw, Lex."

She blinked.

"You're killing me, kiddo! Don't tell me you don't even recognize your Uncle Mort!"

What then escaped Lex's lips was more than a gasp. The sheer force was such that she half expected the nearby trees to uproot and lodge themselves in her throat.

"You deaf?" Uncle Mort moved the sunglasses to the top of his head, revealing a pair of piercing green eyes. "I said get on."

Lex didn't move. "I'm actually not feeling the eviscerated-by-a-creepy-stranger thing today," she said, unable to hide the nervous tinge in her voice. "My vital organs are just fine where they are."

He let out a short laugh. "That's funny. You're funny." He thumped the seat of the bike. "Now get on."

"No."

Her uncle's eye twitched. "You had five hours to change your mind. Get on the damned bike."

Lex's hands grew hot, the way they sometimes did when she got mad. "How do I know you're telling the truth?"

"I wouldn't lie to you. We're family."

"You don't look like family. You look like a freak."

"Okay, Lex," he said, revving the engine once more. "I didn't want it to come to this, but you leave me no — " His eyes widened at some unknown horror behind her. "Is that a *bear?*"

"What?" screeched Lex, twisting around to cower at — nothing.

But that millisecond of falsely placed terror was all Uncle

Mort needed. Deftly grabbing her around the waist, he chucked her onto the seat behind him, kicked the bike into gear, and tore down the road as if blasted from a cannon.

"I can't believe you fell for that!" he yelled over the roar of the engine.

"What the hell is wrong with you?" Lex frantically threw her arms around his chest and screamed so loudly that a nearby flock of birds took to the air to escape the clamor. "Let me OFF!"

He sped up. "You're welcome to jump at any time."

Momentarily forgetting how wind works, Lex tried spitting at him. This failed. She wiped the goo from her cheek, deciding that the time for diplomacy had ended. Keeping one hand around his chest and balling the other into a fist, she exploded into a hysterical fury, pummeling his head, back, and, her very favorite target, kidneys.

Without even looking, Uncle Mort promptly reached back and grabbed her flailing arm, squeezing her wrist with a strength and certainty Lex had never before sensed from an adult. She stared at him with wide eyes as he stopped the bike and spun around to face her.

"You may have gotten away with this childish, petulant bullshit back home, but I assure you, it's not going to fly here," he said, letting go of her arm. "So I'll cut you a deal: you behave like the mature individual that deep down I know you are, and in turn, you will be treated as such. Sound fair?"

Lex sat, stupefied. Over the past two years the various authority figures in her life had scolded, pleaded, lectured, cajoled, reprimanded, and threatened bodily harm, but none of them had spoken to her with anything resembling respect.

Uncle Mort took this brief opportunity of tranquility to toss her a helmet. "Almost forgot. Safety first."

Lex took one look at the scar gashed into the corner of her uncle's eye and quickly snapped the helmet onto her head. "Where's yours?"

"I have a very thick skull," he said, his eyes glinting with the sort of look possessed only by the criminally insane.

Lex stared. "You're crazy."

"Little bit."

The motorcycle sprang to life yet again and shot down the road. Lex squinted against the wind as they rode, the trees a drab green blur, the road a dizzying ribbon beneath her feet.

"You ready, kiddo?" Uncle Mort eventually shouted.

"Ready for what?"

"A little excitement. Hold on!"

He sped up. Just as they approached a particularly grody puddle, he jerked the handlebars to the left. Lex hugged her uncle's torso even tighter, her head lolling about in a comical fashion as the bike leaned into the turn, the mud splattering off the tires and onto her face. Lex briefly thought of her loved ones and prepared for death, pausing only to curse her uncle's name straight to hell for robbing her of all the piercings she would never have the chance to get.

But the bike soon righted itself. "Are you out of your MIND?" she yelled, headbutting him with her helmet as they straightened out onto a narrow, darkened dirt road. She looked up at the impossibly dense trees, whose hostile gray branches now stretched over the road to form a low-ceilinged canopy. It was as if they were entering a bleak, sinister tunnel.

Uncle Mort stopped the bike and turned around in his seat to admire his handiwork. "You've got a little mud on your face."

"No shit, jerkwad," she said with a grimace, wiping it off. "What's next? Will you be setting me on fire?"

"Don't be ridiculous, Lex. The flamethrower shoots forward."

Lex couldn't take it anymore. The madness had to be stopped. "Okay, wait a minute. *You* are my Uncle Mort? My father's brother? A certified biological member of the most boring family on earth?"

"Guilty as charged. And I'm ecstatic to see you, kiddo. When your dad told me that you were becoming quite the handful, well . . ." He glanced sideways, his mouth twitching wryly at some inside joke. "I simply *had* to invite you."

"To suffer through your little ride of death? We could have been killed!"

"*Could* have been killed. You'll note that we weren't."

"Barely! What is going on?

"Relax, Lex. I know it seems strange, but all will be explained in good time."

"Explain it now!" She punched his arm, a healthy dose of rage flowing.

"You *are* a spunky one, aren't you?" he said, ignoring the blow. "Big bro said you were full of piss and vinegar, but I really had no idea." He scratched his chin, thinking to himself. "This'll work out better than I had hoped."

Lex looked at her fist in shock, baffled that she still hadn't inflicted the usual amount of pain. "Fine, be all cryptic," she said in a misguided attempt to use reverse psychology. "I don't care."

"Wonderful."

This infuriated Lex all over again. She jumped off the seat, only to be grabbed around the waist and wrangled back into it. "Let me go!" She tore off a mirror and brandished it in his face. "I mean it! I don't want to go to your godforsaken hellbarn, you retarded psycho farmer!"

He let out an amused snicker. "I'm not a farmer."

Lex stopped railing for a moment and blinked in confusion. "Then what are you?"

"Let's just say I'm in the business of importing and exporting."

She rolled her eyes. "Call it whatever you want. It still involves fertilizer."

"I suppose it does, in a manner of speaking."

Lex gritted her teeth. Among her many other shortcomings, she was not a patient girl. She didn't know how much longer she could stand to be in the dark, irked and befuddled by a blatantly unhinged man who spoke only in riddles.

"Don't worry, Lexington," he said in a warm, avuncular voice. "You've got a truckload of potential, I can tell. You're going to excel here."

"Excel at *what*? Asking pointless questions that never get answered?"

"Oh, absolutely. But in addition to that — " He pried the mirror from her hands and smiled enigmatically. "This is going to be the best summer of your life. Trust me."

As all kids know, it's difficult enough to trust any adult, much less a deranged, life-endangering importer-exporter. As her uncle kicked the bike into gear, the possibility that maybe he really was a mass murderer crept back into her mind. Of *course* he was. Of *course* he had a machete stashed somewhere in the woods. Her small intestine would soon be strewn messily across the road, her head bouncing off into the trees like a kickball.

The tires slogged through more mud as they drove deeper into the very heart of the Adirondacks. The sky had all but disappeared from view. She peered over his shoulder, but could see nothing more than the rise of a small hill.

"We're here," Uncle Mort said as they came to a halt at the top.

"Where?"

He pointed ahead. "The godforsaken hellbarn."

Lex stared. And stared.

Gone was the thick, ugly brush of forest. In its place lay a valley below, with rolling hills of green stretching as far as Lex's stunned eyes could see. Dazzling blue ponds glittered furiously as the sun finally broke through the clouds. A gentle breeze wafted through the leafy trees and up the hill, bringing with it the luscious smell of lavender, vanilla, and freshly cut grass.

Uncle Mort turned to her and smiled.

"Welcome to Croak."

4

"I gotta be honest, Lex," Uncle Mort said as they continued down the hill into town, slowing the bike so they could speak without yelling. "You look just about ready to soil yourself."

Lex shot him a glare, then eyed a sign at the side of the road that read **CROAK! POPULATION: 78.** The number clicked over to 80 as they passed.

She scrunched up her nose. "That was weird."

"But accurate."

Lex gazed at the handful of small buildings as they passed by. "I don't get it. Where's the town?" she asked, searching into the distance.

"You're in it."

"This is *it?*"

"It is small," Uncle Mort agreed. "But it's got heart."

Lex assumed he meant this literally as well as figuratively, since both sides of the street were lined with blooms of brilliantly red bleeding-heart flowers. As she gawked at the short buildings, she got the eeriest feeling that she had stumbled into a historical theme park. The storefronts just seemed so old-fashioned, like they were part of some bygone era of yore, or maybe even yester-year. She had only ever seen places like this on the evening news during election years, when politicians invaded to kiss babies and purchase homemade pies from smiling, toothless bakery owners.

"Please tell me you have running water," she said.

"Of course. Tuesdays and Thursdays."

She couldn't tell if he was being sarcastic.

"Don't worry," he said. "Croak's a pretty modern place. Up there are the Pine Condos, where some of the younger people live, and a few good shops on the right down Slain Lane." He pointed to a side street paved with cobblestones, unlike the smooth pavement of the one they were on. Lex craned her neck and spotted a handful of oddly named stores: a flower shop called PUSHING DAISIES, a mattress place labeled THE BIG SLEEP, and a grocery store with a giant sign reading BOUGHT THE FARM.

At the junction of the two roads, a gravestonelike obelisk rose out of a small fountain. Uncle Mort nodded to the left. "Best diner in the universe right there. Hello, Dora!" he called to the ancient woman sweeping the sidewalk outside. She waved cheerily.

"And the library's up on the left — oh, but check this out, our pride and joy," he said with reverence, looking straight ahead. At a fork in the road stood the tallest building in town, clocking in at a whopping two stories. The Victorian house was painted a sunny yellow, with friendly letters spelling out the word BANK across the façade. The wooden front porch contained a hammock, a small table, and, naturally, a pitcher of lemonade. "We take our investments very seriously."

Lex struggled to take it all in. She had never seen a bank that looked as though it could double as a summer home. Nor could she conceive of a place that didn't seem to have a single traffic light. And the quaint, nostalgic street sign labeled DEAD END rather than Main Street only confirmed her suspicions that the town had surely lost its quaint, nostalgic marbles.

Then, just like that, it was behind them.

The bike veered onto the fork to the left of the Bank and passed a large field on the right. Across that, a dozen or so houses stretched down the other fork, looking like any other suburb in America.

Lex squirmed in her seat. "Are you kidding me? That was *not* a town," she said. "I mean, where's the Starbucks?"

Uncle Mort sighed. "Lex, I know you're from New York, so I'm going to forgive you for that. But let me tell you something right now, something that I don't want you ever to forget: Starbucks is an abomination."

Lex was speechless, for she now believed there was no way in a million years this man could possibly be a blood relative.

"And here are my digs," he said as the bike slowed. "What do you think?"

Lex no longer knew what to think. The house was practically a larger version of Uncle Mort himself—loud, schizophrenic, and potentially fatal. Speckled with all manner of colors in no apparent pattern, it looked as if it had rolled around the country-side picking up random items and whatnots before finally coming to a halt at the top of its grassy hill.

Lex ogled the bizarre devices poking out of each window as the bike rolled to a stop. She took off her helmet and dropped it to the ground. "You really live here?" she asked, her voice tinged with the faintest trace of warmth. This house, in all its chaotic glory, reminded her of her bedroom back home.

Uncle Mort dismounted the bike. "Yep. And now, so do you." He handed her a set of keys. "Your room is the first door on the left."

Lex, who from the moment of her conception had never had a room of her own, snatched the keys out of his hand and tore into the house. If she really was going to be stuck here for the duration of the summer, she might as well become accustomed to the living quarters in which she would undoubtedly be holing herself up. And at least this was an actual house with actual walls and not a crusty, fetid hayloft, as she had feared. It almost seemed — she hardly dared to think it — kind of cool.

She burst into the front hallway. Unsurprisingly, the kitchen was a mess, and the living room was buried under piles of unidentifiable paraphernalia. Useless junk clogged each pore. Empty photograph frames collected dust at every turn, while a large tank of jellyfish stretched across an entire wall, like a live mural. The luggage Lex's mother had sent sat at the edge of it all, blending in perfectly. Lex grinned, her sense of alienation abating. This was exactly the way she and Cordy had always preferred to live: in utter squalor and disarray.

Tingling with anticipation, Lex ran down the hall to her room and flung open the door.

Her face fell.

No bedlam. No eyesores. And not a single useless trinket.

Instead, a beautifully carved armoire stood gracefully in the corner. Next to it, a desk made from spotless white oak. Pink bedding, curtains, and rugs, as if a flamingo had exploded. And worst of all, looming on the wall across from the frilly, perfectly made bed: a *Titanic* movie poster.

Lex shrieked in horror and slammed the door. "What was *that?*"

"What's wrong?" Uncle Mort asked as he entered the house. "You don't like it?"

"I hate it! Were those doilies?!"

"Dammit." He sighed. "I thought I could trust him with this."

Lex glanced at the slightly open door across from hers, on which was tacked a poster of The Who. She peeked through the crack, but all she could see was a massive set of drums. Next to that, another door was wide open and spewing a heavy stream of smoke. She squinted down a set of stairs at several bubbling vials of goo.

"Your basement's on fire."

"Oh, that's just my lab," Uncle Mort calmly replied, closing the door and fanning the sulfuric fumes away. "I like to tinker."

"I see." Lex strayed back into the living room and looked around, confused. "Where's the TV?"

"I don't have one."

"WHAT?" she yelled. "WHAT?"

"After a few days you won't even care. And don't worry about your room, it'll all be fixed by the time we get back."

"Get back? Where are we going?"

"Out. Can't very well have the redecorators come in while you're still here, can we? Besides, we have to talk."

"Yeah, right." She let out a huff, walked into the kitchen, and sat down, throwing her muddy feet up onto the table. "You almost killed me about twelve times in the past hour. I'm not going anywhere with you."

"Ah, but you are."

"Make me."

"Gladly."

And with a lightning-quick swoop of his arm, Uncle Mort grabbed his niece by the waist yet again, flung her over his shoulder, and walked out the door.

As she was lugged upside down through the empty streets of Croak, Lex thrashed with a ferocity that would have impressed even the most seasoned probation officer. Yet Uncle Mort seemed not to notice, and before long, Lex's protests were reduced to nothing more than an occasional groan.

"Almost forgot — I promised your family we'd call when you got here," he said cheerfully as they passed into the other end of town, his shoulder digging into her stomach more and more with every step.

Lex, now fairly nauseated, jammed her elbow into his lower back and propped up her addled head onto her hand. "Here's an idea," she said weakly. "You put me down, I'll use my cell."

"No reception for miles. Hence, the Cuff," he said, indicating the strange band around his wrist.

"Fascinating. Put me down."

Uncle Mort ignored her. "Gotta make a personal call first." He did something to the Cuff — it turned staticky again and stayed that way — then began to quietly scold it. Lex thought she heard him utter a few key phrases like "it's a bedroom, not a Victoria's Secret," but by now she was teetering too closely to the brink of unconsciousness to even guess what was going on.

"I am about two seconds away from vomiting all over every inch of you," she told her uncle in a slurred voice as he hung up.

"And me without a poncho. Pity."

She riskily let out a small burp. "Oh God. Put me down. Please?"

"Was that a magic word I just heard? Did an ounce of politeness just escape the mouth of Lexington Bartleby? I think it did!" And with a surprising gentleness, he lowered his queasy passenger to her feet.

"Good?" he asked, giving her a hard pat on the shoulder.

"Yep." Lex's eyes focused, then unfocused. "Nope. Head rush," she said on her way to the ground.

Five minutes later she woke up and squinted at her uncle's hovering head.

"Hey, kiddo. What's your name?" he asked.

"Lex."

"What month are we in?"

"July."

"Yankees or Mets?"

"Mets."

"Good girl." He yanked her up from the ground and pointed at a nearby hill. "This way."

Lex swallowed a couple of times, clutched her stomach, and followed him through the trees as he began talking into his wrist once more.

"Yep, she got in just fine, no problems to speak of. Lex, say hi to your dad."

"Dad!" She grabbed her uncle's arm and shouted into the flickering metal. "Your brother is a lunatic. He's trying to kill me!"

"Nice try, Lex," her father's tinny voice answered. "You're not getting home that easily."

"I don't think you're fully grasping the enormity of the situation, Dad. He doesn't even have a *television!*"

Uncle Mort jerked his arm away, hung up, and began walking faster. "Enough chat. Let's enjoy us some nature."

Lex tried to keep up. "Good idea. Find me a nice tree to puke on."

They were now ascending the gently sloping side of a grassy

bluff. When at last they reached the top, Lex gaped at her surroundings, which included, among other things, an enormous gray boulder that almost seemed to be keeping watch over the town below. "Where are we?"

Uncle Mort walked to the brink of the precipice and sat down on the cliff's edge. "Best place in Croak to watch the sunset."

Something in Lex snapped. She didn't want to watch a sunset. She wanted to be told what in holy hell was going on here. The rage stirred yet again, spurring her to grab her uncle's arm and twist it behind his back as hard as she could.

Seemingly bored with her antics, Uncle Mort breathed a peaceful sigh and gazed into the distance. The sun, a fiery ball of neon orange, set over the village below them.

"What can you see out there, Lex?" he asked in a tranquil voice.

"Well," Lex said, twisting harder, "I see a pitiful excuse for a town, some trees, a few hills, and an abusive, stark raving madman." She dug her nails into his wrist. "That about cover it?"

"More or less. Hey, would you mind letting go? It's starting to tickle."

Lex dropped his arm with a defeated grunt. How had she not separated his shoulder by now? Why wasn't he begging for mercy?

"Just sit," he said. "You may continue your attempt to detach one of my limbs later. Right now, there are some things you need to know."

Lex sat, defeated, exhausted, but most of all, confused — because despite all efforts to suppress such inclinations, she could not help but feel the tiniest bit of admiration for her uncle, who was now wiping away the few drops of blood that emerged where her nails had dug into his skin.

He caught her sheepish gaze. "Don't worry, I've encountered much worse," he said, his eyes sparkling with either youthful excitement or demented delirium. "I knew you'd put up a good fight. I'd be surprised and frankly insulted if you hadn't."

Lex cocked her head. The wrath that had raged within her only seconds ago seemed to be rapidly melting away of its own accord, like an ebbing storm. What was going on?

"But you're also smart," he went on, "which is why you're going to listen very closely to what I'm about to tell you. Right?"

Lex found herself nodding. How did he do that?

He turned serious, all traces of insanity abruptly leaving his face. "Your parents haven't been entirely forthcoming with you, Lex. Nor have I been entirely forthcoming with your parents. It was my idea for you to come here, not theirs. When I heard that you had turned delinquent, I knew your time had come. So I suggested to your father that you visit me and experience some country living." His eyes turned dark. "But that is not your purpose here."

Lex listened as patiently as she could, tearing a piece of grass into microscopic shards.

"We're going into town tomorrow, and I want you to be prepared. What we do here is important business and should never, ever be taken lightly. We have been blessed — and burdened — with a very grave responsibility, if you'll forgive the pun." He glanced over the valley. "Croak, as you may have gathered, is a different kind of town. All of its citizens exist for a common purpose. Naturally, from time to time we need some fresh blood, which is where you come in. And as I said earlier, you're going to be a natural. Trust me on that one. All you need to do is pay close attention, learn as much as you can, and try not to be scared by anything you see."

"Scared of what?" she said. "How disgustingly adorable your little village is? The perfectly groomed flowers? The — the . . ." Lex trailed off. A national coffee shop chain wasn't the only thing missing from this town. She had seen no firehouses, no police departments, churches, gas stations, schools . . .

A furious outbreak of goose bumps flickered across her skin. Everything was starting to feel very strange.

That same electric crackle shot through the air once more as Uncle Mort opened his mouth to speak. "Lex," he said, "Croak is a portal — one that sits between our world and the next."

A strange noise escaped Lex's lips, something between a stupefied gasp and a dubious snicker. "What?"

"That's why you're here. I'm going to teach you how to do what I do."

"And what is that?"

He leaned in close. She could feel his breath on her face.

"I Kill people."

5

Starving and exhausted, yet unable to fall asleep without the familiar sounds of Cordy wheezing from three feet away, Lex lay on top of her covers that evening and stared at Leonardo DiCaprio's giant head. Other than the poster, everything else had been mysteriously remodeled after she and Uncle Mort left for their chat. Most of the pink items were gone, the armoire had been replaced by a small tank of jellyfish, and a series of satellite dishes and gizmos now stuck out of the window.

The poster, however, had been glued so strongly to the wall that nothing in the house could remove it.

Lex didn't know how many hours she had been lying there awake, painstakingly analyzing every word her uncle had said, but it felt like at least a baker's dozen. And the stomachache produced by the Family Size bag of Doritos she had eaten in lieu of a proper dinner wasn't helping, either. So she simply clutched at her pillow, dazed beyond belief — and not just by Leo's whimsical coif.

"Excuse me?" she had said back at the cliff. "You *Kill* people? What is that supposed to mean?"

"It means that I am one of a very select group of people who are endowed with the power to transport souls from this life to the next." Her uncle looked at her, his green eyes flashing. "That's who we are. That's who *you* are."

A small surge rose into Lex's chest. She almost recognized it as excitement — something she had not felt in a long time — but the rational part of her brain bulldozed it too quickly for her to savor.

"You're nuts," she said to him. "Really. Is Dad aware of your mental deterioration? You need help."

He watched her, amused.

"I mean, listen, I appreciate the effort to make this farm stay thing a little more fascinating than just an exercise in dispensing pig slop, but this is just moronic. Or — wait, I get it, you're speaking metaphorically, right? We butcher the cows and deliver them to a new 'afterlife' on the shelves of supermarkets? Hilarious. Really clever." She got up, dusted off the seat of her pants, and crossed her arms. "Let's just go," she said miserably. "Why did you even drag me up here? Don't get me wrong, the sunset was simply breathtaking, but here's the thing: I'm stuck in this stupid town for the summer no matter what. So I'll clean up as much goat shit as you want to throw at me, fine, but don't bother to make it sound like a higher calling."

He nodded slowly. "Well, a thousand apologies," he finally said with a shrug. "I guess I was wrong about you."

She started to walk away, back down the hill.

"Unless, of course, you've ever seen a deathflash."

Lex turned around. He was standing at the edge of the cliff, his body a silhouette against the sunset.

"A what?"

"Deathflash," he said. "A white, blinding light that flashes when someone dies. Sound familiar?"

"I — " Lex screwed up her face. "On the bus ride here, there was an accident. I saw a light . . . a bunch of lights . . ."

"You want to know why I dragged you up here, Lex?" He pointed out over the town. "Do me a favor. Count how many tractors you see."

Lex walked back to the precipice and scanned the vista, really looked at it this time, and the sudden realization that followed almost short-circuited her brain: the sweeping panorama, green to the farthest horizon, was devoid of even the smallest agricultural endeavor. Not a barn, silo, field, or errant chicken in sight. She turned to him, dumbfounded.

He just smiled.

"Okay," Lex said, compulsively peeling the bark off a twig as they walked back to the house, "let's just entertain for a moment the completely mental notion that what you're saying is true. How come I've never heard of this before? How come *no one's* ever heard of this before? How did a hole to the great beyond just pop up in the middle of the Adirondacks? How did a puny little human like you become entrusted with such a massive undertaking? How does one transport a soul? How does one even hold a soul? And what in the name of all that is disturbing did you mean when you said you're going to teach me how to Kill people?"

He snickered. "You didn't really think you were going to spend the whole summer milking cows, did you?"

"Don't! Change! The! Subject!" she cried, stabbing the twig into his arm with each word until it stuck there.

He effortlessly yanked it out. "I gotta say, Lex, your negotiation skills really leave something to be desired."

She blinked in disbelief at the bloodied splinter. "And even if all that other bullshit were true, why me? What makes you think that a walking calamity such as myself would be even a fraction of a smidgen qualified to Kill people?"

"Well, you did just shiv your own uncle with a stick."

Lex shrank a little. "That's . . . different."

"And you beat up all those kids at school."

"Yeah, but — hey, that's not fair. It's not like I wanted them dead or anything."

He raised an eyebrow. "So what you're saying is that maybe you're not really as bad a kid as everyone thinks you are."

Lex's mouth fell open. There it was, that one steadfast belief she had been clinging to all along, the one thing her principal, her teachers, even her own parents hadn't been able to see. He had just said it. Out loud.

"You didn't end up here by chance, Lex," Uncle Mort said. "If you believe only one thing I've told you tonight, believe that. I know nothing else makes sense right now, but try sleeping on it." He smiled. "And tomorrow I'll show you how to do things that a walking calamity such as yourself has never even fathomed."

|||||||

Lex awoke the next morning with a start.

After a few seconds of disoriented panic she rubbed the sleep out of her eyes, sat up, and immediately clutched her rumbling stomach, cursing her uncle for his paltry dining options. "Sorry for not preparing a welcome feast," he had said when they arrived home, tossing her the Doritos as he descended into the smoggy basement. "Not really my forte."

Lex took a moment to look around the room in the light of day and ponder exactly what his forte was, as it was becoming increasingly evident that it was not, in fact, farming. The weird gadgets poking out of the windows suggested some type of technological occupation, but she couldn't imagine how that could be, seeing as how he lived in the middle of nowhere. And what did the jellyfish have to do with any of it?

Still, the only other explanation he had provided was, in a word, nutzoid. Lex had watched enough Discovery Channel specials to know that conspiracies and secrets of this magnitude did not exist in the real world. And even if they did, the chances that she was smart or talented or Bond-girl-sexy enough to be privy to them were slim to none.

Yet why would he bother to come up with a lie like that? And the deathflashes, as he called them — she had seen those, no question. How could he have known?

She resolved to torture it out of him today. She fell out of bed and threw on a T-shirt, a pair of jeans, sneakers, and her black hoodie, then shuffled down the hallway and pushed open the door to the bathroom.

"HEY!"

"Whoa!" Lex screeched. "Sorry!"

The kid standing at the toilet crumpled in embarrassment just in the nick of time, or Lex would have gotten much more of an eyeful. As it was, she could tell that he was probably a little older than she was, but not by much. His deep brown hair was the color of enriched soil, the kind sold at hardware stores. Like Mort's, but cut shorter, it too stuck out in every conceivable direction, as if suffering an existential crisis over which way it should be going. He seemed tallish and lean, but not lanky; well built, but not bulgingly muscular. He wore a faded blue T-shirt, cargo shorts, and a beat-up pair of high-top Chuck Taylors. But none of these features made a bit of difference, because Lex was floored by only one element of his appearance.

His right eye was brown. His left eye was blue.

Both of Lex's eyes, meanwhile, were blinking maniacally. Her face instantly flushed, though she was unsure whether this was due to humiliation or to the fact that this kid made even the hottest kid at her school look like a bog monster. "Who are you?" she asked.

"This bathroom's current occupant," he said breathlessly, his hands fumbling with the zipper as if they had never operated one before. "Ever heard of knocking?"

In an attempt to suppress any further hormonal shenanigans, Lex shielded her eyes and pawed at the doorknob, her motor skills failing her at the precise moment she needed them most. "I'm sorry!"

The kid, clearly no stranger to hormonal shenanigans himself, kept working at his fly and staring at her as if she were an advancing velociraptor. "And yet you're still here."

"Okay, I know. Sorry." Lex ultimately managed to take a step back into the hallway and regain her faculties. She frowned. Uncle Mort didn't have any kids, she knew that much. "What are you doing here?"

"Isn't it obvious?"

"I mean here in this house."

With a final tug at his pants, the kid straightened up. He flushed the toilet, took a deep, cleansing breath, and walked to the sink in a far more composed manner. "I live here," he said affably, washing his hands. "Nice to meet you, roomie."

Lex didn't know how to handle this. At school, not even the

gym classes were coed, let alone the bathrooms. "I am no one's 'roomie,'" she replied nervously.

The boy took a step toward her. Lex jumped back, her contentious instincts kicking in. "Stop right there," she warned. "I punch, I kick, and I feel compelled to warn you, I can bite harder than the average Amazonian crocodile."

He smirked and leaned against the doorframe. "And I feel compelled to warn *you* that the bathroom we now share has a leaky ceiling," he said, pointing up. "There's an umbrella under the sink, if you're going be in here for a while."

"I mean it," she continued, her voice rising. "I will kick your ass!"

"And the shower faucet sticks a little, sometimes you have to jiggle it."

"Hey! Can't you hear me?"

"I think the whole town can hear you."

Lex sputtered. She was so confused. This was a girl who had once reduced the entire varsity hockey team to a chorus of high-pitched, hiccuppy sobs. She could understand Mort not being intimidated by her, since he was an adult, but this kid was just . . . well, a kid. His unflappability disarmed her, as did his stupid captivating eyes.

"Who are you?" she asked, still yelling.

"I'm Driggs." He grinned and stuck out his hand. "It's an absolute — "

"That's a dumb name."

" — displeasure to meet you." He withdrew his hand, stepped past her into the hallway, then gestured back at the bathroom. "All yours."

Lex watched him walk down the hallway and into the room with a The Who poster. "Wait," she said, following him. "I mean, who *are* you? Why are you in my bathroom? What are you — "

The door slammed in her face.

A loud crash of drumming belted forth from within.

Lex pounded on Pete Townshend's face for a few moments until finally, realizing that the kid was infuriatingly incorporating her knocking into the rhythm, she was forced to admit defeat. She slumped back to the bathroom, concluded her business there, and upon exiting into the hallway heard a rustle of newspaper from the kitchen.

"Time to go, Lex!" yelled Uncle Mort.

She found him sitting at the table. "Who's the prick with the drums?" she asked.

"Driggs," Uncle Mort said evasively, skimming a newspaper titled *The Obituary*.

"Yeah, I got that part. Who is he?"

"My pool boy."

Lex shut her mouth and spent the next few seconds fighting a strong urge to flip over the kitchen table in frustration. Uncle Mort looked at the clock on the wall. "Half the day's over. You sleep okay?"

"Spare me the pleasantries. What's the plan?"

"You'll see."

"When?"

"Soon."

"How soon?"

"Shortly."

"Enough!" Feral in the way that only cranky, overtired youth can be, Lex pounded her fists on the table. "Enough of all this squirrelly, evasive bullshit. You're not a farmer. You're not an importer-exporter. And you sure as hell aren't the almighty Angel of Death. So you better tell me why I'm really here, or I'm leaving. I mean it."

Her uncle leaned back in his chair and scrutinized her. "Why *are* you here, Lex? I know, your parents made you come, but we both know you could have wriggled out of it if you really wanted to. Why give up a summer at home, free to go to the beach, explore the city" — he raised an eyebrow — "hang out with friends?"

A little bit of the fight went out of her. Lex's eyes dropped to the linoleum. "I don't have any friends."

She was not proud of this. As much as she had tried to convince herself otherwise over the past couple of years, the empty hole in her life where her friends used to be felt like a tender bruise. They had abandoned her with good cause, of course, but it still hurt. And it had only gotten worse with time.

Uncle Mort leaned in. "Lex, the reason the things I told you last night are bothering you so much is because there is a very small, very ecstatic, very curious part of your brain that thinks there's a chance this might all be true, that this is the moment your life is finally about to kick in. But the only way I can make that happen for you is if you agree to drop the theatrics from now on, try to keep the sarcasm to a minimum, and start acting like an adult about all this."

The very small, very ecstatic, very curious part of Lex's brain began bouncing around her head like a pinball. She studied him. All she had to do was behave?

"You'll tell me today?" she asked.

"As much as we can squeeze in, yes."

"And you promise full disclosure?"

"I promise," he said, extending his hand.

She hesitated for a moment, then shook it. "Deal."

"Ah, bribery." He grinned at his niece. "Is there anything it can't do?"

She fidgeted irritably. "So now what?"

"Breakfast first. We need to turn you into more of a sentient life form. Here." He handed her a box of Life cereal. "It's ironically delicious."

Lex sat down, poured herself a bowl, and inhaled its contents in about thirty seconds. After gulping down the milk, she smeared a napkin around her face and stared at him expectantly. "Now what?"

"Patience, kiddo," he said, not looking up from the newspaper, "or you'll pass out before we even get there."

"Get where?"

"The Bank."

"The Bank? What's at the goddamned Bank?"

"Lexington, we need to talk about this swearing habit of yours. Personally, I don't give a shit. But it's forbidden for the rest of the summer — that's a direct order from your mother."

Lex grunted. For all she knew, Uncle Mort had been forced to set up an intricate series of hidden microphones to relay every word directly to her mother, who would be waiting at home with a hefty swear bill upon her daughter's return. "Fine," she grumbled, impatiently tapping her spoon on the table.

"And another thing." Uncle Mort grabbed the spoon from her hand and flung it into the sink. "This isn't a vacation. It's a full-time job with ten-hour days. From now on, you'll be getting up at dawn." He walked to the door and opened it. "Let's go. You're here to work, not sleep."

Lex gave him a bitter look as she got up from the table. "Ten hours?"

"Don't worry," he said, holding the door open for her. "Time flies when you're breaching the space-time continuum."

|||||||

Uncle Mort said nothing more as they hurried down the road from the house, a bundle of black fabric tucked under his arm. After five minutes they came upon the large field on the left, behind the Bank.

Lex stopped in her tracks. A handful of people stood in the field, spread out across the grass in groups of two. Lex tried to watch what they were doing, but Uncle Mort pulled her away. "Not yet."

She stewed beside him as they reached Dead End, practically running in order to keep up with his long strides. His marked silence was ripping her insides to shreds. It was almost enough to make her grab the collar of one of the iced-coffee-sipping people bustling around the street and beg to be told what was going on, or why they seemed to be gawking at her in fascination, or, at the very least, where they had gotten their coffee.

They were just about to climb the steps to the Bank when a hefty, sunburned man clutching a wrinkled map tapped Uncle Mort on the elbow.

"'Scuse me," he said in a friendly voice. "Can you tell me where the Happy Spruce Inn is?"

"Back the way you came," Uncle Mort said. "Go for about twenty miles, then . . . I don't know, hang a left or something. Can't miss it. And you might want to hurry up, we've got a tornado warning on the radar."

The man glanced at the clearly unconcerned pedestrians, then up at the cloudless sky. "Uh, okay. Thanks, buddy."

Lex started to walk away, but Uncle Mort remained where he was and cleared his throat. The man screwed up his face. Then, in a flash of understanding, he dug into his wallet and handed Uncle Mort a crisp five-dollar bill.

"Enjoy your stay in the Adirondacks!" Uncle Mort said, shooting him a theatrical grin.

It melted off his face the moment he and Lex reached the Bank's door. "I hate summer," he told her. "Three simple rules for getting rid of tourists, Lex: lie, deny, and bleed 'em dry."

A tiny knot of bells announced their entrance into the lobby, which looked less like a bank and more like someone's fancy living room. Small and homey, it featured two fluffy couches, a mahogany coffee table, cheerful red curtains, and an information counter boasting an array of brochures for local attractions and hotels. An elegant Oriental rug ran the length of the room to the hallway beyond, and the air was noticeably permeated with clashing scents of potpourri, owing to the multitude of bowls dispersed throughout.

Lex crinkled her nose. "It smells like a candle store in here."

"I know, it's disgusting," Uncle Mort said, poking at a pile of dried rose petals. "But it's best not to fight her."

"Who?"

"Good morning, Mort!" A plump middle-aged woman with tomato-red hair popped up from behind the counter, a blinding smile plastered across her face. She wore a peacock-blue business suit and a necklace of shiny pearls. A massive flower corsage took up half her chest. "And who do we have here?"

"This is my niece, Lex," Uncle Mort said proudly. "Our newest rookie."

"How marvelous!" The woman clamped Lex's hand like a vise and shook it vigorously. "I'm so pleased to meet you! My name is Kilda!"

Lex looked to her uncle for help, but he had slipped off into the nearby hallway. She watched as he opened a door and began speaking to a man in a suit — a man who was staring directly at her.

Though fairly certain she hadn't done anything to offend him, Lex could feel his foxlike yellow eyes boring into her own with a distinct animosity. Tall and gaunt, with permanent scowl lines etched into his colorless face, he exuded the air of someone who hated this earth and everything on it and would be much happier if it just broke free of its orbit and hurled itself into the sun.

Lex cringed.

Meanwhile, Kilda was still squawking out a welcome, and though Lex tried to ignore her, it soon became very difficult to do so. She had never met anyone whose every sentence ended in an exclamation point.

"I'm Croak's director of tourism! And its public relations specialist! And to top it all off, its postmaster, if you can believe it!"

Lex thought the hysteria might never end, but at long last her uncle interceded to pry their hands apart. "No time to chat, Kilda," he said. "We've got a busy day ahead of us. And you've got a lost Texan out there about to start asking for souvenirs."

"Well, that won't do!" Kilda hurried outside, her lipstick-smeared teeth flashing. "Off I go!"

Lex grabbed at her uncle's sleeve. "What did I do to deserve that?"

"She's a lot to handle, I know. But Kilda's a genius in her field. You should hear the bullshit she can sell to all the lost backpackers we get here."

"Who's that man you were talking to?"

"Oh, that's Norwood. He was checking you in for your first shift. I'll introduce you tomorrow."

She made a face. "No rush."

"I mean, you were scheduled to have a brief orientation with him today, but you know, you needed your beauty sleep, so we don't have time. Are you aware, Lex, that sloth is a deadly sin?"

She made a face at him, then glanced back at the hallway. She thought she could make out a bustle of activity behind the array of frosted glass tiles that lined its right-hand wall, but Uncle Mort ushered her out the front door too quickly for her to get a closer look.

"Wait, we're done here?"

"Well, I was going to show you around upstairs as well, but —"

"No time. Sloth. I get it."

"Deadly sin."

People often think that trees are boring. These people have obviously never feasted their eyes upon the eerily fascinating Australian Ghost Gum tree, or *Corymbia aparrerinja,* under which Lex now stood. Uncle Mort had led her to the middle of the field behind the Bank and instructed her to stay still while he spoke into his Cuff. The people she had seen earlier were gone.

Lex, correctly of the opinion that trees are awesome, ran her fingers over the dead Ghost Gum's trunk. Instead of a dark, rough bark, the surface was chalky and smooth. Its pure white color blazed in the radiant sunlight, while its crooked, gnarled branches stretched widely across the sky. No leaves adorned the limbs, but a single large nest sat perched atop the highest bough, as if it had been dropped there by a disoriented seagull.

"This is the Field," Uncle Mort said. "The runway and landing strip, if you will."

"Huh?" Lex asked futilely, knowing full well he wouldn't clarify.

He didn't.

Lex wondered what Cordy would have to say about all of this — the bizarre town, the confirmation of their estranged uncle's lunacy, the fact that it was almost noon and she still hadn't consumed a drop of caffeine. She started to make a mental list of things to tell her, in the unlikely event an Internet connection existed somewhere in the Land That Cable Forgot.

She poked her uncle's shoulder. "Can I have some coffee?"

"You're only sixteen, Lex. Try getting high on life."

To keep from strangling him, she turned her thoughts to the weather. A series of fluffy, trout-shaped clouds dotted the sky. She didn't feel the least bit hot in her black sweatshirt, despite the scorching sun. No breeze either — though she could have sworn she saw a nearby shrub rustling of its own volition.

"Okay, we're all set," Uncle Mort said, hanging up and looking at something behind Lex. "Ah, at least someone's on time today."

Lex turned around and gulped. Walking toward them was a girl, maybe a couple of years older than Lex, wearing a tight long-sleeved T-shirt and jeans. She too carried a bundle of black fabric. Slender, tall, and toned, her limbs undulated as if only marginally attached to her body. Though her pale face was angular and serious, her eyes were light and thoughtful. Yet Lex was entranced more than anything by her hair, which was long and thick, with a slight wave to it, and absolutely, unmistakably silver.

Not gray, not white, but silver — as if it had been melted down from jewelry and stretched out into a waterfall of gorgeous, silky strands. Lex tried to tear her gaze away, but couldn't. What was it with this place and crazy hair?

"Lex, this is Zara," Uncle Mort said, pronouncing both syllables in her name with an *ah* sound, which Lex thought was an unnecessarily fancy way to say it. "She's here to help with training."

The girl smiled and extended her hand, all while gazing deep into Lex's eyes, as if attempting to decipher some secret hidden within them. "I've heard a lot about you," she said in a strong voice.

"Really?" Lex numbly shook her hand, then willed herself to stop staring at the girl as if she were a freak. Which she definitely was.

"Okay, Lex," said Uncle Mort. "For your first time, all you have to do is watch. But pay close attention, because it's the only observation run you're gonna get."

"Um — huh?"

Zara laughed. "Don't worry," she said, the intensity fading from her wintry gray eyes. "You'll get the hang of it soon enough."

"All right." Uncle Mort slapped his hands together. "Suit up." Both he and Zara unfolded the balls of black fabric they had been carrying and slid them over their heads. Uncle Mort reached into his pocket. "And for you, Lex, a lightweight, durable, thermo-regulated — oh." He stopped and scrutinized her. "You already have the uniform?"

They looked at one another. All three were wearing identical black hoodies.

Uncle Mort scratched his head. "Did I give that to you this morning?"

"No, this is what I always wear. Actually," she said, a curious memory suddenly occurring to her, "didn't you send this as a thirteenth birthday present?"

"Did I?" he said, his mouth upturning ever so slightly. "How reprehensibly irresponsible of me."

Lex looked at Zara, who shrugged.

Lex clapped her hands together. "Well, let's get this show on the road!" she said in an overly chipper voice. "Bring on the death! These souls aren't going to reap themselves!"

Uncle Mort looked about ready to smack her, but instead stretched a tight smile across his lips. "I can't wait to see the look on her face," he muttered to Zara, who snickered. He turned back to Lex. "You. Hop up onto my back."

Lex's sarcastic smile disappeared. "Huh?"

"Get onto my back and hold on as tight as you can."

She backed away. "Hell no. Last time I did that, you almost splattered me across the pavement."

"I know it's weird, but it's only for training purposes. Come on."

"No way. You're probably going to fling me into a volcano or something."

"If you don't climb up here right now, I absolutely will."

Lex ultimately decided not to test this. She put her hands on her uncle's shoulders, hopped up off the ground, and tucked her legs into his sides. "And no kicking the yarbles," he warned.

"No promises."

He secured her grip around his neck. "We'll take it easy for your first time, start off with a simple geezer. After that, it's full throttle. Like I said, pay close attention, because it'll be over before you even know it. But the most important thing is: don't panic. Don't scream, don't close your eyes, and above all, do not let go of me. Do you understand?"

"Yeah, but — " Lex swallowed, a small lump of nerves now forming in her stomach. What was going on?

Staring at nothing but each other, Zara and Uncle Mort raised their right arms high above their heads — the sun glittering off something shiny in their hands — then brought them down in unison with a quick slicing motion.

Lex, meanwhile, continued to survey the scene in apprehension, trying to guess what could possibly warrant all this melodrama. Here they were, standing perfectly still in the middle of a placid, sun-dappled valley, where it seemed as though nothing exciting had ever happened and probably never would — except there was that rustling bush again. Was there someone behind it? Someone watching?

But it no longer mattered. Lex had been blinked out of existence.

6

Her first sensation was one of dizziness. Lex couldn't tell which way was up, down, in, or out. Her stomach dropped with a lurch, that disquieting but oddly pleasant feeling one gets on the plunge down the first hill of a roller coaster. She sped through the deepest bowels of space, wormholed through galaxies, the whole of the universe swirling around in one unending vortex.

She saw colors — every color, even ones beyond the visible spectrum. The air whipping through her lungs — if one could even call it air, it was more like a gale-force wind that ripped and fought its way down her trachea — stung her nostrils like icy mint. Every inch of her skin prickled, the entire arsenal of its nerve endings exploding into a shivery chill.

But the noise — the noise was deafening. It was as if every sound that had ever been uttered in the history of the world were being played backwards, on maximum volume, at the same time.

Lex fought hard to make sense of it all, tried to focus the distorted images, to extrapolate a single sound from the cacophony (she thought she might have heard a cow mooing), but eventually she gave up and surrendered to the moment. Exhilarated, she screamed into the void, half shrieking, half laughing.

Until everything came to a crashing halt.

Lex couldn't guess how much time had passed. It could have been seconds, it could have been hours. She looked around, disoriented. The only thing she could really be sure of was her uncle's neck, still clenched firmly between her arms.

They were in a dark place. As her vision adjusted, Lex realized that it was a bedroom — cool, quiet, and smelling of musk and chicken soup. Everything seemed blurred around the edges. She scrunched up her eyes.

Lying asleep on a bed in a near-fetal position was an old woman. Framed photos of grandchildren smiled down from the walls, while a veritable pharmacy of pill bottles stood like a tiny city on her nightstand. It was a peaceful scene, what Lex could see of it. She was afraid to breathe, not wanting to disturb anything or wake the woman up — until she noticed that one of the pill bottles had tipped over. It lay on its side, small green pills spilling out over the edge of the table.

But they weren't falling. They were frozen in midair.

Lex's eyes bugged. "What — "

Uncle Mort shushed her. "Watch." He reached out a single white finger and touched the woman on the cheek.

A brilliant flash of white light briefly illuminated the room — the same sort of blaze Lex had seen on the bus ride — along with the strangest noise: a loud pop mixed with a shrill, piercing screech. A sort of mist began to emerge from the woman — a bluish-tinged light gently flowing out of her body, floating through the air like an unearthly aurora.

Lex exhaled. It was the most beautiful thing she had ever seen.

Zara stretched her hand toward the light. It seemed to obey her movements, gracefully swirling into her open fingers as if it were eager to be collected. She carefully guided it into a spherical container — Lex couldn't tell what it was — until the last wisps disappeared and the light was gone, fading from the air with an almost human sigh.

Zara put the container back into her pocket and withdrew the shiny object again. She and Uncle Mort swiped them through the air in unison — drawing them upward this time — and blustered back into the vortex.

Lex let out another screech, every one of her organs flopping in delight. She was still screaming when they landed, minutes or eons later, in the same spot from which they had left. All air gone from her lungs, she slumped down off her uncle's back and began staggering around the grass.

Zara made a face. "Is she going to throw up?"

"Lex?" asked Uncle Mort. "Are you going to throw up?"

"No." Lex coughed. "No, I'm fine. Just give me a sec."

She put her hands over her eyes and tried to breathe evenly. After a beat, she exhaled and dropped her hands to her sides.

"Oh my GOD!" she yelled.

"That's it." Uncle Mort elbowed Zara. "That's the face."

"How did we — where did we — *what was that?*"

"Let me answer that question," Uncle Mort said, reaching into his hoodie pocket, "with a present."

He removed a polished, oblong black rock made of stone so dark it seemed to negate the very idea of light. Riveted, Lex took it from him and ran her fingers over its smooth, impossibly hard surface, ultimately reaching a bump. She grabbed the small protrusion and unfolded it like a penknife, her heart beginning to race as she realized what it was: a curved, razor-sharp blade made out of the same pitch-black stone. It pivoted noiselessly outward and came to a stop at a ninety-degree angle to the handle, forming a crooked *L*.

She held the weapon as if it were made of the brittlest glass, turning it over and over in her hands. She never would have thought it possible to fall in love with an inanimate object, but in this case, as in many cases, love didn't follow any particular set of rules.

"What is this? A knife?"

"Nope," Uncle Mort said, his eye glinting. "A scythe."

Lex just stared.

"Allow me to explain." Uncle Mort sat on the ground and leaned against the Ghost Gum. "The nothingness — or rather, everythingness — from which we just returned is called the ether," he said as the two girls joined him on the grass. "It is the method of transportation that we use to transfer souls from this life to the next."

Lex listened, engrossed. She hadn't blinked in minutes.

Uncle Mort was pleased with her reaction, as it was finally not one of disgust or outrage or both. "We always work in pairs, because there are two types of Field jobs — Killers and Cullers. You and I are Killers," he said plainly. "With a single touch, a Killer officially ends the life of a human being by releasing the Gamma, or soul, from the body."

"That was a soul?" Lex said in awe.

"Zara, on the other hand, is a Culler. It's her job to collect the soul, place it in a secure Vessel, and provide safe passage back here to Croak, where it's processed and put into storage, so to speak."

"Vessel?"

Zara handed her a small white sphere about the size of a baseball. Lex cupped her hands around its soft surface and marveled at the silky strands that were woven together to form its shape.

Lex gave it back to Zara, then scanned Uncle Mort's face for an explanation. "So wait," she said, her mind numb. "I actually have to Kill people?"

"Have to? No. You don't *have* to do anything. But you're here because you're special, and you're special because — well, I don't like throwing around words like 'destiny,' but let's put it this way: this job chose you. Whether or not you reciprocate is completely your call."

Lex didn't know what to say. Her throat was dry.

She flicked open her scythe again and began absent-mindedly pitching it from one hand to the other, but Uncle Mort quickly snatched it out of the air. "A scythe is not a toy," he scolded. "It's your closest friend, most valuable tool, and a handy lockpick in a pinch, but never a toy." He gingerly placed it back in her hand. "Scything is how we break into the ether to get to our targets. In order for us to do our work, we need to get in and out as quickly and effectively as possible. That's where the scythe comes in." He pulled out his own scythe, a slightly larger weapon made out of —

Lex nearly choked. "Is that *diamond?*"

"Yes. Each scythe is made from a different metal, rock, or mineral. The material of your scythe says something about your personality . . . or something. I don't know, I don't really buy into any of that hippie crap." Zara stifled a laugh. "Suffice it to say that your scythe is tailored to you, and you alone," he said. "Treat it right, and it'll serve you with the utmost faith and loyalty to the bitter end."

"But how did you get diamond?"

"Beats me. It's the hardest naturally occurring mineral, right? And I'm . . . hardheaded? A hard nut to crack? Hard on the eyes? I don't know, pick your favorite. Check out Zara's."

Zara held up her scythe, made from a brilliant silver. "Self-explanatory."

"What's mine?" asked Lex, running her fingers over the cold stone.

"Obsidian," said Uncle Mort. "One of the smoothest, sharpest blades known to man. Used in surgeries, actually."

Lex interrupted before he could launch into what was undoubtedly a creepily vast knowledge of medical supplies. "But what does it mean?"

He scratched at his stubbly chin. "Obsidian is a type of glass formed from igneous rock, found in lava flows around volcanoes. Fiery and explosive — I'd say that's you in a nutshell."

Lex turned her scythe over in her hands once more, unable to take her eyes off it. "It's amazing."

"And so dark, too," said Zara. "I've never seen one that dark before."

Uncle Mort rolled his eyes. "So it's agreed, the scythe is totally dreamy." He stood up and grinned that unglued smile again. "But it's nothing more than a butter knife until you put it into action."

"Um —"

"Unfortunately," he continued in a voice that suggested there was nothing unfortunate about this at all, "there's no such thing as a practice run when it comes to scything. You just have to jump right in and pray that all of your body parts make it with you."

Lex got to her feet, her knuckles blazingly white against the ebony of the scythe. "Now?" she said nervously. "Just like that?"

"I thought you wanted to be spared the pleasantries."

Zara stood up. "Try to visualize the air around you as a viscous, fluid substance that can be physically ripped," she told Lex. "Grasp the scythe firmly in your hands — you'll want to use both for your first time — then bring it down as hard and fast as you can in a sort of hacking motion and give your wrist a little flick at the end, like you're throwing a Frisbee."

"Then jump through," added Uncle Mort. "Simple."

"Wait," Lex said. "Jump through what?"

"Be ready to go in a couple minutes." He twirled his own scythe like a pistol, shoved it into his pocket, and walked a few feet away, poking at his Cuff. "I just need to call the Bank, tell them you're ready to go."

Lex turned to Zara. "What does the Bank have to do with anything?"

"Well, the Bank isn't really a bank," Zara said. "It's more like command central for all of Croak. The people who work there are like air traffic controllers, programming our scythes for transport routes to the appropriate targets. Each time a new death is put into play, they relay it out to whichever team is free to grab it."

They were silent for a moment. Lex looked up at the ghostly branches of the tree. "This can't be real," she muttered to herself.

Zara looked at her. "Doesn't get much realer."

"But seriously. We really have the power to whack people?"

Zara let out an exasperated huff, as if she'd been over this countless times before. "We're not hit men, Lex. We don't *cause* death. We're just there to pick up the pieces."

"Huh?"

"Okay, a guy's head is chopped off. He's dead, right? But his soul isn't. Our job is to remove that live soul from the dead body. In the space of a yoctosecond — that's one septillionth of a second — after death, we jump in through the ether to within an arm's length of the target, Kill and Cull, then leave."

"Then why is the term 'Killer,' if the targets are already dead?"

Zara looked almost surprised at the question. "Gammas are our entire *lives*. Everything that's happened to us, everyone we've met, every feeling we've ever felt. A body — even a physically dead one — is technically still alive if the soul is inside. So what a Killer really does is remove the very last part of what makes a person human. If that's not Killing, I don't know what is." She eyed Lex. "Souls live on without their bodies. But bodies without souls are nothing but compost."

With that, Zara settled into a patient stance and looked at her fingernails, her silver hair blinding in the sunlight. Lex, on the other hand, felt strongly that she should start screaming. The very curious part of her brain that Uncle Mort had talked about had swelled and expanded so pervasively that Lex feared she'd have to bore a hole in her skull to relieve the pressure.

Zara turned to her. "Are you having fun?"

Lex was thrown. "Am I supposed to?"

"I don't know," said Zara with a quizzical stare. "But I bet you'll do really well here. You're . . . different."

Lex narrowed her eyes. "Different how?"

"Ready, kiddo?" Uncle Mort interrupted as he approached. "You're good to go. You'll do a short shift of five targets with Zara, and then tomorrow we'll set you up with your new partner."

"Zara's not my partner?"

"Nope, she's a sub, just here today to help with training," he said as Zara removed a Cuff from her own pocket and put it on. "Now, under most circumstances, threesomes aren't allowed, but

I'll be jumping in for the first target to observe your work. Pay no attention to me, just concentrate on what you're doing. Zara will call for help if you run into any problems." He tapped his Cuff. "Cooperate with her, follow her lead, and never lose focus. But most important of all," he said, his voice lowering, "you must believe with every fiber of your being that these people's lives have come to a close. Trust that you're doing the right thing by touching them, because you are — no matter what."

Lex gulped. "What happens if I don't?"

"Then their souls will be trapped in their bodies forever. Believe me, you do not want to be the one responsible for obliterating someone's right to an everlasting afterlife." He leaned in almost threateningly. "But that's not going to happen, is it? You have a job to do now, Lex, and you sure as shit are going to do it. Do you understand?"

"Yeah, but — " Her mouth felt like a desert. What was wrong with her? Back home, Tyrannosaurus Lex would have had no problem with dishing out this sort of destruction. She would have jumped into the ether in an instant, breezing past these two without a care in the world and maybe even giving them concussions on the way.

But Lex knew how hollow that badass part of her really was. All those little outbursts of violence — they seemed so empty and meaningless now that she faced a task of such profound importance. Nothing had prepared her for this.

Lex gazed up at her uncle, the weight and reality of the situation finally sinking in. "I don't know if I can do this."

He nodded warmly, sensing the change in her. "I think you can."

Lex licked her lips, looked around at her small circle of compatriots, and tightened her grip on the scythe. Inhaling deeply, she raised it above her head and sliced it down through the air just as Zara had instructed.

Her body immediately tensed. She hadn't expected to meet resistance — in the middle of thin air? Still, she kept tearing, remembering to cut the scythe at an angle toward the bottom, until a rip in the fabric of space eerily appeared before her — a defined yet wavy line, like the blurred wetness rising from a highway in the scorching sun.

"Slide in," Uncle Mort said.

Lex eyed the breach. Unsure, she leaned closer and closer until the laws of gravity imploded once more. A whirlwind of invigoration washed over her like a monsoon, drenching every atom of her body.

Eventually the chaos screeched to a bizarrely silent halt. Frozen in front of her was a middle-aged man on a gurney, his chest cracked open and exposed in all of its shiny, disgusting glory. Lex peered through the smudged air at the sterile white walls, the kind that could only belong to an operating room. A team of doctors and nurses surrounded the man, their faces locked into expressions of worry and determination. One surgeon had cupped his hands around the patient's heart to massage it back to life.

His efforts had obviously been fruitless. "Do it!" Zara said to Lex. "It's safe, go ahead!"

Lex swallowed, the image of the glistening heart searing itself into her memory. She'd never seen anything so terrifyingly real.

Wincing, she held up her hand, slowly extended her finger, and touched it to the man's shoulder.

A jolt shot through her body with the sheer force and brilliance of an exploding supernova.

Lex gasped.

This wasn't like the ether.

The ether was giddy and fun, but this — whatever it was — this was *excruciating*.

Both body and mind were racked with an electrical current the likes of which Lex had never experienced — an almost otherworldly sensation pulsing up and down her twitching nerves, tearing into the very depths of her —

"Lex?" Uncle Mort said.

She blinked hard as the surge subsided. She threw a desperate glance at her uncle, who for some reason looked impressed rather than concerned. Zara's expression, on the other hand, was the strangest conglomeration of awe, horror, surprise, jealousy, anger, and the slightest hint of — was it curiosity?

But it passed just as quickly as it had surfaced, her face melting back into a look of concentration as she finished Culling the glowing Gamma and placed it in the Vessel. "Scythe, now," Zara instructed.

Lex could barely breathe. "Wait — I can't — "

"Come on." Zara grabbed Lex's hand as they simultaneously scythed back into the ether —

— and out just as fast, this time without Uncle Mort. They now stood in an alley. A homeless person of indeterminable gender lay slumped on the ground.

"Go," Zara said.

"But it burns," Lex gasped.

This time Zara's face gave away nothing. "Come on, hurry up."

Lex shot her a pained, pleading look, but she knew now that

it wouldn't get her anywhere. She had a job to do, and she sure as shit was going to do it. So she closed her eyes, held out her finger, and entered the world of pain once more.

Once Zara finished Culling and they had scythed to the mangled wreckage of a car accident, Lex didn't even bother to glance at the blood splattered across the broken windshield before jabbing her finger into the driver's arm. Anything to get it over with as soon as possible. Upon their arrival at a hospital, she barely noticed the sobbing family members alongside the cancer patient's bed as she extended her touch. And when they landed in a posh living room where a young man lay splayed out across a couch, it wasn't until after she had rapped him on the noggin that she registered the gleaming red bullet hole in his chest. And the startled look on his face. And the —

"Good job," Zara said in a voice that sounded less than sincere. "Let's head back."

Zara prepared to scythe, but Lex had not joined her. She was staring at the door to the kitchen.

A figure was standing there, watching them.

And aiming a gun.

7

"Who is that?" Lex asked.

Zara looked up. "Who?"

"That woman over there — she's watching us!"

"No she's not, no one can see us. Come on, scythe up-ward — that'll always automatically return you back to Croak."

"But she has a gun!"

"It doesn't matter! She's frozen in time, she can't shoot it."

Lex felt a stab of relief, one that quickly melted into dread. "She murdered him."

"Let's go, Lex."

Lex's hands suddenly grew very hot. "But we can't just let her get away with it!" she protested, lunging toward the woman. Something had taken hold of her. It was similar to the inexplicable rage she felt all the time, but — no, it was so much more than that —

"Lex!"

Without missing a beat, Zara grabbed her arm, slashed the silver blade up through the air, and yanked her back into the ether.

|||||||

Whereas Zara landed back in the Field with a graceful hop, Lex crashed to the ground like a newborn giraffe. She was about to begin yelling, and maybe even punching, but Uncle Mort started in before she could ball her hand into a fist.

"Damn, Lex!" he said as she jumped to her feet, his face beaming with pride. "That was the smoothest first Kill I've ever seen! How do you feel?"

Her rage briefly subsided at this generous outpouring of praise, though her hands still felt abnormally warm and tingly. "I feel . . ." She was at a loss for words. What exactly should she be feeling? Guilt over the lives she had just ended? Lingering pain from the brutal shocks? Rage over the woman who had gotten away? Or — and she suspected this was the most appropriate option — shame over the fact that she was apparently so good at it all?

"Conflicted," she finally said.

"I knew it from the start, you're a natural." He patted her on the back. "How did you do on the others?"

"Actually — "

"Fine," Zara said.

Lex's jaw dropped. She started to object, but the look Zara shot her could have silenced a pack of screech monkeys.

"Overdose, car wreck, cancer, GSW," Zara rattled off. "Great job, all around."

They were interrupted by Uncle Mort's Cuff. "That'll be Norwood. Hang on a sec," he said, walking away to yell at his wrist.

Zara looked at Lex. "You're welcome."

"Are you out of your mind? We just let a murderer off the hook for no reason!"

"We have plenty of reason," Zara said under her breath. "Do you have any idea how much trouble you could have gotten into?

I just saved your ass back there! Just stick to the plan from now on, okay?"

Lex opened her mouth to tell Zara exactly where she'd like to stick such a plan, but Uncle Mort had finished his call, so she was forced to let it go. But she continued to glare at Zara, who now had a smug look on her face.

"Getting late," Uncle Mort said. "You ready to head home?"

"Already?" Lex glanced up in disbelief at the darkening sky. Hadn't she eaten breakfast only a little while ago?

"I told you time flies." He turned to face Zara. "Thanks for your help, Zar."

"No problem. And good luck tomorrow," she told Lex. "You'll need it."

"Why?"

"Oh, no reason," she said as she walked back toward town. "Your partner is just an acquired taste, that's all."

Lex snorted. "Who around here isn't?"

||||||

The second she entered the kitchen, Lex realized she was famished. "I'm about to gnaw my arm off," she said to Uncle Mort. "What's for dinner?"

"Dinner?" He seemed confused. "I already gave you breakfast."

"Well, on most planets, guardians feed their kids three meals a day."

"That seems excessive."

"What are your feelings on frozen pizza?" a third voice asked.

The boy from that morning stood idly in the doorframe, once again wearing that maddening smirk. "Mort doesn't really believe in cooking," he said, swinging into the room. He opened the freezer door and nimbly transferred a pie from the box to the microwave. "He calls it a waste of time and sulfuric acid."

Lex attempted to disguise the mangled expression of intrigue and annoyance that had involuntarily appeared on her face. "And you would know because you're his . . ."

"Pool boy."

"There is no pool!" She turned to Uncle Mort, the ire rising once again. "What is he *doing* here?"

Uncle Mort heaved an overdramatic shrug. "What are any of us doing here, really?" he said, waving his hands philosophically.

"Jesus. You're both evil."

"That's no way to talk about your uncle," her uncle said.

"Or your partner," Driggs added.

"What?" Lex squawked, a whole new stew of emotions bubbling over. Not knowing what else to do, she grabbed the salt shaker and hurled it at him, followed by the pepper. "*You're* my partner?"

Driggs caught both items and began to juggle. "Yes, he is," said Uncle Mort. "And in case you've forgotten, you still have a full week of training left — training that I can easily cancel and turn into a one-way ticket back home if you keep acting like a troglodyte." Lex frowned, but lowered the sugar bowl she had readied. "So you two better find a way to get along. Now hug it out."

"No way." She eyed Driggs. "I'm not hugging that."

"Oh yes you are." Uncle Mort was enjoying this little show. "Befriend or else."

She had no choice. Careful to avoid Driggs's gaze, Lex reluctantly entered into the frosty embrace.

"You have no intention of befriending, do you?" Driggs whispered.

"I'd rather take a bath with a toaster."

Oblivious to their murmurs, Uncle Mort gave a satisfied nod as they withdrew. Driggs, a mischievous look in his blue eye, removed the half-cooked pizza from the microwave, sliced it into two sloppy halves, and gestured for Lex to follow him. "We're gonna go do some trust falls, okay, Mort?" he said, disappearing with the plates out the door.

"Yeah, okay," Uncle Mort muttered as they went outside. "Go bond."

Lex watched Driggs clamber up a ladder with their dinner. "Climb," he said.

There comes a time in every young girl's life when she is instructed by a complete stranger to scale a tall ladder for dinner atop a roof, and in almost every case the best thing to do is refuse and run home to call the asylum from which the stranger escaped. But after a day of ending people's lives and slicing through space and time with a magical switchblade, Lex figured another heaping dose of absurdity couldn't hurt.

So she grabbed at the rungs and flung herself up onto the gently sloped surface. "Here," Driggs said, tossing her a slice.

Unfortunately, Lex and projectiles had never gotten along very well. She caught it, fumbled, and watched as it sailed gracefully to the ground.

Lex, who had hoped to keep her athletic incompetence a secret for at least more than a day in this new town, sat down to stew and reflect on this maddening situation. Here she was, throwing her dinner off the roof in front of a strange kid with whom she'd soon be working in close proximity on a daily basis and who, for reasons she still couldn't ascertain, was immune to her usual threats. How could she be partners with a boy who had so whimsically inserted himself into her life and who had the audacity to ignore her belligerence?

Peeved, she gazed down into the valley at Croak's few sparkling lights. She could just make out the craggy branches of the Ghost Gum in the moonlight, its nest a small dot against the dark sky.

Driggs silently handed her the remainder of his own pizza, then watched with amusement as she wrestled with how to humbly accept it. Eventually she gave up on decorum and shoved the whole thing into her mouth in about two bites, a messy decision that she instantly regretted.

"You've got sauce in your nostril," Driggs informed her.

Lex sighed. "Of course I do." She grabbed a nearby leaf and tended to the situation. "Better?"

"Radiant." He smiled, leaned back on his elbows, and watched her expectantly.

Lex stared back, confused. She grabbed the leaf and dabbed at her face again, but he still wouldn't look away. "What?"

"Don't you have any questions? I mean, Mort loves his secrets, and Zara never elaborates on anything, especially not to rookies. Which means that if you want any answers, I'm your guy."

"What could you possibly tell me that I can't learn from the back of a children's menu?"

He sat up. "I know why you were brought to Croak. Do you?"

Lex inhaled sharply. She had craved nothing but information since she arrived, and now here it was, dangling in front of her like a tantalizing venti caramel macchiato. "No, why?" she said hungrily, forgetting all rules of personal space as she grabbed at his shirt. *"Why?"*

"Relax, spaz." He laughed, rocking back onto his elbows. "You're here because of a textbook spike in misanthropic tendencies and violent behavior. The one thing we all have in common."

There it was, spelled right out for her. An explanation. Lex's heart leaped so high, she wouldn't have been surprised if it jumped out of her chest and started tap-dancing across the shingles. After all this time, all the questioning, all the detentions — a concrete answer. She couldn't wait to tell Cordy —

She grimaced. Cordy. They'd gone a whole day without talking.

This was a first.

Lex put it out of her mind. She'd book the guilt trip later.

"All of us used to be holy terrors," Driggs went on. "The wild streaks fade as soon as we get here," he said, eyeing her clawing hand, "though in some cases, it may take longer."

"Sorry," Lex stammered, letting go of his shirt. She cleared her throat. "Is that what happened to you?"

"Yep. I have not always been the bastion of virtue I am today. One minute I was an immaculate child, the next, a savage little criminal. Got into fights, did drugs, stole stuff. Got caught a few times, but I didn't care."

"What about your parents?"

"They didn't care either."

Lex thought this was very sad, but she decided not to say so. "How did you end up here?"

He brightened. "That would be Mort's doing. Showed up one

night and offered me the chance to do something productive with my life."

"And you went with him?" Lex asked, doubtful. "Willingly?"

"Mort's a persuasive guy."

"What did your parents say?"

Driggs looked away and was silent. "They didn't object," he said after a moment.

Lex winced. She had never been any good at that whole consolation thing. "Good pizza," she uttered instead, immediately loathing herself.

"Yeah," he said sardonically. "Mama Celeste is a culinary genius."

Lex swallowed this indignity and pressed on. "But why do you live with Uncle Mort?" Her eyes bulged in terror. "We're not related, are we?"

"No!" he said a little too quickly. "I mean, no."

"So . . . no?"

"Right. No." He ran a hand through his hair, the roof's atmosphere rapidly sinking into a cesspool of embarrassment. "Uh, due to extenuating circumstances, Mort recruited me when I was fourteen, and not sixteen like everyone else. I couldn't really live in the dorm with the older kids yet, so he let me stay at his house — and four years later I still haven't left. I like to keep the guy company," he said with affection. "His demented ramblings warm the cockles of my heart."

"So wait a minute. How many other kids are here?"

"There are seven of us Juniors in training — now eight, counting you."

"And you all do the same kind of stuff I learned today?"

"Yeah, more or less. Think of it as an internship. Lasts five years, until you turn twenty-one. Then you become a Senior."

Lex looked back at the Ghost Gum tree again, her mind swimming. Here they were, talking about all this as if it were a fun little summer camp, when in reality Lex had encountered people today in the very last moments of their lives and then proceeded to *end* them. It just didn't feel right.

But it didn't feel wrong, either.

"I don't get it," she said. "I mean, why teenagers? Why pick the most immature people on earth to handle such a huge responsibility?"

Driggs looked up at the stars, then back at Lex. "You know *Charlie and the Chocolate Factory*?"

Lex stared.

"The world of pure imagination?" he added.

"I'm familiar with the world of pure imagination," Lex said dryly. "I'm just skeptical as to how manufacturing candy is in any way similar to reaping mortal souls."

"You know how at the end, Willy Wonka gives Charlie the factory?" Driggs went on. "Do you remember the reason he chose a child?"

"Yeah, he said adults would want to do everything their own way, whereas a child — "

"Would learn all the secrets," said Driggs, "and keep them secret." He flicked a pebble off the roof. "I mean, now that you've seen what really goes on here, have you thought for even a second of ratting us out?"

"No, but — " The wordless anxiety that had been pumping through her veins ever since Uncle Mort touched that old woman came spilling out all at once. "I just find it disturbing that people — we ordinary, mortal, dumbass people — are in charge of all this. And we've covered it up for, what, millennia? You really expect me to believe that?"

"Just because it's the biggest secret in the history of the world doesn't make it any less true."

Even Lex couldn't think of a snarky answer to this.

"Did I just blow your mind?" Driggs asked. "I think I just blew your mind." With that, he pulled out a handful of at least a dozen Oreos from his pocket and shoved three into his mouth. "Tho, whatthu thik of theeeetha?" he asked, spraying her with cookie bits.

Lex picked a crumb out of her hair. "Pardon?"

"Sorry. The ether," he repeated, giving her a cookie. "What do you think of it?"

"I don't know," she said, chewing thoughtfully. "Loud? Turbulent? Really outstandingly fun?" She thought back to the swirling void. "Why is it like that?"

Driggs shrugged. "I think it has something to do with the fact that you're traveling through every bit of humanity that's ever existed, but all at once. Unfathomable profundity plus weightlessness plus pretty colors equals highly enjoyable."

"And highly addictive. I could fly around in that thing all day. It's heaven compared to the torture of Killing."

Driggs sat up abruptly, spilling a couple of Oreos onto the shingles. "What torture?"

Lex looked at him, perplexed. "Touching the targets. When it happens, that shock you get."

He frowned.

"You know what I mean, right?" Lex continued, concerned.

"Feels like electrocution? Trust me, I touched an exposed wire when I was ten, and it was nothing compared to this."

"That's — " Driggs looked worried. "That's not supposed to happen."

Lex's neck prickled. "What do you mean? I'm not making it up."

He studied her more seriously now. "I'm not saying you are."

Lex tried to wipe the anxiety off her face, but her wiping mechanism seemed to be broken. "Maybe it's different for Cullers."

Driggs shook his head slowly, never breaking his gaze. "No, it's the same for everyone, whether Killing or Culling. You only feel a tiny pinch in your finger, like a static shock."

"Oh," said Lex. Should she go on? Or drop it? Maybe this was one of those things that people should keep to themselves, like a hatred of baby pandas or a passion for polka music. Everyone needs a secret or two.

But what made her so different?

Driggs was still staring her down. "Why didn't you say anything about this before?"

"You mean, why didn't I bring up this one ludicrous thing amidst the billions of other ludicrous things that happened today? I don't know, good question. I'll get back to you on that."

"It's just kind of a big deal, is all."

"Well, I'm kind of a big deal."

A smile spread across his face. "I can see that."

Lex exhaled irritably, dying to change the subject. "Forget it, okay? God, you're worse than Zara."

He laughed. "I doubt that. Nobody's worse than Zara. What did she do to you?"

Lex shrugged. "Nothing. I mean, she was nice at first, then sort of a bitch, then — I don't even know what."

"Don't take it personally," he said. "This happens every year. The girl hates rookies. She's the best Junior in Croak, so she gets all huffy and competitive when new people invade her turf. And since you've already gotten so much attention, the jealousy is probably eating her alive."

"Attention?" Lex let out a small breath of disbelief. "From who?"

Driggs looked startled, as if realizing he had said more than he should have. "Nothing big, just little rumors here and there. Everyone's curious about how you'll do — you know, since you're Mort's niece and all."

As if on cue, a large puff of smoke mushroomed out of the basement window and drifted up past the roof.

"Yeah, lucky me," Lex said, sniffing the air.

"He makes it hard to tell, but Mort's actually a certified genius. You should see the lab he's got down there. Tons of gadgets, experiments, satellite dishes, who knows what else. He's the one who invented Cuffs — brilliant idea, using ether-infused iron to get around the dead reception zones. And he knows more about Croak than anyone. Plus, he's in charge of scouting out new Juniors — I have no idea how he finds them, but every year he does, hones in on them like a laser beam. It's a gift, I guess."

"Yeah, well, it doesn't make up for his lack of sanity. Or parental instincts. Or decorating skills. Did you see that hideous display of girlish vomit that was supposed to be my room?"

"Oh? You didn't like it?"

"Hell no."

"Why not? *Titanic* is a timeless classic. The ultimate love story. One of the most towering achievements in cinematic — "

"Wait a damn minute," Lex interrupted as his straight face began to crack. "*You* did that? On purpose?"

"Don't girls like *Titanic*?"

To her credit, Lex really had tried. She had actually managed to converse with someone her own age for an extended period of time without feeling the need to hurl him off the roof.

But this — this was unforgivable. So she balled her hand into a fist, reared back her arm, and slugged him right in the blue eye. She gulped down a breath of cool night air. That felt so *good*.

Until another heavy *smack* echoed into the sky. A spasm of pain ripped through her face, her vision bursting into stars.

"You hit back?!" she shouted.

Driggs was gaping in disbelief at his own hand. Slowly, he recovered and looked into her good eye. "I had a feeling you'd be more insulted if I didn't."

Lex stared back. He couldn't have been more right.

"You can't hit a girl," she said, rubbing her face.

"You hit me first."

"So?"

"So I was defending myself."

Lex huffed. This was going terribly. "You can't do that!"

"It seems I just did," he replied with a stilted laugh.

She scowled. "You are *not* normal."

"Neither are you," he said with a wry smirk. "And don't worry, Lex — now that you're one of us, no one'll make the mistake of thinking so ever again."

8

The next morning, while Lex snuggled comfortably in bed, a crash of cymbals exploded in her ear. She opened her eyes to behold Driggs clanging them vigorously, a mischievous grin on his face and a large bruise surrounding his eye.

"I hope, for the sake of your fertility, you're wearing a cup," she warned through clenched teeth.

"Come on," he said, jumping onto the mattress. "It's time for work."

Lex moaned. "How are you so awake already?"

"If you recall, I eat a lot of chocolate."

Ten minutes and two fights over the bathroom later, they slid into their seats at the kitchen table. Uncle Mort took one look at their matching black eyes and nodded.

"Yep," he said to himself, drifting back to his newspaper. "That's about what I expected."

||||||

After breakfast, the trio headed out into the fiery morning sun and made their way into town.

Lex yawned. In addition to the pain in her swollen eye, the faces of those she had Killed kept her up half the night. Haunting images — the exposed heart, the yellowed-newspaper skin of the old woman, the gunshot in the man's chest — churned through her head like a nightmarish whirlpool. Plus, she still couldn't get used to sleeping in a room all by herself. She thought about Cordy, who was undoubtedly ready to throttle her by now. Lex hadn't called, she hadn't written, she couldn't even email. Unless...

"Do you have Internet here?" she asked as they neared the Bank.

"For what?" Driggs asked.

"E-mail."

He gave her a sideways glance. "Who are you e-mailing?"

"My sister. Any more questions, Dad?"

"Knock it off," Uncle Mort told her as they climbed the Bank stairs. "And pay attention. You're starting a typical Junior work-day. Five hours in the morning, hour break for lunch, then five more in the afternoon."

"Good Lord."

"Enjoy it while you can — Seniors get fourteen-hour shifts. But it's not that bad," he said upon seeing her dumbfounded face. "Time gets lost in the ether, remember? Five hours only feels like two." He stopped on the porch to take a swig of lemonade. "So here's the drill. Every morning you'll come here to the Bank to check in with the Etceteras."

"Wait, what?"

"Etceteras. ETC stands for Ether Traffic Controllers, and the nickname just evolved from there."

"What does that make us, then?"

"Well, technically," said Uncle Mort, "we're called Gamma Removal and Immigration Managers — "

"But are more commonly known as Grims," Driggs said.

"Can't say I approve of the term." Uncle Mort flourished his razor-sharp scythe and smiled. "We're not that grim, are we?"

Lex snickered.

Uncle Mort finished his lemonade and opened the door to the Bank. "Hi, Kilda," he said hastily as they walked through the foyer.

Kilda beamed. "Good morning! Wonderful to see you!"

"Sorry, terrible hurry."

"Have a resplendent day!"

Once they got to the hallway, Uncle Mort opened a door on the right to reveal a large, sleek office, its atmosphere wildly out of place compared with the rest of the folksy Bank. Buzzing and whirling in a form of controlled chaos, it reminded Lex of an ul-tramodern secret government facility — or at least the ones on television. A man in a suit was barking orders, and a handful of other people sat at machines that looked sort of like computers, but not quite. A large aquarium spanned the far wall, the jellyfish within glowing a bright blue, as if fiercely trying to do their part to contribute to the futuristic feel of the place.

"This," Uncle Mort said, gesturing to the room, "is the hub, where all of our scything is controlled and monitored. The peo-ple who work here are very good at what they do, so do not — I repeat, do not — get on their bad side."

"Who, me?" Lex said in an innocent voice.

"Don't start, Lex. Norwood!" He walked over to the yelling man in the suit. "Lex, this is Norwood, director of Ether Traffic Control. Norwood, this is my niece, our newest Killer."

The man assessed her with a cold glower, the same look he had given her the day before in the hallway. "Scythe," he said gruffly, holding out his hand. Lex looked at Driggs, who handed his over. She reluctantly did the same, then watched as Norwood plugged them both into the side of his computer.

"And here's his lovely wife and codirector, Heloise," said Uncle Mort. "Morning, Hel." An equally loathsome woman approached, slender and severe, wearing an expensive suit and a fierce scowl.

She nodded. "Mort." Her auburn hair, pulled into a tight bun, didn't move an inch. Disarmed, Lex backed up against the desk, knocking a stapler to the floor.

Norwood grunted. "They get more incompetent every year, don't they, Mort?" He ran a hand through his dry, gray-streaked brown hair. Lex half expected a puff of ash to dust up out of it. "Sooner or later, one of 'em's bound to burn down the town as soon as they set foot in it."

"Oh, I don't know," Uncle Mort said distractedly, thumbing through a stack of papers. "I don't think Dead End is very flammable."

Norwood leaned in to Lex, close enough to audibly sniff at her. "What'd you do to your eye? Get too close to a mirror?"

Lex narrowed her eyes at him. "Well, aren't you a bucket of sunshine."

Heloise walked to her husband's side, her sharp heels rapping ominously across the floor. "Destructive *and* sarcastic," she said, clicking her tongue and flashing Lex a hollow smile. "Lucky us."

Uncle Mort jumped in before things got any hairier. "Orientation, Norwood. Go."

Norwood took a deep breath, then flew through his prepared speech in a disinterested monotone. "For your first week, you must check in for all shifts with either myself or Heloise. No complaints, no whining, no special requests. After checking in, head directly out to the Field for your first shift. No detours, no chitchat, no coffee breaks."

He sat down at his desk and began to peck at the strange keyboard, which contained a jumbled series of symbols rather than letters and numbers, as well as several oddly shaped buttons. Lex followed the machine's cables down to the floor, where they merged with others and wound their way through the various workstations, finally connecting to the bottom of the large jellyfish aquarium on the far wall of the office.

"What's with all the —"

"Jellyfish detect death," he continued, anticipating her question. "All incoming Gamma signals arrive through them and only them. They work in a gigantic global network, each one able to communicate with any other on the planet, no matter the species. We use this system for two reasons: jellyfish exist in every ocean, and their range is infinite. A single jellyfish off the coast of South Africa can pick up a death as far away as Alaska. The energy they exude is so pervasive that it even extends into the ether, thereby powering our ability to scythe to the designated targets. As for the jellyfish tank, no tapping, no thumping, no disturbing."

Lex was once again finding it unbearably difficult to believe a word she was hearing. "And what does this do?" she asked, reaching out to the strange machine. "Does it get Internet?"

"This is a Smack," Norwood said, slapping her hand away. "If I ever catch you touching one, you lose a finger."

Heloise gave Lex a harsh look. "Smacks track and code all incoming Gamma alerts so that we can reroute them to you out in the Field. Without them — and us — you'd be nothing more than a couple of knife-wielding brats playing make-believe."

"And thus concludes Etcetera orientation," Uncle Mort added before any more insults could be hurled.

Norwood glared at him, tapped at a few more keys, and yanked the scythes out of the Smack. "All set," he said, handing them back.

"Thanks. Come on, kids." Uncle Mort gestured at them to follow as he walked out of the room.

Lex started for the door, but once Uncle Mort was out of view, Norwood seized her arm and pointed a finger into her face. "Let's get one thing straight, princess," he growled. "If you ever give us anything less than absolutely stellar work, I'll make you sorry Uncle Nepotism ever smuggled you in here. Got that?"

Heloise leaned in to whisper in her ear. Lex could feel her hot breath on her cheek, as well as Norwood's icy gaze.

"We are watching you."

"Come on, Lex!" Uncle Mort yelled from the hall.

She broke away from his grip and joined Driggs out in the hall. "What crawled up their butts and died?" she asked him.

"Who knows?" he said as they followed Uncle Mort outside. "But they're like that all the time, so try to space out your contempt. It's healthier that way."

Lex had never been skilled at doing anything with her contempt but causing bodily harm. But strangely enough, Norwood's threat hadn't prompted a single desire to bloody his nose, scratch his eyes out, or follow through on any of her usual violent impulses. In fact, she could even feel the anger dissipating before it could surface, seeping away from her body in calm, measured waves. She contemplated this newfound serenity with a distinct wariness. Driggs had said her ferocity would fade, but overnight?

She thought back to the anger she had felt at the gunshot scene yesterday. Maybe her rage was just becoming more focused on those who deserved it.

But she could sort through all that later. "Is all of that crap he just said about jellyfish really true?" she asked as they made their way to the Field.

Uncle Mort nodded. "You bet."

"And you're the only ones who have discovered this? The scientific world is still in the dark about the mystical powers of death-knelling invertebrates?"

"Biologists don't have access to the same knowledge that we do," said Uncle Mort, "and therefore don't have the technology to fully realize the abilities of our dear gelatinous friends."

Lex opened her mouth, then closed it. What was the point?

"That's why the machines are called Smacks," Driggs said, "because 'smack' is the technical term — "

"For a group of jellyfish," Lex finished.

He looked at her in disbelief. Or admiration. It was hard to tell. "How did you know that?"

"It's not very nice of you to just assume I'm a raging idiot such as yourself."

"Oh, I would never assume what I already know to be true."

"Don't think I won't blacken that other eye."

"Don't think I won't laugh heartily at your futile attempt."

"Kids," said Uncle Mort. "Coexist, please."

Lex scratched her head. "So really, how has this place been kept secret for so long? Are you guys not allowed to leave?"

"Well, Croak isn't a prison," Uncle Mort said. "Grims are free to quit the profession whenever they want. Only one catch: they won't remember a thing about it. And, of course, they can never return."

"That's two catches."

"Hey, the kid can add," said Driggs.

"What happened to *your* old partner?" Lex asked him. "Suicide, I take it?"

He frowned. "Worse — business school. Can you believe it? Two years of Croak, then one day the kid decided he wants to be the next Donald Trump. So we threw him in a car, dropped him off near Woodstock, and now he thinks he spent the past two years in a drug-addled haze at some hippie commune."

"Nice severance package."

"It's for our own protection," Uncle Mort said. "Same fate awaits any Grims who refuse to Kill or Cull their targets, or who breathe a word of any of this to the outside world."

Lex bristled. Total confidentiality? What was she supposed to tell her sister, that she'd been shearing sheep this whole time? Cordy would never buy it.

"Yeah, zero tolerance policy," Driggs said. "One wrong move and you're gone. And not just banned from Croak — from the entire Grimsphere, too. Memory wiped clean, and it's back to your miserable old existence. But that's really rare. A lot of people are in this for life. It's a pretty sweet gig."

"Oh, definitely," Lex said with a bitter edge, thinking back to the uneasiness she had felt while Killing, the faces of yesterday's targets. "Ending people's lives is such a hoot."

Uncle Mort stopped walking and grabbed Lex's elbow. She looked up at him, startled, as he spoke. "Veterinarians don't delight in putting sick animals to sleep, but that's part of the job, isn't it? The alternative would be inhumane." His face was inches from hers, his eyes fiery. "Lex, if you're not just being a smart-ass, if you really do have a problem with all this, now's the time to say so. If you're hesitant, you're a liability, and if you're a liability, you sure as hell are never going to be a Grim."

Lex instantly felt very small. No matter how morally ambivalent she was feeling, one thing was for sure: she didn't want to leave. "No, I — the smart-ass thing. I'm fine. I'm okay with it."

"Good." Uncle Mort let go of her arm and started walking again.

Lex, cowed, followed him. "Except I'm really not okay with that shock that comes with Killing people."

"Oh, the little pinch?" Uncle Mort said, seemingly in better spirits. Lex couldn't keep up with these mood swings of his. "That's nothing. You'll get used to it. I barely even feel it anymore."

"No, I mean the massive shock that feels like I'm jabbing my finger into a power line."

"Really?" Uncle Mort shot her a curious look. "Interesting."

"Actually, no. Painful. Why is it happening? And why only to me?"

He furrowed his brow, lost in thought for a few moments. "I don't know." He shrugged. "Though I'll bet it has something to do with those natural abilities of yours. I've never seen anyone Kill so fast, especially on the first try."

"Huh?"

"Most Killers have to hold their fingers to the target for a second or two, but you Killed instantly. And I can't even count the number of times I've had to jump in to finish the job of a rookie because they couldn't release the Gamma completely. But you did, every time." He glanced at her. "Best rookie Kills I've seen in . . . well, ever."

She swallowed. "What do you think that means?"

"No idea. At the very least, I'd say that it hints at a slew of further potential. Who knows where you could go from here?" He patted her on the back. "I had a feeling you'd be gifted."

Lex crinkled her face. He was making her sound like a nerd.

"Anyway, with talent like yours — Croak isn't the only game in town, you know," Uncle Mort went on, his eyes glinting as they arrived at the Ghost Gum. "There are other cities, other positions. Ladders to be climbed, places you can really go, if you so possessed the ambition."

"Maybe I do."

He looked at her. "Well, that's all a long way off," he said, waving his hand to dismiss the thought. "First you must establish a firm understanding of the fundamentals. It takes a lot of hard work to ascend to a position like mine."

"Why, what are you?"

Driggs let out a snicker as he donned a Cuff. "He's the mayor, Lex."

"What? You never told me that!"

"Details, details," Uncle Mort said. "I'm only in charge of the town and all of the Grims' operations within."

"Oh. Only that."

He gave a modest shrug. "It's not as glamorous as it seems. I miss working out in the Field," he said, touching the Ghost Gum. "So have some fun out there for me. If you run into any problems, I'll be at the library. And remember, you're partners now, so try not to give each other concussions, okay?"

Agreeing to no such thing, Driggs and Lex dug into their pockets and took out their scythes. And since Croak was no different from any other culture — and therefore contained its own equivalent of a pissing contest — the two partners immediately sized up each other's scythes as they tore them through the air.

"Sapphire," Driggs said, waving a gleaming blue weapon.

"Obsidian."

Uncle Mort smirked. "Adorable."

The two rolled their eyes in unison, then disappeared into the ether.

|||||

"For future reference," said Driggs as he Culled the soul of a man trapped under a tractor, "I wouldn't go around telling people about these shocks of yours."

"Why not?" Lex asked.

"It's like announcing to the world that you have crabs. It's embarrassing, and no one'll ever shake your hand again."

"But these feelings are not ones of crotchal itching," she said as they scythed to the bottom of a gorge. She tapped their target, a fallen hiker impaled on a jagged rock, and flinched as the charge coursed through her body. Driggs watched, unnerved. "Why should they be embarrassing? Uncle Mort just said they're from an overdose of talent or whatever."

"They're different. People don't like different. And if Zara found out — trust me, she'd make your life a living hell."

"I think it's too late for that," she murmured, remembering the look Zara had given her.

Lex tried to suppress the shocks for rest of the morning

(which, as Uncle Mort had promised, flew by faster than she could have imagined), but nothing worked. Over the next five hours of Killing, she saw enough death to last for a lifetime of nightmares — car wrecks, geezers, heart attacks, diseases, drugs, suicides, a hodgepodge of other fatalities — and the currents that shot across her nerves seemed to intensify with every target she touched.

And Driggs's reactions certainly weren't helping. By the end of their shift, the looks of bewilderment flashing across his face whenever she Killed were making her want to gouge his eyes out with a melon baller.

"I'm trying, okay?" she finally snapped as they scythed onto the deck of a cruise ship. "But I can't help it! It's rooted in my nervous system or something, it feels like fireworks exploding through my body—" She jabbed the target, jerked back, sucked on her inflamed finger, and looked at Driggs's aghast face. "See? You're staring at me like I'm drowning sackfuls of kittens."

"I'm not—I mean, partly, but it's mostly because you're—" He scratched his ear and seemed almost shy. "You're *really* fast."

"Oh. Um, thanks," she muttered, suddenly very aware of the last time she'd been complimented by a boy (never) and the current condition of her hair (pure chaos). She smoothed it out and tried to change the subject while Driggs Culled the target, a woman nearly burned to cinders in the hot midday sun. "Death by tanning?"

"Nah. Her drink was spiked."

Lex looked at the empty margarita glass sitting next to the lounge chair. "How could you possibly know that?"

"GHB. Date rape drug. Salty taste, almost impossible to detect in a salt-rimmed margarita glass."

"How did you —"

"Experience. Once you've got enough of it, determining cause of death becomes second nature."

The urge to search the ship for the guilty party quickly arose, but Lex remembered what Zara had told her the day before, and she reluctantly held it in check. "Oh, really?" she said nonchalantly as they scythed into the stands of a jam-packed baseball stadium. "Then how did this guy die?"

She pointed at the target, a man bent over his souvenir program. Lex looked around, dazed. There was just something eerie about the silent scene of thirty-eight thousand screaming fans fixed in mid-cheer, players hovering in petrified dives toward the bases, and stationary beer splashing its thick globules across the stands.

"Experience," Driggs said, frowning, "can also be a fickle mistress." He peered at the field, then dropped to the ground.

"What are you doing?"

"Looking for a ball," he said from underneath the seats. "Maybe he was hit by a line drive."

"Yeah, right. I loathe sports as much as the next marginally intelligent being, but even I know a ball could never reach all the way up here. And even if it could, it wouldn't be fatal."

"True." He straightened up to examine the man more closely. "No visible signs of injury, doesn't look like he's having any health problems. Go ahead, touch him." Lex obliged, though something about this scene was starting to feel very off.

Driggs's concern grew as he Culled the Gamma. "It's like he just . . . stopped living. Maybe —"

He stopped abruptly, dropping to the floor once again. He

peered up at the man's face. "Look at this," he said, his voice strange.

Lex crouched down beside him. "Whoa."

The man's eyes were completely white.

Lex frowned. "What's wrong with him?"

"I don't know." Driggs nervously shoved the Vessel into his pocket as they scythed once more, this time automatically returning to the Ghost Gum.

Lex looked in surprise at the sun, directly overhead. Their shift was over already? She'd never be able to get used to this time-warping business.

Driggs, meanwhile, was pacing back and forth. "I've never seen anything like that."

"What do you mean?"

"I've been doing this for four years, and I've been able to find the cause of every single death." He swallowed. "But that guy — I have no idea."

Lex thought. "Heart attack?"

Driggs shook his head. "You can't die from a heart attack that fast. There would have been at least some sign of distress."

"Poison? Drugs?"

"No chemical works that instantly. You saw the guy — it looked like he was still reading his program."

"Then what, magical fairy dust? Vulcan death grip?"

"Focus, Lex. Wake up that lonely brain cell."

"Well, what are you trying to say? He wasn't supposed to be dead?"

"That's what it looked like, but — "

"But how is that even possible?"

"It's not."

They were silent for a moment. Lex stuck her hands into her voluminous hoodie pocket, only to quickly yank them out again. She had forgotten about the heaps of Vessels Driggs had given her to store there.

"Are we going to unload these things?" she asked, a trace of nervousness creeping into her voice. "They're starting to gross me out."

"They're just souls."

"But they're warm. Like eggs. I feel like a spawning salmon." Driggs laughed. This only made her voice get higher. "And they're people's souls, and they're kinda important, so shouldn't we maybe, I don't know — dammit, what are we supposed to do with them?"

"Hey." Driggs put his hands on her shoulders and caught her manic gaze. "Relax, spaz. I'll show you."

||||||

Over at the Bank, Kilda was terrorizing a pair of uneasy French-women seated on the lobby sofa. "Of course black sweatshirts are in style here, they're the rage everywhere in America!" She leaned in ominously, her gigantic corsage almost touching their noses. "Now, let me give you some dining options for the next town over!"

Driggs led Lex down the hallway and up the flight of stairs, coming to a halt at the top upon a small landing. In front of them was an unmarked door. He turned the knob.

Lex had expected something a little more illustrious to exist on the only second floor in all of Croak, but disappointment ensued as they stepped into the room. It contained nothing more than a potted plant, a black door on the left-hand wall, a steel bank vault door in front of them, and a desk, behind which sat a bored-looking kid about Lex's age with a head of moppy, fluorescent orange hair. He was staring fixedly at a computer and pounding at its keys.

"D-bag," he said without looking. "What up?"

Driggs closed the door behind them. "I brought you a present. This is Lex." The kid did not respond. "Hey."

"What? I'm trying to work here."

"This is Lex," he repeated. "She's training today."

He gave her an unenthusiastic thumbs-up, his eyes still fixed on the screen. "Stupendous."

Driggs crossed the room, sat on the desk, and glanced over the kid's shoulder. "Level sixty-three, nice. Who's the hot elf?"

"Wait a minute," Lex said, glancing at the game on the screen. "Does that get Internet?" she asked the kid.

"Not for you."

Lex crossed her arms.

"Lex," said Driggs, "meet best friend Ferbus."

"Seriously?" she said with a glance of skepticism. Driggs and this nerdlinger? "You guys are best friends?"

Ferbus looked up briefly to give her a smug look. "We prefer the term heterosexual life mates."

Lex rolled her eyes. Driggs stood up and knocked on the enormous circular vault door, which was made of spotless brushed metal and extended all the way to the ceiling. At its center was a large wheel, the kind that looked like the helm of a pirate ship. "How's the weather in there today?" he asked Ferbus.

"Partly rowdy with a chance of gunfights."

Driggs grinned at Lex, but all she could do was give a listless shrug. She had no idea what was going on. Plus, she felt a little uneasy in the room, as if something were slightly wrong with the physics of it. But she couldn't figure out what it was. She glanced at Ferbus, then at the window behind him, then at the vault door. She frowned. That couldn't be right . . .

"Okay, first stop on the tour," Driggs said. "Check this out." Her eyes followed his finger to something she hadn't noticed before: a miniature version of the vault door, about the size of a grapefruit, fixed into the wall beside its massive counterpart.

He began to twirl its little wheel. "This is where we deposit the souls." The door swung open to reveal nothing but darkness. Lex leaned in to inspect it further, but she saw only more of the black space, with a tiny pinprick of white far off in the distance.

"At the end of every shift," he said, taking a handful of Vessels out of his pocket, "we run up here, pop open the tunnel, and deposit all collected Vessels. Just place them in this hole, and then — " The first Vessel was gone, sucked into the tunnel before he could finish his sentence. "That's it." One by one, he fed in the rest, each disappearing as quickly as the first. "Now do yours."

Lex dug into her pockets and eagerly deposited the white globes into the hole, glad to be rid of them. When they were all gone, she gazed down the tube. "Where do they go?"

"To our next stop on the tour. Are we okay to go in, Ferb?"

"Not sure. Burr and Hamilton dueled it out again this morning. Last time I checked, Abe was still cleaning up the mess."

He picked up the phone, his eyes still on the screen. Lex noted that he didn't punch any numbers into the keypad before he started talking — if one could even call it talking. His side of the conversation was more like a series of monosyllabic grunts.

He hung up and resumed tapping at the keyboard. "All clear, head on in."

"Awesome." Driggs shut the little tunnel door and turned to Lex. "You ready to see something really crazy?"

"It's about time," she deadpanned.

Ferbus typed a code into the computer, prompting a series of whirring, clicking noises to sound from behind the vault. Driggs grabbed the heavy wheel on the door and spun it counterclockwise.

And that's when Lex realized what had been bothering her about the room. By all rational accounts — according to her mental floor plan of the building — that vault should have opened straight into the nothingness of sky, two stories above the Field.

But, of course, that's not even close to where it actually led.

9

The rational part of Lex's brain surmised that she had not been thrust *exactly* into the center of the sun, but in terms of brightness, she must surely have been within a dangerous proximity. The blinding luminescence could be felt even through her closed eyelids. As she groped in the direction of Driggs, her feet bounced and wobbled over a plush, cushiony surface. And yet, despite all of the very good reasons to panic, an overall feeling of peace began to settle through her frayed nerves.

"Takes a minute to adjust at first," Driggs said. "You'll get used to it."

"This is the eight hundredth time you've said that," she said, blinking. "Is there anything here that I'll never get used to?"

"Probably these guys."

Lex opened her eyes.

For a moment she could have sworn she was standing in one of those history-comes-alive museums — the kind that feature animatronic robots, the narration stylings of James Earl Jones, and the sort of exhibits that invade children's nightmares for years to come. But instead of a cyborgish John Wilkes Booth discharging his deadly bullet into the back of a plastic Lincoln's head, a very real version of the assassin was engaged in a furious arm-wrestling match with Elvis Presley.

Lincoln was watching the tussle, amused. "Come on, John," he said. "You can do better than that."

"He's all talk," Elvis whispered back.

"Silence!" roared Booth. "I'm trying to concentrate!"

Lincoln rolled his eyes.

Lex was stunned. "What. The. Hell?"

"Not hell," said Driggs. "Just the Afterlife."

|||||||

After narrowly escaping a biplane containing the Wright brothers and receiving a hearty welcome from a bombastic Teddy Roosevelt on behalf of the entire gang of former presidents, Lex demanded an explanation.

She tried to follow Driggs as he took her aside, but it was hard to walk normally, as the strange substance that formed the floor was too bouncy and uneven to navigate. Fortunately, they soon came upon a hammock made of the pillowy white stuff. As Lex climbed into it, Driggs grabbed a couple of handfuls for himself, sculpted them up into a seat, and plopped down next to her.

"So," he said, spreading his arms wide, "this is the Afterlife. See, there are our targets from this morning." He pointed to a confused-looking mass of people. Lex recognized the drugged woman from the cruise ship. "The tunnel flings the Vessels into this space, the atrium. Think of it as a big entrance hall. Once here, the Vessels dissolve and the souls are released and take bodily forms again. They are then welcomed by an ambassador." He gestured at George Washington, who shook the woman's sunburned hand. "The ambassador fills them in on the situation, then leads them out of the atrium and into the Void."

Lex shook her head, as if to free up more space to comprehend all of this. "And that's . . . heaven?"

"Not exactly. It's more like whatever you want it to be. You can do anything — hang out with all your dead relatives, eat donuts all day, go skiing for months at a time — "

"Rue the day you were born," moaned a thin man with a black mustache, digging through a nearby pile of debris and seemingly carrying on a conversation with the sleek, dignified raven sitting on his shoulder. "I *told* you it wasn't here, Quoth. Has anyone seen my cravat?" he shouted to no one in particular.

Lex fell right out of her hammock. "What the — are you *Poe?*"

"Regrettably." He sighed, smoothing his pants. "Call me Edgar. Or the Tell-Tale Fart, that's Teddy Roosevelt's favorite." He shot a distasteful glance at the crowd of presidents. "Jerks."

"Wow." Lex blushed, starstruck for the first time in her life. "Um, how are things?"

"Lamentable."

Lex looked at Driggs. He shrugged.

"O . . . kay," she said, reboarding the hammock and looking around for walls or a ceiling, neither of which she could find. "How big is this place?"

"Huge," Driggs said. "Bigger than anything you can imagine. It contains almost everyone who's ever died — "

"Almost everyone?"

" — and has room enough for everyone who eventually will die. It has to be gigantic. But you can live wherever you want — "

Edgar let out a snort.

"Sorry, *go* wherever you want," Driggs said. "Deserts, oceans, glaciers, the Land of Oz, outer space — anything you can dream up. Some souls have even created entire planets just for themselves."

"Like Mozartopia," Edgar said, sulking. Quoth resentfully ruffled his feathers.

"Can I see them?" Lex asked.

"No," Edgar told her. "You're still alive."

"We can't physically go past the atrium," Driggs said, pointing. "Only the dead are allowed into the Void."

She followed his finger into the distance, where the light intensified too brightly to see anything. "Why?"

"We'd get lost pretty quick. With billions of souls warping the space, it would be impossible for any of us mere mortals to find our way around. Plus, if we tried to stay even in the atrium for more than ten hours or so, we would start to, uh . . . how to put this lightly . . . die of exposure."

She gave him a dubious look and was about to press further, but she got sidetracked as Thomas Jefferson walked by wielding a pair of homemade nunchucks. "They're very nice, Tom," Driggs told him. The founding father nodded proudly and scampered away.

"Why are there so many presidents here?" Lex asked.

"Because we're the Grim town closest to where most of them died. Some volunteer to be ambassadors, and the rest just like to hang out in the atrium solely for the reactions. The looks on new souls' faces when they meet dead presidents in the flesh, so to speak — those guys just eat it up."

"So there really are other Grim towns?"

"All over the world," said Driggs. "In the U.S. alone, there's DeMyse on the West Coast — which I'm told looks like one big Oscar party — and Necropolis, the capital, in Kansas. Croak's jurisdiction only covers the eastern third of the country."

Lex shivered all over for a moment, the sort of shiver a person experiences when they realize how little they really know about the world.

She studied the Void. "So wait, what about religion and the Devil and all that?" She turned to Edgar. "Is there a God?"

Edgar's face went blank. His mustache twitched.

"If there is, no one's telling," Driggs said. "The souls are very secretive about all that meaning-of-life stuff. That's another reason the living aren't allowed in any farther."

"You'll just have to wait your turn," Edgar snipped.

Lex swung the hammock a little and looked up at the sky, or whatever it was. "So if this is heaven — "

"It's *not* heaven," Driggs said. "And it's not hell. It's the Afterlife. Completely neutral. It's whatever you make of it."

"Much like life," Edgar said.

Lex thought for a moment. "But if there's no hell," she said, sitting up, "if there's no chance of punishment afterward, then why even bother trying to be good while you're alive? Isn't there at least a pit of hungry snakes or something?"

Driggs shrugged. "Maybe. But we won't find out until we get there."

Lex angrily pointed to the crowd. "John Wilkes Booth! What is he doing here? And why do those people seem to actually like him?"

"I don't," Edgar said. "He stole my favorite quill."

"But . . . no fire and brimstone for the bad guys?" Lex sputtered. "That's just not fair!"

"Well, life's not fair," Driggs said quietly. "Why should death be any different?"

Lex fell silent.

"I should go," Edgar said, giving Quoth a gentle pat. "Roosevelt's probably turned my cravat into a pirate flag by now. Ingrate."

"Okay," Driggs said. "Later, Ed."

Lex grumbled. "Sorry we weren't better company."

Edgar gave her a stately nod. "I enjoyed when you fell out of the hammock."

Driggs watched him trudge away, then turned to a troubled Lex. "It's a lot to digest, I know," he said. "But it'll sink in." He stretched and got up from his makeshift seat, which melted back down into the ground. "We should probably take off, too. I still have to show you the Lair." And it was just as well that they decided to leave, because by then an angry, frizzy-haired Mark Twain had arrived to chase them out of his hammock.

As they neared the vault door, Lex noticed a desk sculpted from the fluff, which the sudden blindness had prevented her from seeing before. "Omigod! Hi!" exclaimed the perky blond girl who sat behind it.

"Crap," said Driggs.

"You're Lex, aren't you?" The girl jumped up and grabbed Lex by the shoulders, which her head barely reached. She wore a green sundress, a gold necklace, several bracelets, and a huge smile. "I'm Elysia. Sorry I couldn't greet you on the way in, I was dealing with another one of Taft's hissy fits. But I'm so glad you're here! We've been waiting for you for forever. What happened to your eye? Have you already started Killing? I know you were going to stop by yesterday but then you didn't so I've been wondering what you were up to. I manage the front desk in here, so I'm stuck inside all day. This is your first time to the Afterlife, huh?

What do you think? Pretty cool? I told the presidents to behave when you arrived and it seems like they all acted okay. Ugh, except for McKinley. Bill!" She scolded into the distance. "He's just so enchanted by the invention of boxer shorts that he can't help showing them off. Personally, I think he might be a little retar — "

"Elysia!" Driggs interrupted. "Slow the hell down."

She grinned at Lex. "Sorry. I talk a lot when I get excited."

"That's okay," Lex said with an impish nod. "We all have our flaws. Driggs here loves *Titanic*."

"Really??"

Driggs folded his arms and studied the girls. "I can already see the ramifications of an alliance between you two. And they are troublesome."

"Oh, shut up," said Elysia. She took Lex's arm, her warm hazel eyes aglow in the brightness. "I'm so glad you're here. These guys can be such idiots sometimes."

A loud rapping clamored from behind the vault door. "I heard that!" Ferbus's muffled voice rang out.

"Well, it's true!" She gestured at the door. "He's the grumpiest of all. The only thing that cheers that kid up is some quality alone time with his precious Nintendo."

"Xbox!"

"Whatever!"

"Listen, shorty," said Driggs, "we gotta run. I want to show her the Lair before lunch."

"Ew." A look of disgust spread across Elysia's face. "Well, have fun with that." She opened up the vault for them. "I get off for my break in a few minutes, we can go to lunch together! I can show you the Morgue, it's really — "

"Yeah, we'll be there, okay, bye," said Driggs, shutting the door.

Lex frowned at him.

"What?" he said innocently. "Hey, I love the girl to death, but if you don't actively stop her, she'll talk herself right into a case of laryngitis."

"Which makes her talk even more," said Ferbus in a tone suggesting that he knew this all too well.

"I like her," Lex was surprised to hear herself say. Driggs and Ferbus stared in disbelief.

As everyone knows, the only population more catty than a pack of actual cats is a clique of teenage girls. Back home, it sometimes seemed to Lex as though her violent beatings couldn't cause nearly as much pain as the popular crowd's sharp-tongued wickedness. Eventually it got so bad that she had come to forever swear off the possibility of friendship with another girl, aside from Cordy. But Elysia's congeniality was infectious. It had been so long since Lex was on the receiving end of such well-intentioned exuberance from a female that it was impossible not to get excited about it.

"Anyway," said Driggs, eyeing her strangely, "the Lair's over here." He walked across the room to the shiny black door, turned the handle, and stopped. He looked at Lex.

"If I've been reading you correctly — and I like to think that I have — I'm gonna guess that you're not the type of person who will scream when we enter this room. But just in case I'm wrong — don't scream. It disturbs them."

"Them? More jellyfish?"

"Elysia screamed," Ferbus said from his desk. "Even though you told her not to. Remember?"

"Hey!" Elysia's muted voice came through the wall.

"In fact, if I recall correctly," continued Ferbus, "I think she almost cried."

"So?" the voice shot back. "Most sane people would! Seriously, you should put a warning sign on that room or something. One of these days it's going to give some poor rookie a heart attack, because I know mine almost friggin' exploded — "

Ferbus had begun slamming his head down on the desk. "Just go," he said between pounds. "It could be a while."

Driggs pushed the handle forward to reveal a dimly lit room. Draped in what looked like a terrific amount of velvet, the walls almost seemed to be pulsating, though Lex couldn't quite tell why — until Driggs snapped on the lights.

Covering the room from floor to ceiling were thousands of black widow spiders.

10

Lex wasn't scared. She wasn't even grossed out. She was transfixed, hypnotized by the rhythmic writhing of the massive colony, its shape heaving more like one gigantic organism than heaps of minuscule entities. Their shiny black bodies glimmered menacingly in the harsh fluorescent lighting.

"You okay?" asked Driggs, closing the door behind them.

"Yeah," she whispered.

"You mind if I turn down the lights now that you've gotten a good look?" he said, returning to the dimmer. "They don't like it so bright."

"Sure, whatever," Lex said, barely hearing him. The buzzing bulbs above them softened to a dull glow, and indeed, the spiders seemed to relax. Test tubes full of a pale liquid lined the wall next to the door, and a pile of Vessels sat in the corner. In the new lighting, the silken webs surrounding the hordes gave the room an ethereal, dreamlike quality.

"So these are my lovely ladies," Driggs said, affectionately gazing around the room. "What do you think?"

"I think you must be a very lonely boy."

He reached out his finger, allowing a large spider to crawl onto it. "You sure you want to mock the guy in charge of the venomous spider room?"

"Who in their right mind would put you in charge of anything?"

"Mort did, as soon as he started noticing I was hanging out with them all the time. Love at first sight, I guess."

Lex snorted. "What are they for?"

"Here," he said, casting a white blur into the air. "The fruits of their wee labors."

Lex caught it and gave him an incredulous look. "Vessels are made from spider silk?"

"One of the strongest materials in the world."

"Cool." She picked at the soft fibers of the ball. "Is that it?"

"Is that *it*? A roomful of spiders toiling twenty-four hours a day to make thousands of Vessels per week, and you're asking if that's *it*?"

"Yeah."

He grinned. "Actually, no, it's not. We also extract their venom."

"Why?"

"So we can isolate and make airborne the chemicals in it that induce memory loss. That's how we confuse any outsiders who wander into town. We show them a good time, take advantage of their travel budgets, and send them on their way with only a marginal recollection of their visit and an eerie feeling that they should never return." He pointed at the test tubes. "Kilda's our main line of defense — she douses herself in Amnesia every day. One whiff of her brooch and tourists forget their own phone numbers."

"But why doesn't it affect us?"

"We build up immunity. You've been breathing it in small amounts ever since you got here." He leaned into a web and let a spider crawl onto his nose.

She winced. "Don't you ever get bitten?"

"Nah, they love me," he said with a certain warmth that even Lex found endearing. "I wouldn't touch them if I were you, though. They can sense ineptitude."

Lex ignored this. She carefully blew another strand of silk aside and examined the crawling walls, noticing that among the thousands of black, lustrous eyes, the colony was also speckled with a bunch of tiny red spots. She inspected a spider within a nearby cluster. Sure enough, centered directly on the underside of its bulbous abdomen was a large crimson marking in the unmistakable shape of an hourglass. "How frighteningly appropriate."

Driggs nodded. "Nature is not without a dark sense of humor." He gently picked the spider out of his hair, placed it on the wall, and opened the door. "And that's the whole Bank," he said as they exited into the office.

Elysia was sitting on Ferbus's desk, waiting for them. "Gross, huh? You guys ready for lunch? My replacement just headed in, but we're still waiting for Ferbus's. Oh, and he still needs to slay this dragon or whatever." She looked at the screen. "Left! Down! Stab!"

"Shut up, woman!"

They didn't have to wait for long. After a few more minutes of frenzied keyboard pounding, a man entered the room and walked over to the desk. "Great, he's here," Elysia said, snapping off the computer screen. "Let's go!"

Ferbus's howls echoed for miles.

Elysia apologized all the way to the diner. "I'm sorry! How was I supposed to know it was a really important dragon?"

"Silence," said Ferbus, his face still white. "You're dead to me."

They arrived at a beaten screen door, which Driggs held open for the group as they walked in. Ferbus made a beeline for the jukebox and started playing "Everybody Hurts," while Elysia berated him for being so melodramatic.

Driggs steered Lex toward the counter. "Welcome to the Morgue," he said.

She took a moment to assess the eatery, which, as decreed by the American Diner, Soda Fountain, and Greasy Spoon Preservation Act, had stubbornly clung to the décor of the 1950s in every conceivable manner. A long, stainless steel counter with blue cylindrical stools spanned the far wall, while scores of hooded Senior Grims conversed with one another in shiny red leather booths, strains of "tumor the size of a barn!" and "crushed by a refrigerator!" wafting through the delicious, burger-scented air.

"Dora!" Driggs yelled across the sunny restaurant. An old woman — in fact, the same witchy-looking lady Uncle Mort had pointed out to Lex when she first arrived in Croak — beamed at them from behind the counter.

"My goodness," she cackled as they approached. "Driggsy finally managed to secure a broad. How much is he paying you, dear?"

"Calm down, Dora," Driggs said, poking at a nearby plate of chocolate chip cookies. "Or you'll jog that smallpox right out of remission."

"Zing!" yelled Ferbus from across the room.

"Get your grimy paws out of there!" She slapped Driggs's fingers away with a pale, liver-spotted hand. "Last thing *you* need is another acne breakout." Lex stifled a giggle. Driggs's ears reddened. "His face used to look like the Pacific Ring of Fire," Dora told Lex, her wrinkly features glowing with glee.

"Lex, this is Pandora," Driggs speedily interjected in a not-so-subtle effort to change the subject. "Uglier than a troll and older than dirt. Any questions about the Mesozoic era may be directed straight to her."

"Pleasure, Lex," Dora said, giving her a squeeze on the shoulder. "I hope this one hasn't been giving you too much troub — Oh, for Pete's sake, Driggs." She spit on her hand and smushed it into his face. "It's like you were raised by badgers." She wiped a smudge off his cheek, then, nimbly avoiding his futile swipes of defense, tackled the far trickier challenge of his ruffled hair. "What do you wash this stuff with, boy? Maple syrup?"

Driggs struggled in vain, yelling, "Burn the witch!" and, "Unhand me, you hag!" until finally she released his scalp, pinched his cheek, and pulled it close to her gnarled nose. "What a mug," she said. "Even with a shiner. Just look at those eyes!"

Driggs wrenched his face away, then relaxed and lovingly patted her on the elbow. "Thanks, Dora."

"We like to josh," she said to Lex. "But don't listen to an old poop like me. He's quite the catch."

Lex's smile instantly turned to a grimace, while Driggs's face flushed a spectacular purple.

"Ah." Pandora clucked. "I see. Well. What can I get you?"

"A pile of burgers," Driggs said, running a hand through his now hopelessly chaotic hair. "And — "

" — Oreos. And for you, sweetheart?"

"Um . . ." Lex cringed as she pondered the menu board, which featured items such as Mad CowBurger, E. Coli Cola, and the gag-inducing Salmo-Nilla Ice Cream.

"Don't let the name fool you," Pandora said. "It's actually frozen yogurt."

Twenty-four hours ago Lex would have sold her soul for a cup of Coffin Coffee, but compared with the rush of the ether and the jolts of the shocks, caffeine now just seemed so . . . weak. So she ordered some Pox Chicken and a large glass of something called HomiCider. After Dora plated their meals, Lex grabbed her tray and followed Driggs to the largest booth in the restaurant. A red, horseshoe-shaped monstrosity, it seemed dingier and more well worn than the other tables, and JOONYEЯ GЯIMS was written in what appeared to be ketchup on a wooden plaque hanging from the ceiling — though the label hardly seemed necessary, as the table was clearly populated only by Grims of the teenage persuasion.

Ferbus, now somewhat recovered, grabbed a burger from Driggs's tray and sat down at the table. Elysia joined him, followed by Driggs, then Lex, who could feel the eyes of the other kids boring through her. One was a muscular Asian boy whose black hair faded to a peroxide blond in the center to form a skunklike fauxhawk. Next to him sat a tall chocolate-skinned girl with hair woven into a dizzying maze of braids.

"Guys, this is her!" said Elysia. "This is Lex!"

The boy nodded and downed half of his burger in one bite. The girl snapped her head around to face Lex, whacking the boy in the face with her braids. "Hi! I'm Kloo," she said warmly. "And this is Ayjay."

"What happened to your eye?" he garbled, his mouth full. Kloo elbowed him. "I mean, hi."

"So," Elysia said, "Kloo is the one you want to go to if you cut yourself on your scythe or if you get another black eye or you fall down a flight of stairs because you tripped on an untied shoelace." A quick, disapproving glance at Ferbus suggested that this might be a frequent occurrence. "She's practically a doctor, she can fix you up in no time and even throw in a week's worth of subsequent care and worry. She's like our mom."

Kloo nodded at Lex in an indescribably maternal way, somehow cramming a lifetime of compassion, support, and tenderness all into one slight bounce of the head. "It's true," she said. "Anything you need, hon."

"And Ayjay is — um — "

"I eat. I sleep. I Cull. I lift." Ayjay smiled and gestured at the gym across the street called Dead Weight, showing off a well-sculpted bicep. He took another bite. "That's about it."

Elysia nodded. "Ayjay's a man of few words."

Ayjay turned to Kloo. "You gonna drink that?" he asked, pointing at her glass.

"No. I'm gonna pour it down your pants."

"Sexy."

"Yeah? You think?"

They then proceeded to make out.

"Great, they're at it again," said Ferbus loudly, as if this were not obvious to everyone in the restaurant. "You'd think it would get old, but apparently it does *not.*"

"And this is Zara, who you trained with yesterday, right?" said Elysia, determined to continue with her introductions. "How did she do, Zara?"

Zara shifted in her seat. "Fine," she said with a small scowl.

Elysia exchanged an exasperated glance with Driggs. "But not as good as you, Zara. Right, we know. Oh, and this is Sofi. She's an Etcetera."

A mocha-skinned girl approached the table, her hair slick and brown with badly bleached highlights. "Holy bananas!" she squeaked when she saw Driggs. "What happened to your face?"

"Bar fight."

"Oh, you," she said, squeezing into the empty seat next to him. She turned to face Lex and winced at her matching bruise. "Wow, chica, you too? You guys, like, fall off the roof?"

"Something like that," Driggs said.

Sofi giggled and flicked at her dangly earrings. Lex imagined that this was the sort of girl who kept a notebook full of signatures combining her first name with cute boys' last names.

"This is Lex," Elysia said to her.

"Wait, don't tell me." Sofi looked Lex up and down. "Toootally a Killer. Like, a hundred zillion percent."

"How do you *do* that?" Driggs asked.

"Born talent." She batted her eyes and took a sip of his soda. Lex internally retched.

"Hey, guys," Driggs said to the table. "Have you seen anything strange out in your shifts lately? We got this really weird guy today — I don't know what happened to him. I couldn't figure out the cause of death."

"*You* couldn't?" Ferbus said in amazement. "What's that make your record now, one out of a million?"

"What did he look like?" Kloo asked. "Where was he?"

"Baseball game," Driggs said. "No injuries, no disease, no substance abuse, no signs of a struggle. He looked normal, except for — well, his eyes were completely white."

A general murmur of confusion swept through the table. "What do you mean?" said Elysia.

Lex saw her opportunity to contribute to the discussion instead of continuing to sit there like a lump. "Solid white," she said. "They looked like hailstones."

Driggs nodded. "Which means that it can't be poison, either, because there's nothing I know of that can blind *and* kill a person that fast without the victim even flinching. Unless — " He let out a weird gasping noise, choking on his own epiphany. "Guys, what if a Grim did it? Maybe it's a Crasher!"

His suggestion was met by fits of laughter. "Or a leprechaun! Or a mermaid!" said Ferbus, flicking a fry at him.

"What's a Crasher?" Lex asked.

"Nothing," said Ferbus. "Driggs is out of his tree, that's all."

"So I've gathered."

"See, D-bag? Even the rookie knows better."

Lex nibbled at her chicken fingers, shocked at how she seemed to have been accepted into the group so swiftly and completely, without so much as a derisive whisper. She couldn't even remember the last time she had sat at a lunch table with people her own age. Back at school, she had been forced to spend much of the last two years sitting with the teachers, who didn't trust her not to douse the cheerleading squad with ketchup again.

"Well, I don't know," said Driggs with a shrug, slightly deflated by Ferbus's ridicule. "Keep a lookout on your shifts, I guess."

"Wish I could," said Ferbus. "Almost makes me want to jump back into the Field, just to watch you lose your mind."

"Why *do* you two work in the Afterlife?" Lex asked Ferbus and Elysia. "Why aren't you out in the Field?"

"I was a Culler last year," Elysia said. "And Ferbus was a Killer. We were partners." They exchanged disgusted glances. "But once you finish your first year, you can decide what area you want to try within the Grimming community. Sort of like a college major."

"Like me," said Sofi. "I was a Killer for like only a few months before I started begging to work with the Smacks."

"Kloo and Ayjay are full-time Field Grims," Elysia went on. "They're the oldest Juniors, almost graduated. And Zara's on hiatus from Field work — except when we need a sub — because she's doing her swiping internship at the butcher shop this summer."

"I don't want to talk about it." Zara shuddered. "It's disgusting."

"Swiping internship?" Lex said.

"The owners of all the shops and restaurants in town — mostly retired Grims and Etceteras — are called swipers," Elysia said, all too happy to have more stuff to explain. "It's their job to take things from the outside world for our own purposes, like food, clothes, medicine, toiletries — "

"Veal, tongue, gizzards," Zara said with a look of revulsion.

"Swipers use their scythes a little differently," Elysia continued. "They open up small windows into the ether — just large enough for them to reach through — and take supplies that generally go unnoticed from places like large warehouses, back rooms of grocery stores, Laundromats — "

"Laundromats?"

"You should see our sock inventory," Driggs said. "Massive."

Elysia nodded. "We're pretty isolated out here, so it's a really efficient system."

Lex was dumbfounded. "I had no idea petty theft was such a noble endeavor."

"Well," said Zara, "when you think about the gracious services we provide to the citizens of this world, it's only fair. People should be thankful we don't charge more."

"But don't you ever get caught?"

"Nope," she said, combing through her staticky silver hair with the long, bony fingers that everyone in Croak seemed to possess. "We only take enough to sustain our small population. People out there never notice their things are missing, and if they do, they blame themselves anyway."

Lex longingly thought of her mother, and of all the clothes she had complained about losing over the years. Now, definitive proof that the washing machine wasn't a "ravenous, blouse-eating monster," as she put it.

"As for me, I'm currently trying out Afterlife Liaisons," Elysia said. "And Ferbus, well . . ."

"Ferbus wanted to hone his defensive skills," said Ferbus. "So Ferbus took up the Vault Post."

"Right, defensive skills," Lex said. "Bet those come in real handy on dragon raids."

Ferbus narrowed his eyes. "My job may seem pointless," he said testily, "but if any unauthorized individuals come upstairs, it's my job to make sure they don't get into the Lair or Afterlife."

"And how do you do that?"

"I can't tell you. Suffice it to say that Mort trained me, and in the time it'd take for any intruder to say 'Who's that handsome devil?' I'd have already broken their neck in three places."

"But he still can't tie his shoes," said Driggs.

Everyone laughed. Elysia laughed the hardest.

"I guess you have to learn how to entertain yourselves around here, without TVs or anything," said Lex.

"Oh, we have a TV," Elysia said.

Lex grabbed her arm. "Say that again?"

She laughed. "At the Crypt. That's our dorm. And what's ours is yours, come over whenever you want. We all live there, except for you and Driggs."

Driggs nodded. "Best not to mingle with the dirty peons."

"It's only because Uncle Mort is my uncle," Lex said, rolling her eyes. "My parents would shit a brick if I had to live on my own."

Had this exchange taken place in a cheesy comedy movie, a record needle scratch would have sounded at this moment to denote the stunned silence that Lex's statement had produced, followed by an uncomfortable cough or two. But in a noisy diner, the sudden hush of a small group of people went largely unnoticed, and Lex became aware that she had said something wrong only when she realized that all of the Juniors were staring at her, their mouths agape. Driggs swore under his breath.

"What?" Lex asked, perplexed. "What's wrong?"

"You — you have parents?" choked Elysia.

"Um, yeah."

"Two of 'em?" Ferbus asked.

"How many should I have?"

Ferbus eyed Lex with a furious glower. Elysia bit her nail and looked like she was about to cry. Everyone else stared at the table.

Driggs lightly touched Lex on the elbow. "Lex," he said, his blue eye flashing sadly, "the rest of us don't have parents."

Elysia sniffed. Zara wore a hard expression.

"Sorry, guys," he said to the group. "I didn't tell her."

Lex awkwardly shifted in her seat, not knowing what to do or say. She felt ill.

"Mine left when I was ten," Kloo said bitterly, breaking the silence. "Dumped me at my senile grandmother's and never looked back."

"Mom overdosed," Ayjay said. "Dad's in jail."

"Kicked me out of the house," said Elysia.

"I got bounced around every foster home in the state." Ferbus was seething. "Ask me how many parents *I* have."

Lex looked down. "I didn't know," she said in a barely audible whisper.

After a moment Kloo spoke up. "It's not your fault, hon. We've got better lives now, anyway. That's why we're here."

"But then what — " said Sofi to Lex, her eyes still troubled, "what are *you* doing here?"

"Yeah," said Ferbus with a sneer. "If you've got such a loving family?"

Driggs sat up a little taller. "Hey, she turned delinquent just like the rest of us," he said defensively. "And remember, it was *Mort's* decision to bring her here. So if any of you have a problem with that, I suggest you take it up with him."

That seemed to do it. The rest of the group softened, though the sour look on Ferbus's face never quite went away.

"Omigod!" said Elysia, looking at her watch. "I have to go. I promised Ben I'd watch his next kite experiment. I keep telling him that electricity is a pretty well-known concept by now, but that doesn't stop him from trying to one-up Thomas Edison all the frickin' time." She turned to Lex. "Seriously, sometimes grown dead men act like children."

Lex let out a nervous laugh as the Juniors gathered their trash and got up to leave. Pandora shot Lex a friendly wink as they piled out the door. She limply waved back.

"So I guess we'll see you later," said Kloo once they got outside.

"Right," Lex carefully replied as the group separated. "Have a good day?"

No one answered.

After they had walked a considerable distance away, Lex jabbed Driggs in the rib. "Why didn't you tell me?"

"I honestly forgot to," he said. "I mean, you were actually having a good time and getting along with everyone. Imagine my shock."

"Well, I hope you enjoyed the ride, because now they hate me."

"I thought you wanted to be hated."

"Only by you."

He snickered. "They'll come around. I wouldn't lose sleep over it."

"I only lose sleep when you bang on those goddamned drums."

"Good. It is my mission to annoy."

"Mission accomplished."

Driggs threw a lingering smile at her, which Lex, to her surprise, returned.

Luckily, she caught herself, and quickly followed it with a scowl.

11

Lex picked at her lips as she leaned against the Ghost Gum tree and watched pairs of Senior Grims swapping out for their lunch breaks, emotions swirling through her mind like unflagging hurricanes. So many unanswered questions, moral debacles, social insecurities, and mysterious feelings, both hormonal and otherwise . . .

She dismissed those last ones easily enough. Lex had never taken any interest in the moronic half of the human race, and she didn't plan on starting anytime soon.

Her eyes wandered up the trunk of the tree, where the craggy branches scratched at the sky like skeletal fingers. She then glanced at Driggs's hands and snorted at the similarity.

"What?" he asked.

"Nothing. Your bony hands of death amuse me, that's all."

"Wait until yours look the same," he said, preparing to scythe.

"Wait — what?" She batted the sapphire blade out of his hands. "What do you mean? Is that why everyone around here has such creepy fingers?"

"Yeah." He bent down to pick up his scythe. "I don't know why it happens, though. Probably the same weird reason our hair goes all wonky."

"What?" she barked, knocking his scythe to the ground once more.

"Stop that!"

"What happens to our hair?"

He gestured at the disaster atop his head. "You think I want to look like a drunken hedgehog all the time? It's from hanging out in the ether so much. It messes with your follicles or something. Doesn't happen to everyone, but I can assure you that Ferbus's wasn't always the color of a prison jumpsuit, Zara wasn't born Silvylocks, and Mort's been rocking the electrocution look for years. Look, yours has gotten straighter already."

Lex ran a hand through her hair. It *had* lost some of its poofyness. There had been so many other circuses of insanity to deal with that she hadn't even noticed. It was calm, manageable, even — she shuddered to think it — sleek and shiny.

"Oh my God," she said in disgust. "I'm a shampoo commercial."

"And you'll soon get a nice pair of death claws to boot." He wiggled his fingers at her nose.

"Get those spindly things out of my face," she said. "What about my eyes? Are they gonna morph into monstrosities, like yours?"

"Nope," he said, twirling his scythe. "These are a hundred percent ugly, mutated me."

Lex snickered, though she begrudgingly conceded to herself that of all the words to describe Driggs, "ugly" wasn't one of them. She pulled her hood up over her flushing cheeks and readied her scythe. "Well, they nicely complement the rest of your hideousness," she overcompensated.

Uncle Mort wasn't kidding when he promised Lex that she'd be going full throttle. Their afternoon shift was just as intense as the morning one, if not more — though her unsettling feelings were starting to dissipate now that she had seen the Afterlife. If she really was sending souls to such a wonderful place, what she was doing couldn't possibly be all that wrong.

Unless not all of them got there.

"Hey," she said to Driggs as they landed in a large corner office. She tapped the elbow of a man who had just blown his brains out all over the windows. After the deathflash, the Gamma flowed from the man's body, curling into the air like an iridescent vapor. "You said before that *almost* everyone gets to go to the Afterlife when they die. So who doesn't? I know that if I don't do my job, the soul gets trapped, but what happens if you don't do yours?"

As an answer, Driggs pointed at the Gamma diffusing through the room.

"Um, okay," she said, her voice edged with panic as she stared at the escaping light. "What if you don't catch it?"

Driggs's face clouded. "You believe in ghosts?"

"No."

"Might want to start." The Gamma flickered as it flowed into Driggs's waiting hands.

Lex let out a breath she hadn't realized she was holding. "Oh."

She worked in quiet reflection for the next couple of targets until they landed in a thin forest next to a playground. Lex took one look at the ground and gasped. A young girl, bruised and bloodied, lay across a fallen tree. A red-spattered teddy bear sat in the crook of her arm.

Driggs looked away. "Just do it," he said. "Better to get kids done fast, especially the brutal ones."

Lex, still staring in horror, bent down and inspected the girl's face. Her skin was smooth; she couldn't have been more than eight years old. Lex felt the contempt welling up once again, the same kind that had arisen when she was with Zara and had seen that woman with the gun . . .

She stood up abruptly and scoured the area. "Driggs — "

"What?"

"The guy's still here."

Blinded by fury, Lex could no longer see anything but the man retreating through the trees, hardly ten feet away. Hatred engulfed her body, her hands grew white-hot, and her tongue detected the metallic taste of blood. Emitting a faint growl, she gripped her scythe and stalked across the grass toward the man — closer and closer, until the blade was mere inches away from him. "That pervert, that sick f — "

"STOP!" Driggs shouted, grabbing her arms and wrestling her back to the target. "Touch her. Now," he said, holding her hand over the child.

"But she's only a kid!"

"She's already gone! You want her soul to be trapped?"

Lex resisted a moment longer, then looked away as she bitterly poked her finger into the little girl's skin.

Driggs somehow managed to Cull with one hand as he continued to restrain Lex. "We're leaving." Tugging on her wrist, he ripped his scythe upward through the air and pulled her back through the ether to the Field.

This did not go over well. Lex erupted into a flurry of punches, madly flapping about like a wounded ostrich, but Driggs — now a tad wiser — put his hand on her head and held her at arm's length, rendering her swings futile.

"Are you done?" he asked after a couple dozen swipes.

Lex dropped her hands. Unfortunately, Driggs followed suit, affording her the perfect opportunity to kick him in the crotch. Which she did.

"That . . . was . . . unnecessary," he groaned from the ground.

Lex blew a tuft of hair out of her face.

"I disagree."

||||||

Lex looked at her hands as Driggs dragged her down the street. They felt like they were on fire. She inhaled deeply, shoved them into her pocket, and blinked back the hot tears stinging at her eyes. Sure, she'd gotten mad before — the past two years of feral outbursts were proof enough of that. But they were nothing compared to this.

"To what do I owe the pleasure?" Uncle Mort said as Driggs dragged Lex into the Croak Public Library.

"She cracked out in the Field, tried to go after someone," Driggs said, seating her at a large wooden table. "You'd better go over the Terms."

"I thought this might happen," said Uncle Mort, staring pointedly at his niece. "I'll go get the slides."

As he bumbled into the closet, Lex glanced around the room. In addition to an army of hulking bookshelves stacked with hundreds of dusty, forgotten tomes, the walls of the library also boasted a sweeping display of old-timey photographs of old-timey people, all unsmiling and wearing heavy black cloaks. She scowled back at them.

"I didn't do anything wrong," she said to Driggs. "I reacted the way any decent human being would. Okay, I get that the girl was already dead, fine. But that guy — how could you just ignore him? Did you *see* what he did to her?"

"Lex —"

"First Zara, then you. You people are sick."

"Wait — what about Zara?"

"When we were training yesterday, the same thing happened. This woman shot her husband or lover or whatever, so I tried to go after her, but Zara stopped me and told me not to tell Uncle Mort because it would get me into a lot of trouble."

Driggs sighed and rubbed his eyes. "There are so many things wrong with that sentence."

"Like what?"

"For one thing, Zara should have known better. She knows the protocol for rookie training. That's the sort of thing we'd report right after it happens."

"Which would make this all part of the jealousy-sabotage thing, right?"

"Right. But that's not the point." He leaned in. "You can't just go around doling out vigilante justice, Lex. If you ever lose your temper like you did back there and end up attacking a nontarget — trust me, you have *no* idea how severe the consequences are for executing whatever plans your spiteful little mind is concocting."

"Enlighten me, then."

"That's his job," Driggs said as Uncle Mort emerged from the closet.

"I found the slides," he said, stuffing them into a projector. A myriad of flow charts appeared on the wall before them. Uncle

Mort uselessly grappled with the focus until the text became clear, then blurry, then unreadable.

"Okay, forget it," he said, hurling the entire contraption back into the closet. "You're a smart kid, you don't need pie graphs." He grabbed a weighty book from a nearby shelf and dropped it onto the table, where it landed with a resounding thud. A cloud of dust puffed up into the air, through which Lex could read *Terms of Execution* embossed in gold lettering across the cover. Uncle Mort loomed over them.

"The Terms of Execution are the guidelines that all Grims adhere to," he said. "They are strict — some of the strictest laws ever written — and anyone who chooses to break them does so with the knowledge that punishment will be swift, severe, and astronomically unpleasant." He indicated the book. "Of course, it'd take years to properly teach you each and every one of the rules the Grimsphere has devised over the centuries, so I'll save both of us the trouble by saying that they all boil down to essentially the same thing: do your job, and only your job. Kill the target. This needs to be done with as little judgment as humanly possible. Just because time is stopped and murderers are powerless to defend themselves doesn't mean you can run around like a maniac and exact vengeance on them, no matter how evil you think they are. We are objective, unbiased third parties, Lex." He leaned in, that scary gleam in his eyes again. "It is not up to us to decide who lives and who dies."

"But that monster in the woods, with that girl — he's just going to do it again!"

"It's an awful thing to turn away from, I know," Uncle Mort said sadly. "But whenever those feelings surface, you've got to repress them. It's not in our job description to impose justice. It's unfortunate, yes, that people kill each other, but that's how the world works. And we have no right to change that. We can't interfere with human nature and free will any more than we can meddle with the fundamental laws of the universe. It's not our place."

Lex shook her head. "That's so messed up. If we have the chance — the power — to stop someone from killing again — "

"Let me ask you this," Uncle Mort said. "You're a New Yorker. How often do you give spare change to homeless people?"

"Um — " Lex was thrown. "Hardly ever."

"See? It's easy to ignore the injustices of the world. People do it every day. And that's precisely what you'll be doing here."

"Or else what? Memory wipe and exile?"

"For lesser offenses, yeah. But for harming a nontarget . . ." He and Driggs exchanged somber glances. "Let's just put it this way: the Grimsphere crime rate is virtually nil. Draw your own conclusions."

"But — "

"Enough, Lex," Uncle Mort said, gruffly taking his niece by the shoulders. "It comes down to this: violating the Terms is the fastest way to obliterate your career, life, and any happiness you ever hoped to achieve from either. You decide to attack a nontarget, you better damn well be prepared to pay the consequences. Got it?"

Lex's shoulders fell. She nodded.

"You're done for the day. Go home, clear your head, and we'll start fresh tomorrow," he said, a stab of disappointment in his voice.

But as Driggs and Lex got up to leave, her eye lingered for a half a second more on her uncle's face, which she could have sworn bore the unmistakable expression of someone extending a dare.

|||||||

"This is bullshit," Lex said, stomping down the street. "Letting murderers and rapists off the hook because of some idiotic rule. Letting them go on killing for your own entertainment."

"Jesus, Lex. It's not like that."

"But it would be so easy to stop them! I'd recognize that guy's face again in a second; all we'd have to do is find out where it happened, track him down, and bam — no more dead kids!"

"There's always going to be dead kids, Lex," Driggs said in a softer tone. "And there's always going to be unspeakable crimes. Who are you to decide who gets punished and who doesn't?"

Lex screwed up her face. Back at school, she didn't even need an excuse to lash out at people — and now she was expected to withhold her wrath in the presence of actual criminals?

Things were so complicated here. If only she could talk to her sister, Cordy would fix everything. And Mom would bake her two dozen cookies. Hell, even Dad would know what to say to make all of this feel right, instead of so, so wrong.

"This sucks," she said in a small voice.

Driggs made a couple of awkward movements as they walked, as if he were trying to touch her in a reassuring way, but eventually he gave up. "It gets easier," he said in a sympathetic voice. "I promise."

Lex remained silent.

"Hey," he said, brightening. "I know what'll cheer you up."

He would say nothing more until they got to the house. Once inside, he led her into the living room and sat her down at a small table, its bulky contents covered by a drop cloth. "Why don't you play with this for a little while?" he said, removing the cover.

Lex's heart stopped mid-beat. "There is a God," she whispered, staring at the ancient computer. She clawed at Driggs's shirt. "Internet?"

"Ow. Yes." He turned it on. "But I don't know how great the connection is. We hardly ever use it."

"What is *wrong* with you people?" she grumbled, pounding at the keys. "How can you not care about what's happening in the world?"

He gave her a sad look. "Wait until you've seen as many blood-soaked teddy bears as I have. The world is highly overrated." He grabbed a box of Oreos from the top of the refrigerator and headed to his room. Minutes later, a crash of drumming erupted from within.

Lex watched him go, then signed into her email account. Her heart sank into a puddle of guilt as she studied the screen. Eleven messages, all from Cordy.

hey dingus,

where ARE you? does uncle mort live in the stone age or something? or maybe he locked you up in his dungeon basement. how many other bodies are down there?

michael thorley came into the store today. i was too busy staring at his eyes to listen to his order so when he said he wanted extra nuts, i started laughing uncontrollably for some reason, until he just sort of left without taking anything. so yeah. i'll pretty much never be able to go to school again.

write back, idiot.

cordy

p.s. mom found the mountain of dirty laundry you left in the closet. she is not pleased.

Lex couldn't type fast enough. She poured her heart out — from Uncle Mort and the town to Juniors and the Afterlife. She told her about the way she felt when she Killed, about the painful shocks. She described the situation with the girl in the woods in graphic detail, followed by a desperate plea for advice. And she closed with the very true statement that she missed Cordy more than anything in the known galaxy, including television.

When she finished, Lex read back over what she had written. Her heart sank. "I can't send this," she told the screen.

She couldn't tell Cordy what Croak really was, not unless she wanted them both to end up with giant holes in their memories. But she couldn't make anything up, either. Cordy would see right through her and start asking questions, which would only lead to more lying.

Lex swallowed hard. There were no other options — she'd just have to ignore her. She went to click Discard, then changed her mind and hit Save. Maybe she'd think of something.

Frustrated, she stood up and began pacing around the living room. She stopped short in front of the jellyfish tank as their graceful, eerie beauty caught her eye. The gelatinous blobs quivered and drifted through the water, their ghostlike tentacles stretching across the glass like paint strokes on a canvas. She shuddered, marveling at the visions they had the power to see, imagining a life that consisted of nothing but nightmarish revelations of death.

It came to her in a flash, then disappeared just as quickly: a sudden urge to break the glass and set them free.

"Whoa," Lex said a few days later as she and Driggs scythed into a dingy-looking bathroom. They looked at the target, a middle-aged woman in skintight leopard print leggings, slumped over a toilet. "There's something you can't un-see."

Driggs did not reply. He squinted at the woman, then wedged himself in next to the toilet and grabbed a hunk of her peroxide-blond hair.

Lex recoiled. "Driggs, ew."

He ignored her and continued to lift the woman's head. "I *knew* it! No injuries, no trauma, and voilà." He angled the head at Lex.

Two lifeless white orbs stared back at her.

"So it wasn't an anomaly," she said.

"Nope."

She pointed at the empty vodka bottle on the counter. "Think that has anything to do with it?"

"Since when did alcohol miraculously evolve the ability to erase eyeballs?"

The past few days had been interesting, to say the least. As Driggs had promised, the Juniors were quick to become friendly toward Lex again — though there was no denying the truth that she was different from them and always would be. As for Lex's newfound Killing career, she continued to impress Uncle Mort with her speed, skills, and overall kickassery as a Grim — although she was still bitter about the clash over the girl in the woods. Violent deaths popped up at least once a day, and although thus far she had tried very hard to do as he instructed and control her vengeful impulses, the question of how long she could keep it up was never far from her mind. And the shocks that still racked her body with each Kill weren't showing any signs of weakening, either. In fact, a red, bubbling blister was beginning to form on her finger where they had burned her raw.

But none of these headaches were enough to squelch the overall sense of fulfillment that had taken root in Lex. Almost everything had gotten easier (again, just as Driggs had promised), and instead of feeling uncomfortable about being the one to pull the plug, Lex was now beginning to truly appreciate the responsibility with which she had been trusted. Being so close to people who had been alive only a yoctosecond ago — there was a sad, haunting beauty to it all.

It couldn't be denied any longer: Lex had fallen in love with Croak. She loved the people, she loved the town, she loved that she belonged, and she loved being a part of something significant. Lex had finally found her purpose in life, and it wasn't, as previously thought, to drive her principal to early retirement.

Still, each day held the promise of a new curveball. After the white-eyed woman, Lex and Driggs scythed out of the bathroom and into the whooshing ether. The roaring din soon ceased, as well as the whirl of incomprehensible images —

But the weightlessness remained.

Lex looked around shakily, seeing nothing but blue sky. Open and peaceful, it almost reminded her of the Afterlife. Until she looked down.

At clouds.

And birds.

And finally, miles beneath her floating body, the ground.

Lex sucked in a breath. Then she screamed. Then she swore very loudly. Seven hundred miles away, her mother unwittingly glanced at the money-filled jar in her kitchen for reasons she would never be able to ascertain.

Driggs watched in amusement as Lex wriggled helplessly in the air, clawing at nothing. "Relax, spaz," he said. "We're not dealing with Wile E. Coyote physics here. If you haven't fallen by now, you're not going to. Turn around."

Lex embarked upon the odd task of rotating herself in midair, paddling her limbs through the troposphere in a comical attempt to accomplish what Driggs was so irritatingly performing with ease. With one final push, she twisted far enough to witness the reason for their impromptu swim through the heavens.

A colossal explosion loomed before them, suspended mid-blast in the center of the sky. The smoldering fuselage of the plane had cleaved into two pieces, the metal torn apart into long, jagged strips. Orange sparks arced out in every direction. A black cloud had begun to form, as well as clusters of smaller dots floating around the wreckage, which Lex recognized as bodies.

A lot of bodies, she thought somberly.

She twisted a little more until the scorched figure of a woman came into view. Lex held her breath, looked away, and gently touched the woman's forehead. As the Gamma began to emerge, Lex gaped at the plane.

"Hey!" she said as more deathflashes flickered in the distance. "Is that —"

Driggs followed her gaze as he Culled. "Kloo and Ayjay, yeah." He nodded toward a bunch of other Senior Grims dispersed throughout the havoc. "This is a multiple, so a lot of our people are on it." He stuffed the Vessel into his pocket and raised his scythe. "In fact, we'll probably have to — "

They scythed through the ether, then ended up on the opposite side of the wreck.

" — stay here for a couple of swipes."

They hit about five more targets at the site, all of whom had suffered injuries Lex never could have thought possible. With each swipe, a new nightmare: charred-black skin, severed limbs, errant viscera —

And then it stopped.

She had just torn her gaze from a brutally disemboweled flight attendant when she found herself back in the Field, under the Ghost Gum. The afternoon sun shone happily overhead.

Lex swayed where she stood, gazing at the pale skin of the tree, her mind a wasteland. She couldn't even begin to process the images she had just seen, the sensations she had just felt, the vomit she had almost discharged. Driggs watched her with an unreadable expression on his face. The eerie, naked branches of the tree rocked in the gentle breeze.

"Hey," he said tenderly after a moment, catching her troubled eyes. "You want a corn dog?"

Corn dogs are rarely the solution to anything, but Lex was starving and shaken, and a hot, deep-fried meal is usually a fine remedy for both. And so she found herself at the Morgue, squished into the Junior booth between Ferbus and Ayjay, who were engaged in a healthy debate over how many sugar packets Ferbus could fit up his nose (five).

"D-money," said Ferbus through a noseful of sugar, "you make the stuff yet?"

"No, I've been working. A concept you may be unfamiliar with," Driggs said, dodging the french fry Ferbus threw. "I'll do it after work." He turned to Kloo. "We saw another weird death today, one of those white-eye things. How about you?"

"No, not yet," said Kloo. "I'm starting to think you're making the whole thing up."

"He probably is." Ferbus snickered. "Still think a Grim is doing it?"

"Actually, I do," said Driggs. Ferbus laughed harder, a mist of sugar spraying out of his nose.

At the moment, Lex couldn't have cared less about the white-eye deaths. The image of the plane crash and the woman's charred remains was still pounding through her rattled head. Her stomach turned as she recalled the mutilated victims, the last moments of their lives a nightmare of —

"We helped them," Kloo whispered. Lex snapped out of her trance and stared at her, wondering how the girl knew what she had been thinking. Kloo gave her a warm smile. "Multiples, explosions, natural disasters — they don't get any easier, but they're not so bad if you keep in mind that you're setting those targets free. No matter how much they suffer in those last few seconds, the end does arrive — and with it, relief. What comes next in the Afterlife is a blast, and you're the one who brings them there."

"That's . . . true." She smiled at Kloo, a calm settling over her. "Thanks, Mom."

Kloo gave her an affectionate tap on the arm. "Any time, hon."

Now in slightly better spirits, Lex perked back up to what Driggs was saying.

" — And odds are, it'll happen again." He leaned in to the group. "So here's the plan. Kloo and Ayjay, triple-check all of your targets. Look for white eyes. And if you can't figure out the cause of death, try to remember all the little details of the situation. Sofi, let's take a look at the logs, see if the Smacks turn up anything weird. Elysia, Ferbus — watch for anything strange going on in the Afterlife. And Zara, take any extra Field shifts that you can. Got it?" Everyone nodded. "Oh, and you know the drill — don't tell any Seniors."

"Why not?" Lex asked.

Sheepish looks abounded. "We got in big trouble last year for doing this sort of thing," Elysia said.

"Huh?"

"The suicides," Ayjay said between bites.

"There were a bunch of kids at a high school in Connecticut who started hanging themselves," Kloo said. "All alone in their bedrooms, one by one, every few days or so."

"Hey, I remember that," Lex said. "It was on the news."

"Right," Ferbus said, "but no one could figure out why they were doing it. We thought that if we poked around their rooms a little, we could figure out what was going on. But someone ratted us out." He shot a scornful glance at Zara.

"I've told you a hundred times, it was for our own protection," she said, pursing her lips. "And if you want my opinion, I don't think it's right to keep quiet about this either. Mort would want to know."

"I *don't* want your opinion." Ferbus made a face at her. "Quit being such a teacher's pet, Bizarra."

"Shut up, Fungus."

"*You're* a fungus!"

"Anyway," Elysia said, "we got in a ton of trouble."

"Why?" asked Lex. "You weren't doing anything wrong."

"Grims aren't allowed to get personally involved, remember?" Zara gave her a pointed look. "Under any circumstances."

Lex let her gaze drift out the window. "So I've heard," she murmured.

"Turns out it was all a virginity pact gone wrong, or something lame like that," said Elysia. "But Norwood got real mad at us for even investigating in the first place."

"Hey!" a loud voice blared through the diner.

"Great," Driggs groaned. "You've summoned the beasts."

Norwood and Heloise marched toward the Junior table, their thin nostrils flaring. "You. Mongrel." Heloise pointed at Lex. "I just completed the first-week review of your logs. Why did you leave in the middle of your shift the other day?"

Lex inhaled sharply. The girl in the woods — now everyone would know what Lex had almost done.

She ventured a glance at Zara, who was staring straight back. Not with a look of contempt, but rather one of mild interest, as if Lex had something large and possibly hilarious stuck in her teeth.

"Calm down, Hellspawn," Driggs said to Heloise. "It was no big deal. Why don't you go back to the hub? I'm sure there are other, more important people who need to be yelled at."

Norwood put his hands on the table and loomed over Driggs. "Listen, you little pissant," he said icily. "One day — and I pray that it's not far off — this deluded arrogance of yours is gonna get you into a lot more trouble than your ignorant excuse for a brain could ever imagine. All of you." He motioned to the table. "Nothing but goddamned punks. Mort sees potential in you? All I see is a swarm of reckless imbeciles who shouldn't be trusted with a toothbrush, let alone the responsibility of harvesting the dead. If it were up to me — "

"But it's not up to you," Driggs pointed out.

Heloise briskly grabbed her husband before anyone could throw a punch, which is undoubtedly what would have happened next if she hadn't intervened. Norwood straightened up, his lip still curled in a malevolent sneer. "Degenerates," he muttered.

Driggs eyed them as they left. "*That's* why we're doing this," he told everyone. "To prove to those asshats that we're not as useless as they think we are. So keep your mouths shut."

The rest of the Juniors nodded, even Zara. Seemingly uninterested in the source of Norwood's accusations, they soon finished lunch without another word about it. Lex exhaled, relieved.

"So I'll see you . . ." Driggs said, giving a queer, suggestive nod to the crowd as they walked out of the diner, "tonight?"

Ayjay grinned, forming his hand into the shape of a gun. "Definitely."

As Driggs and Elysia headed up to the counter to buy some milkshakes to go, Lex hurried out the door. Unfortunately, Zara was outside waiting for her.

"You did something stupid again, didn't you?" she said in a quiet voice. "Nice job, rookie."

Lex simmered irritably, but said nothing. Zara's attempt to

mark her territory was so obvious, Lex wouldn't be surprised if she had peed all over the Ghost Gum tree.

"Onion ring?" Zara said, handing her a leftover carton.

As everyone knows, the offer of an onion ring is not to be taken lightly. Onion rings are far more valuable than their throwaway side dish counterparts — french fries and potato chips — and, as such, have brought about numerous reconciliations throughout history.

So Lex was torn. Zara wasn't exactly a friend, as evidenced by her snooty attitude and incessant dirty looks. But neither was she an enemy, really, and this certain brand of gray area was foreign to Lex, who had previously categorized people into two groups: those to be pummeled, and those to be pummeled harder.

Cautiously, Lex took a greasy ring from the carton and placed it in her mouth. "What's your problem, Zara?"

"Oh, come on. You're the new kid. I'm allowed to have a little fun with you."

"Yeah, except no one else seems to have gotten the hazing memo, so you're the only one coming off as a major bitch."

"Hey," Zara said with a sudden ferocity. "Golden child. Let's get one thing straight. You can swoop in here on your uncle's coattails, and you can win the hearts and minds of all these hopeless ignoramuses, but the one thing you are *not* allowed to do is talk back to me."

Lex felt her knuckles instinctively tighten. "I can talk back to anyone I want."

"Wrong," Zara said, her eyes flashing. "And here's why. You know that feeling you get when you Kill people? That lightning-grade shock?"

Lex's mouth fell open. She thought back to her first day of training, to that look on Zara's face after her first Kill. So much for keeping the shocks a secret.

Zara held up her hand to reveal a matching red finger. "Well, I get it too, when I Cull," she said, softening. "So we need to stick together, because the thing is . . ." Her voice dropped even lower. "We're the only ones."

Lex was stunned. She'd been so wrapped up in her own shocks that day that she hadn't even noticed Zara's. She opened her mouth, but Elysia and Driggs were now exiting the Morgue, milkshakes in hand. Zara shot one last glance at Lex. "We'll talk later," she mouthed, taking off down the street.

Lex became lost in her thoughts as she and Driggs walked back to the Bank with Elysia, who talked the whole way. "This week is destroying me," she said, taking a sip of her milkshake. "Ford won't shut up about his stupid assembly line, Emily's weeping all over the place, Grant and Lee are at it again — oh, and Dewey will *not* stop poking Truman in the eye. He keeps saying it's an accident, but I know better." She sighed. "I wish for once they'd act as dead as they are."

They parted ways once they arrived at the Bank. "Bye, Lex!" Elysia said, heading up the stairs to the Afterlife. "See you tonight!"

"What? Why?" Lex turned to Driggs. "Huh?"

"You'll see," he said.

She crossed her arms. "You do realize that stringing me along across all these little mysteries is one day going to come back to bite you in the ass, right?"

"I fail to see how that could possibly stop me from continuing."

In the hub, Lex grumpily found herself sitting in front of a desk adorned with several pictures of dolphins, a collection of Hello Kitty toys, and a pink iPod. Sofi sat in the middle of it all, beaming at Driggs.

"Now that you've been here for a week," Driggs told Lex, "we don't have to check in with Norwood or Heloise anymore." He plugged his scythe into the Smack and sat on the desk. "We can pick whoever we want."

"And I'm your favorite, right, Driggs?" Sofi said.

"That's right."

Lex watched this little exchange with something resembling unbridled vexation. Sofi's relentless reapplying of her lip gloss and fluffing of her hair and smoothing of her skirt (which Lex estimated to be about two sizes too tight) were just too much. She plugged in her own scythe, then looked over at the jellyfish to distract herself. One of them had its tentacles raised in a friendly wave.

"Lex?" Driggs said moments later, in a way that suggested he had already repeated himself several times. "Care to join us?"

"Hmm?" she said. "Oh, sorry. Did I miss your fascinating conversation?"

Driggs and Sofi exchanged mystified glances. "Sofi's looking up the toilet woman from this morning."

Sofi pounded at the Smack's incomprehensible keys. "Susan Karliak," she read off the screen. "Ten twenty-seven a.m., Richmond, Virginia." She let out an alarmed squeal. "Cause of death: unknown."

Driggs went pale. "What?"

Their faces were so flabbergasted, Lex almost burst out laughing. "What's wrong?"

"I've never seen an unknown before," Sofi said in awe.

"Me neither. I didn't think they existed," said Driggs. "Look up the baseball guy from the other day."

"What's the big deal?" Lex said as Sofi typed. "People die of unknown causes all the time."

"Unknown to medical examiners," Driggs said. "Not to the Smacks."

"Arnold Scadden," Sofi read off the screen. "Eleven fifty-four a.m., Boston, Massachusetts. Cause of death: unknown."

Driggs looked across the hub. "I wonder if Norwood and Heloise know about this."

"Doubtful," said Sofi. "Causes of death are just listed as a formality, Etceteras never look at them. Up until now, there hasn't been a reason to."

Driggs thought for a moment. "Is there any way to route these kinds of targets out to just us Juniors?"

Sofi twisted her mouth. "I'm not supposed to do special requests, but—" Driggs gave her a pleading look. "Fine. You're lucky I like you." Her fingers danced around the keyboard. "Okay, I created a filter," she said proudly.

"Genius," Lex said in a flat voice. She stood up, yanked their scythes out of the Smack, and looked at Driggs. "Let's go."

Sofi pouted her watermelon-flavored lips in a hurt expression. But her smile reappeared when Driggs jumped off the desk, whispered, "See you tonight!" and patted her on the head. Giggling, she tried to swipe back but missed by inches.

Lex, suppressing the urge to throw up, turned wordlessly and headed for the door.

Driggs followed her, stopping only to dump a salt packet into Norwood's unattended cup of coffee. "What's wrong with you?" he asked once they were in the hall.

"Nothing," she said. "I guess I just don't like that . . . place," she finished unsurely. But the truth was, Lex was just as bewildered. Sofi had been nothing but nice since they met, yet Lex couldn't stop picturing her head mounted on some sort of trophy wall.

As they walked out onto Dead End, they spotted Uncle Mort, who stood lecturing a trio of behatted women clutching matching binoculars. "Yeah, fifty-dollar bird-watching tax," he said. The ladies exchanged puzzled glances as they handed over the money. "Hands tied, it's the damned government. What can you do?" He shrugged innocently, sneaking a wink at Lex.

After a chorus of thanks, the women hurried to their car. Uncle Mort waved them off, then counted the money. "With a little left over for inebriation." He grinned, stuffing it into his pocket. "Hey, one week, huh, Lex?" he said, tossing her a Cuff. "Here's your graduation gift."

"Sweet." She slid it onto her wrist. It felt cool, with a slight vibration to it. "Thanks."

"So, you feel all trained up? Driggs teach you everything he knows?"

"Yes. I'm now fully qualified to operate a can opener."

Driggs let out a sigh. "What a lovable scamp you've bestowed upon our fair town, Mort."

"My pleasure," he said to Driggs. "You make the stuff yet?"

"After work," Driggs said out of the corner of his mouth.

"Great." He hopped onto his motorcycle. "Come straight

home after your shift, okay? Especially you, Lex," he said, rubbing his hands together in a diabolical manner.

She watched him leave. "That doesn't bode well."

IIIIII

It didn't bode well at all. As soon as she and Driggs set foot in the driveway later that afternoon, Uncle Mort bounded out the front door. "Into the house, Lex."

"Why?"

"Because I said so. And because Driggs is wildly gesturing for me to get rid of you."

Lex whipped around. Driggs stopped whatever form of exaggerated sign language he had been attempting and gave her an innocent wave as he headed for the backyard.

"Come on, kiddo," Uncle Mort said, holding the door open.

Lex reluctantly allowed herself to be dragged into the kitchen and seated at the table. "What's going on?"

"You've got a date with the telephone."

He slammed an avocado-colored chunk of plastic down in front of her. She eyed him, apprehension slowly icing through her body. "Excuse me?"

"Call your parents."

Lex froze. The inevitable had arrived. All her plans of isolation — which had been working so nicely up until now — were about to come crashing down into a giant pile of remorse and useless apologies.

It wasn't that she didn't miss her parents. She really did. She'd never gone so long without speaking to them, and the guilt was eating her alive. She knew how much they missed her and loved her — and how hard it had been for them to let her go. But now that she'd gotten a taste of where she truly belonged, her old life might as well have been situated on another planet. She couldn't bear to hear the hurt in their voices when it became obvious that she was so much happier here than she'd ever been at home.

"I . . . can't," she sputtered.

"Malarkey," Uncle Mort said. "Don't go into detail, just let them know you're okay."

"I don't want to."

"Too bad."

"But I don't even know how to work this thing. Where are the buttons?"

"It's a rotary phone, Lex."

"A what?"

"LEX! Call your damn family!" He dialed the number and shoved the receiver into her hand. "And don't forget to lie your ass off."

Lex covered the mouthpiece. "What am I supposed to talk about?"

"I don't know. The weather?"

She was about to shoot him a vulgar gesture when a voice trilled on the other end of the line. "Hello? *Hello?*"

Lex sighed. "Hi, Mom."

"Sweetheart! Are you okay? How was the trip? Did you get there safe?"

Another click announced her father's arrival. "Lexy, how's it going? How's Mort?"

"Are you eating well? Why haven't you called?"

"What have you been up to?"

"Did you pack enough underwear?"

"Mom!" Lex shrieked in embarrassment.

"I have to ask. I'm your mother."

"Yes," she said, getting flustered. "Yes to all of your questions. Everything's fine."

Her uncle leaned in with a devilish look. "Tell them how many people you Killed today."

"Uncle Mort says hi." She shoved him away. "Look, I can't talk long. I've got lots of, uh . . . hay to pitchfork."

"He's not making you shovel cow poop, is he?" her mother screeched.

"Sure he is," her father said. "It's part of the job."

"But that's disgusting!"

"How's she ever gonna learn to behave unless she gets knee-deep in manure?"

"Hey, guys?" Lex interrupted desperately. "I gotta go. The goats are getting restless. And the cock is crowing—or something. I'll call again soon, okay?"

A lengthy goodbye ensued, ending with a fervent promise to never get within ten yards of a functioning wheat thresher, as Mom had seen a special on *Dateline* and had grown Concerned.

"Okay, bye!" As her parents clicked off, Lex exhaled for the first time in minutes. She had been evasive, she had been robotic, and she had somehow managed not to spout out a full-blown profession of her love for Croak. "*That* was—"

"Painful," a voice sounded through the phone.

Lex nearly dropped the receiver. "Cordy! What are you doing?"

"Eavesdropping. And having quite the chuckle at your attempts at lying."

"I'm—" Lex snuck a glimpse at her uncle. "Doing no such thing."

"Yeah, right. Why aren't you answering your phone? I've called like a hundred times."

"There's no reception here. But—"

"What's Uncle Mort got you doing up there? Forced labor? Drugs?"

"Yes, Cordy. Plus a lobotomy just for fun."

"What else would explain your sudden enthusiasm for agriculture?"

Lex glanced out the window at the yard, where Driggs was aiming a hose at something on the ground. "Cordy, listen. Just—trust me, okay? I'm fine. Everyone here is nice and not on drugs and extremely normal." The hose had gotten away from Driggs and was now prancing around the yard, soaking him. Uncle Mort, meanwhile, was rooting around in the toaster with a fork. "Or close enough."

"Oh please, Lex. How dumb do you think I am?"

Lex hesitated. For a moment she thought about telling her everything, spilling each and every forbidden bean right there in front of Uncle Mort. She couldn't keep lying to her sister, especially since Cordy was the one person it never, ever worked on.

But Cordy would easily detect the excitement in her voice. She'd realize that Lex liked it there, even preferred it to being stuck at home all summer. Cordy already felt miserable for getting ditched; how would she take the news that Lex was having the time of her life?

She wouldn't take it well, that was for sure. "I really can't talk," Lex said, deciding to postpone the confessions for another day. "I'll call soon, okay? Eat gobs of ice cream for me."

"But —"

"Bye," Lex said, slamming the phone into the receiver.

From the counter, her uncle let out a snort. "So how's the fam?"

She glared at him. "You truly suck."

That night, after a paltry supper of Chef Boyardee's finest, Lex tore herself away from the online news about the airplane explosion (apparently caused by faulty wiring) and banged on Driggs's bedroom door. He didn't answer.

"Hey!" she yelled. "Wake up!"

Nothing.

She knocked again, glancing down the basement stairs to Uncle Mort's lab. Through the smoke she could just make out a series of marked-up maps tacked on the walls. "If you've lapsed into an Oreo-induced coma, I'm not reviving you."

Still nothing.

She walked into the kitchen and noticed that the front door was slightly open. Furtively, she pushed it open to find Driggs sitting on the front steps of the porch between two covered buckets, his head bowed.

She snuck up behind him and noticed that he was smiling down at something. The closer she got, the more distinctly she could make out an item in his hands: a photo of someone . . . a girl . . .

"Who's that?"

Driggs practically jumped into another time zone. "What the hell is wrong with you?" he yelped, crumpling the picture in his hand.

"Who is it?" she repeated, her voice rising. "Your girlfriend?"

His cheeks turned a lovely shade of crimson. "No," he said, scowling. "It's no one. Forget it. Shut up."

He shoved the photo into his pocket. Lex frowned. She'd never get to it now. Then again, why did she even care? "Isn't it time for us to go to this mystery thing?" she said testily.

"Yes, it is," he said, picking up the buckets.

"If you can tear yourself away from your betrothed, that is."

Driggs gritted his teeth. "What are the odds of you dropping this completely?"

"Slim to none."

"Great." He glowered for a moment. "Unless . . ."

"Yes?"

"Can you be bribed?"

Lex raised an eyebrow. "I'm listening."

"Are you a fan of intoxication?"

"What self-respecting sixteen-year-old isn't?"

He took out a wad of dollar bills and fanned them in front of her face. "Then how about I just buy you some drinks and we forget this whole thing ever happened?"

Lex stifled a laugh. "Don't you mean *steal* some drinks and chug them behind a Seven-Eleven? Last time I checked, we're still underage."

Driggs threw an arm around her shoulder. "Not in Croak."

13

As Driggs led her into town, Lex became convinced that all his claims of bars and drinking were complete fabrications. Lying, after all, is what eighteen-year-old boys do best.

"You're gonna love this place," Driggs told her, stopping just past the Morgue at an unmarked wooden door and turning its knob. "Corpp's is the best pub in the Grimsphere. It won an award."

"For what? Invisibility?"

Her skepticism turned to confusion as they stepped into what appeared to be the unholy union of an old-fashioned Irish pub and a schizophrenic art gallery. Every single surface was coated in varying shades of thick, goopy paint. A gigantic mural — depicting what Lex could only guess was the ether, as it featured a whirlpool of colors, shapes, people, and hundreds of other abstract designs — stretched across the canopy of the vaulted ceiling. The walls ranged in design from vast patches of color to long, winding stripes, from speckled flecks to swirling spirals. A *Starry Night* motif seemed to be forming in one corner, whereas the scribbled beginnings of a novel sprawled across the floor of another. A warm, sweet smell pervaded the tavern, which just so happened to be incredibly welcoming and packed with laughing patrons.

Lex stood gawking in awe. This was not at all how she had imagined the only bar in a town full of executioners.

"Evenin', Driggs," said the dark-skinned elderly man behind the bar as they approached. "Evenin', Lex."

"How do you know my name?" she asked.

"Pandora's my wife. I get all the gossip, whether I want it or not," he said, his freckles dancing. He pushed a bowl of peanuts toward them. "Plus, your uncle never stops jabbering about you."

"This is Corpp," Driggs told Lex. "Bartender extraordinaire for fifty years and counting."

"Hi," Lex said shyly. Something about the man's face was very kind. She liked him immediately.

Driggs heaved one of the buckets onto the counter. "For safekeeping."

Corpp grabbed it with a knowing smile and stored it behind the bar. "Ah, yes. Been here a week already?" he said to Lex.

She raised an eyebrow as Driggs lifted the second bucket. "What's in there?" she asked him.

"A human head."

"You're delightful, you know that?"

"What can I get for you kids?" Corpp asked after putting away the buckets, wiping his gnarled hands on a dishrag.

"Two Yoricks." Driggs pulled a wad of bills out of his pocket and began to thumb through it. "Here's your paycheck," he said, handing Lex a few twenties. "One hundred dollars for Juniors, three hundred dollars for Seniors."

"One hundred dollars for a billion-hour workweek? What are we, slave labor?"

"Pretty much. But Grims aren't really in it for the money. Plus, libations are cheap."

"Here we go." Corpp set down two enormous mugs that looked like hollowed-out skulls.

Lex recoiled from the thick brown swill within. "Uh, I'm more of a beer fan."

Driggs made a loud gagging noise. "Beer is disgusting. Trust me, once you've had a Yorick, you'll never touch any of that piss again." He handed her one of the bulbous skulls and then grabbed his own. "Cheers," he said, clinking his mug with hers and downing a gigantic gulp.

Lex did not follow. She gazed into the muddy goop, wishing that she had not prefaced this evening with the ever-perilous combination of milk and SpaghettiOs.

"It's not a real skull," Driggs reassured her, a frothy mustache now on his upper lip. "And even if it is, I'm sure Corpp gave it a thorough cleaning."

They glanced at the venerable bartender. He waved, a peanut shell ensconced within his bushy eyebrow.

Lex eyed her mug. "This is weird and gross."

"As are you. A winning combination."

"Lex, Driggs!" A chipper voice rang out from across the room. "Over here!"

Lex made her way through the crowd to find a smiling Elysia and an unsurprisingly dour Ferbus nursing their own Yoricks. Kloo and Ayjay were making out behind them, while Zara and Sofi played a drinking game called Skulls, Driggs informed her.

Lex stared quizzically at Zara, yet said nothing. She was dying to know more about what Zara had said earlier, about the shocks, but bringing it up in the middle of a crowded pub probably wasn't the best way to keep her dirty little secret under wraps.

"Congratulations on your first week!" Elysia said with spirited jazz hands, her fingernails painted a festive purple. "And welcome to Corpp's!"

"Thanks," said Lex. "Is this what you guys were whispering about all day?"

"Uh . . . sure. Hey, guess what?" She whacked Ayjay on the elbow, despite his obvious focus on other things. "Ayjay, tell them!"

Ayjay wiped a fleck of spittle from his lips. "We saw one of those white-eye death things."

"I did too, actually," said Zara, looking up from her game with Sofi. "I subbed in for a shift this morning."

"My filter worked!" Sofi said, nudging Driggs.

"So this is officially a thing," Driggs said. "Which *means* — " He gestured for them to come in closer. "Which means that whoever's murdering these people *is* a Grim," he finished, his face serious. "I told you!"

"Hang on a sec," said Ferbus, still skeptical. "What filter, Sofi?"

Sofi told them how she had rerouted the white-eye deaths to Juniors only. "But you know what's *really* wackadoodle?" she said in a scandalized voice. "The causes of death for all of them have been listed as unknown."

A buzz of confusion arose from the group. "That's impossible," said Elysia.

"Sure as hell looked unknown to me," said Ayjay. "Driggs was right — no sign of injury, disease, foul play."

"It's like they just stop living," said Kloo. "Whatever's killing these people is doing it instantly — even though that's medically impossible."

"Not to mention incredibly disturbing," said Zara.

Elysia shivered. "Yeah."

"Now do you believe me?" Driggs asked the group. "It's *gotta* be an inside job. Who other than Grims could sneak in and out in the space of a yoctosecond?"

"Shit. I think he's right," said Ferbus, looking disappointed. And worried. "But come on, Driggs, you really think we're dealing with an honest-to-God *Crasher?*"

Lex put her hand up. "Again I ask, what is a Crasher?"

Ferbus looked around, then lowered his voice. "A Grim who's found one of the Loopholes."

"A Loophole is an ancient, obscure document," Elysia told Lex. "Only a few were made, and they were scattered all over the world, so they're really hard to find, only popping up about once a century. Probably because no one is sure what they look like — could be books or charts, or who knows what."

"Whatever they are," Driggs said, "each Loophole is an identical set of instructions for a secret procedure that, when followed exactly, will give a Grim the ability to Crash the system, to scythe outside of the Etceteras' jurisdiction and off the radar, not just to programmed targets."

Lex looked around the circle. "Why is that a big deal?"

"*Why?*" Ferbus looked scandalized. "That's like — like — "

"Think of it this way," Kloo said. "When we're working a shift, it's like we're riding a one-way train. And the targets that the Etceteras assign us to are the different stations we stop at. But

Crashers are able to jump around to other stations, onto other tracks, even to places where there are no tracks."

"The thing is," said Elysia, "Crashers aren't able to control where they scythe to. So a Grim can search his entire life for the Loophole, find it, and become a Crasher, only to end up scything randomly and wildly and getting himself killed by Crashing into the middle of a pack of hungry wolves or something."

"Which is what makes this case so special," Driggs said. "This is *directed* Crashing."

"Sounds a lot like — " Ferbus broke off as he gave the others a meaningful look. Apparently he wasn't alone in his thinking; soon everyone was looking at one another with such terrified expressions that a wave of goose bumps rushed over Lex's skin.

"What?" Lex asked. "What am I missing?"

"It's nothing." Driggs looked a bit embarrassed. "Just an old legend, really. Supposedly in the fourteenth century there was this psychopath named Grotton who went down in history as the only Grim ever to figure out how to Crash to specific places — and specific people."

"Interesting. What did he do once he got there?"

"Killed them," said Ayjay. "Snuck them some poison, stabbed them with his scythe, blew their heads off with a crossbow — "

"We get it, hon," said Kloo.

"Why didn't he just touch them?" Lex asked, a nameless craving stirring inside of her.

Zara let out a snort. "It's not like you can walk through the streets and zap anyone you want," she said. "Killers can only release souls from bodies that are already dead. They can't *cause* death — at least not by touch alone."

"So let me get this straight," Lex said. "This Grotton dude would scythe to the village washer wench who had pissed him off earlier that morning, smash her head in with a rock, and scythe back out, all before the Grim team got there to Kill and Cull the poor thing?"

"Exactly," said Driggs. "Directed Crashing allowed him to instantly murder whoever he wanted, whenever and wherever he wanted, all while escaping detection. The most efficient homicidal maniac of all time."

Silence fell upon the circle.

"Unless — " Lex started. They eyed her. "I mean, how do you know for sure that he was so evil?"

Ferbus bristled. "Did you not hear what we just said?"

"I mean, maybe the ones he was killing were bad people, or . . ." She trailed off at the sight of the disgusted faces surrounding her.

"They weren't," Ferbus said curtly.

"How do you know?"

"Because — " Elysia looked around, then whispered, "Because a bunch of them were Grims."

Lex's eyebrows shot straight up. "He went after his own people?"

"Eventually, yeah."

Lex looked around the bar at the individuals who could now be described as her own people. Uncle Mort had arrived and was already lighting someone's drink on fire, much to the merriment of those gathered around him. She also couldn't help but notice the curious stares coming from some of the Senior Grims; a few of them even pointed at her, mouthing "Mort's niece." Most seemed friendly. A few, predominantly gathered around Norwood and Heloise, did not.

"Well," Lex said slowly, "Grims could just as easily be bad people. Doesn't Grotton's very existence prove that?"

"It doesn't matter whether they were good or bad," Driggs said. "What matters is that he ruthlessly slaughtered a shitload of people using a power that humans were never meant to possess."

Lex was quiet for a moment. "No offense," she said, "but all this sounds pretty far-fetched."

"Duh," said Sofi. "That's why it's called a legend."

"But what are you saying here? That these targets are being murdered by an allegorical bogeyman?"

Driggs gave her a disparaging look. "Come on, Lex. Grotton's been gone for centuries, if he ever existed at all. But the myths live on, and they still scare the crap out of Grims to this day. The thought of someone learning how to Crash with direction — it's pretty unsettling, don't you think?"

"But Crash in to do what?" Lex said. "There weren't any crossbows sticking out of these people's heads."

Driggs looked thoughtful. "Grotton wasn't exactly a paragon of subtlety. There are a lot more modern ways to murder people now, better ways of covering your tracks — though I don't know of anything that can end a life instantly. Or white out someone's eyes."

"Neither do the Smacks," Sofi said.

After a moment of contemplative silence Driggs shrugged. "Just keep looking out for them, I guess. Not much else we can do."

"Except get shitfaced," Ayjay said.

And just like that, the shadow lifted. Zara left for the bar to get more drinks, and Kloo and Ayjay dove right back into each other's tonsils.

Lex took Elysia aside. "Seriously, Lys," she said. "Is this Grotton thing really true?"

"Oh, yes," Elysia said with wide eyes. "He's like the Grimsphere equivalent of Hitler."

Lex really liked Elysia, so she tried very hard not to laugh at that. "But why?" she asked. "I mean, I can see why he was a threat to people in the outside world, but aren't Grims protected by the ether?" After the plane crash Driggs had explained that the reason they didn't lose consciousness at thirty-five thousand feet or get wet in water or burned in a fire was that every time they scythed, their bodies became surrounded by a thin layer of ether that shielded them from the elements.

Elysia cocked her head. "Not from everything, Lex."

"So — wait, we're not bulletproof?"

"No," Elysia replied. "We can die just as easily as anyone else."

A sliver of fear darted through Lex's body. She wasn't sure why she had assumed that Grims were invincible, but the sudden realization that they weren't hit her like an icy splash of water. "Which means," she said, "that if this murderer ever decides to stop targeting baseball enthusiasts and drunken cougars and go after Grims like Grotton did . . . we're completely defenseless?"

Elysia nodded.

Rattled, Lex glanced at her beverage. A large, grimy bubble had erupted onto the surface.

"Why aren't you drinking?" Ferbus piped up. "That's a waste of a perfectly good Yorick."

"I don't know, I guess I'm just not in the mood for raw sewage."

"Shhh," Driggs said worriedly, putting his hand over the brim of her drink. "It'll hear you."

Lex could see no reason not to fling all the contents of the mug directly into his face.

Driggs sensed this. "What I mean is, you must respect the Yorick," he said. "Come on, Lex, you're sixteen and you're at a bar. Drink already."

It was hard to argue with this logic. And so she drank already.

The first thing to bombard her senses was the taste — a rich, creamy, delectable sweetness that was so deeply satisfying it felt like it flowed through every vein in her body, right down to her toes. Like a chocolate-vanilla-malty-caramel-honey-cocoa-ecstasy milkshake, the buttery potion lingered on her tongue long after it had cascaded down her throat. A sumptuous aroma filled her nostrils, stinging her lungs with its potent decadence, blazing hot and icily cool at the same time.

But that wasn't all. Lex realized that in addition to the liquid-candy flavor, she was physically tasting the feeling of *elation*. All her troubles melted away; indeed, it was hard to imagine that she had ever had any troubles at all. A soft glow settled around the edges of her vision as her friends laughed at her stupor. She didn't even care. She loved them. She loved them so much . . .

"Whoa," yelled Driggs, grabbing her shoulders and giving them a hard shake.

"Yummm," she gushed.

Ferbus and Elysia laughed. Driggs finished off his own mug and flashed a silly grin. "Be right back," he said, stumbling to the bar.

"What's *in* this stuff?" Lex sucked down another gulp, not wanting to waste a precious second with frivolous talking.

"Elixir," Elysia said. "It's made from the white fluff in the atrium. There, it's in its rawest form — strictly functional and architectural. But when you remove it from the Afterlife, it condenses down into a liquid state and gives you the most amazing feeling in the world. All Corpp does is mix it with his special blend."

"Of what, crack?"

"Who knows?" Elysia smiled. "Yoricks are different wherever you go in the Grimsphere. The ones in DeMyse have a fruity taste, and in Necropolis they're much more bitter. Each place has its own secret recipe, but I personally *loooove* ours. It's like dessert."

"Like a rainbow," mumbled Ferbus.

The girls stared at him.

"Anyway," Elysia continued, "they're popular wherever you go. The Grims' international drink of choice. And the best part is — "

"No hangover!" Driggs returned with another round. "It doesn't stay in your system as long as alcohol, it'll never make you puke, and the next day you'll wake up feeling like you just won all of the Olympics."

Lex slurped down the rest of her mug and reached for another. "It can't be that easy," she said. "If this got out into the public, it would be outlawed in seconds."

"Actually, there *is* a three-drink maximum." Elysia pointed to a sign hanging over the bar. "And that's strictly enforced. But that's all you need. It's potent stuff. Whatever's in Elixir isn't really meant for this world. A few pure drops could drop you in a flash. That's why it's diluted so heavily for drinking purposes, and that's why there's a cutoff. Drink any more than that, and you tend to stop breathing," she said brightly.

"But Grims have been pounding this stuff for centuries," Driggs said, "so we've gotten pretty good at it. The only way you could get hurt under its influence would be if you went to hug a coat rack and poked your eye out."

"It's all fun and games until someone loses an eye," Ferbus said too loudly. "Then it's one-eyed fun."

Elysia put a napkin over his head. "That's why there's no drinking age here. You can hardly outlaw something that cheers people up, especially with the line of work that we're in."

Lex pointed at the walls. "Is the décor supposed to cheer us up, too?"

"Yep! Corpp used to be an artist," Elysia said. "So when he retired from Culling and opened up this bar, he couldn't help himself. He repaints it every few days." She took another gulp. "See, Corpp always wanted this to be a place for Grims to come and just have fun. You know, let off some steam from the morbid work we do and hang out in one big, unifying, satisfying, creative, artistic masterpiece."

As Elysia drunkenly giggled into her drink, Lex glanced at the old man behind the bar. He smiled at her. She smiled back. And as the night wore on, she continued to smile so often and so hard that by the time last call rolled around, she feared her face would be stuck that way forever.

She even cracked up when Ferbus spilled his drink all over her shirt.

"You frickin' klutz!" Elysia screeched.

"Hey!" he said. "I'm the victim here! That was my last drink!"

Laughing despite her wretched state, Lex made her way to the bathroom to clean up. She held her shirt under the hand dryer until it was mostly dry, then stole a glance at the mirror. The face that looked back was almost unrecognizable.

It was happy.

The giddiness waned, however, as she exited the bathroom to find only an empty corner where the Juniors had been. "Where'd everyone go?"

Driggs, the only one left, shrugged. "The Crypt has a curfew. If they don't get back by midnight, it locks them out, so they had to run."

"Without saying goodbye?" Lex asked warily. She tried in vain to catch his eyes, but they seemed to be unwaveringly fixed on her sodden chest.

"What?" He looked up. "Yeah, you look fine." Now he looked confused. "Uh, let's go home." He dragged her through the crowd, placed their empty mugs on the bar, and headed for the door.

"Wait, what about the buckets?" Lex asked, shooting Corpp a questioning look.

He gave her a pleasant smile. "Have fun!"

Lex tried to decipher this as they walked down Dead End. "Have fun with what?"

"Oh, I don't know. Maybe . . . this," Driggs said as he ducked down a narrow alleyway. Lex blindly followed, her hands feeling along the walls until they emerged at the edge of the forest. She stopped.

Driggs gave her a devilish look, his attention now back in full. "Come on," he said, plunging into the trees.

Lex looked around nervously, her courage fading ever so slightly. She gave her head a determined shake. Surely a fearless ruffian such as herself couldn't be scared by a little darkness.

And a lot of creepy shadows.

And the thickest forest she'd ever seen.

Driggs called out for her once more, so she timidly stepped into the woods, felt her way down the path, and tried not to look at the impossibly black spaces between the trees.

Until something white caught the corner of her eye. She watched the figure — a hunched form moving slowly through the wood. For some reason, she thought back to her first time in the Field, when she'd felt someone watching from behind a bush. Panic gripped her throat. Surely it was a deer or an especially large rabbit — but no, Elysia had told her that animals usually steered clear of Croak, too spooked by the omnipresent air of death.

Lex moved a little faster now, nervously glancing at the figure, which by some small miracle was making no attempt to come any closer. She glimpsed down the trail, desperately searching for Driggs, but the path had taken a sharp turn and he'd disappeared from sight. She broke into a run, willing herself not to look back, but after a mere five seconds she couldn't help it. She whirled around and swung —

At nothing. The wood was empty.

Now even more spooked, Lex turned back — only to slam

into something solid and Driggs-shaped. "Jerk!" she screamed at a hysterical pitch, punching him.

"Ow!" He rubbed his back. "Kidneys again? Ever feel like changing things up? Maybe go for a non-vital organ?"

"I see no need to mess with tradition," Lex said, gulping air and trying to return her voice to its normal octave.

"God, you are so . . ." He looked at her with an expression she couldn't quite decipher. In their flushed, drunken states, it was difficult to tell where this loss of inhibition might lead. But his face was coming closer.

Lex held his gaze and didn't back away. "What?"

His nose was inches from hers. "So distracting."

A maelstrom of butterflies crashed through Lex's stomach. She swallowed and licked her lips, her brain trying to anticipate what was about to happen, whether she should put a stop to it, and how to avoid looking like an inexperienced idiot if she didn't.

Luckily, a heretofore unseen low-hanging branch spared her the decision. It poked Driggs squarely in his already-bruised blue eye, causing him to jump back and flail wildly at the air. "Dammit! See what I mean?"

Lex blinked a few times, then found her voice. "Bad week for the eye, huh?"

Driggs shot her a Look, then took off down the path and dissolved back into the darkness, grumbling. Lex followed him, snickering at her temporary insanity. What exactly had she expected to happen? Those Yoricks must have been more potent than she thought, for her to even consider the idea of jumping aboard the horny teenager bandwagon.

She continued to follow him down the path a little farther,

clearing her mind of all that foolishness and instead pondering what an awesome band name Horny Teenager Bandwagon would be, until eventually the trees began to thin. Lex scoped out the clearing. The moon, peeking out from a blob of clouds, reflected faintly off the ripples of a large pond.

"Where are we?" she asked, approaching the water's edge.

Her question was met by silence. "Driggs?" she called, frantically looking around the small beach. He had disappeared. Again.

Lex tried not to freak out. The shadows were just shadows. The white thing was gone. She was in a safe place. All she had to do was find her way back up the path, go home, and quietly murder Driggs in his sleep. Easy.

The trees began to creak, an otherworldly chorus of eerie moans. Lex blindly faced the menacing forest, her back to the water, vulnerable and trapped. Vowing never to leave her scythe at home again, she grabbed a nearby stick, as if this could possibly defend her from the horrors materializing in her imagination. She had just begun to calculate how many jabs in the eye it would take to bring down a chupacabra, when —

A twig snapped.

Someone yelled.

And seven well-aimed water balloons hit Lex directly in the face.

Instantly drenched, she let out a shrill cry not unlike that of an angry, bathtubbed cat. She shook the water from her eyes, flung her useless stick into the void, and growled as the army of laughing Juniors emerged from the trees.

"What the hell??" Lex shouted, struggling with the logistics of how to punch seven people all at once.

"Sorry, Lex, nothing personal." Driggs grinned. "Rookie always gets clobbered on their one-week anniversary. No need to mess with tradition, right?"

Lex lunged at him, but Ferbus held her back. "Hold that thought," he said, plopping a bucket of slippery ammo at her feet. "Water balloon fight to the death. Grab as many as you can and show no mercy." He stuffed about a dozen balloons into the front of his shirt and scampered off into the forest.

Lex fished a rubbery shard out of her hair and let out a short laugh. "Are you serious?"

"Dead serious," said Elysia, scooping up balloons. "I'd stock up if I were you."

Lex caught a glimpse of Ayjay taking aim at her from across the beach. Devoid of a better plan, she quickly grabbed a handful of balloons and took shelter behind a nearby log. Another cry rang out, and chaos ensued.

The carnage was unspeakable. Balloons torpedoed in every direction. Clothes were soaked. Peals of laughter echoed off the wall of trees into the inky sky. And before long, everyone ended up in the pond, clothes and all.

Except for Lex.

"Careful!" Kloo yelled at Sofi and Zara as they shoved each other under the water. "I'm not doing CPR this time, I mean it!"

Lex gaped at a stark-naked Ferbus as he swung from a rope into the pond. "You're all cracked," she said to no one in particular.

"Lighten up, Lex," Driggs said as he ran by, splashing into the water and drenching her completely.

She couldn't resist it any longer. "You are so dead!" She dove after him into the abyss. The cool water instantly soaked through her clothes, dragging her down into the murky depths. As her lungs got close to bursting, she kicked up to the surface and popped her head out of the water, only to find herself looking directly at a single blue eye.

"Oh," she said. "Hello."

Driggs smiled. "Your nose is all snotty."

"Sucks to be you, then," she said, slurping some water into her mouth and spitting it at his face.

Driggs gave her a reproachful look, but she didn't care. She threw herself backwards, did a little flip, then floated to the surface and gazed up at the star-filled sky. How was it possible that only a week ago she had been trapped in such a crappy little life? And now here she was, the happiest she had ever been, surrounded by people she liked and who miraculously liked her back, and possessing a crapload of talents she'd never even known she had.

Once again, her mind flooded with thoughts of the little girl with the teddy bear, of the man who'd done such inhuman things to her and the heat that had pulsated through Lex's hands. What could she have done to him if Driggs hadn't stopped her?

Lex knew she was here for a reason. She felt it every time she Killed, with every blinding shock. What other talents lay hidden within? Her future was full of limitless possibilities. Even Uncle Mort had said she'd go far.

Her lips curled into a sly grin.

Just how far could she go?

14

A lot can happen in a month. Hideous caterpillars morph into beautiful butterflies. Christmas trees go from symbols of holiday cheer to naked, shriveled cadavers doomed to the woodchipper. And one month after arriving in Croak, Lex too had undergone a curious transformation. She had delved into a state hitherto unknown, been introduced to a foreign territory, and changed into something she never could have imagined.

Lex had become popular.

In fact, she had risen so quickly through the social ranks of Croak's Junior Grim population that it seemed as though no one could remember a time when she hadn't been at the top.

"So we're at this really nice restaurant for our birthday, and Cordy takes the biggest bite of steak I've ever seen," she told the group, sitting outside around the fountain as they ate lunch. "It's roughly the size and shape of a golf ball, I kid you not. Unsurprisingly, she starts choking. So my dad grabs her around the waist and does the Heimlich, the wad of beef soars out of her mouth, and bam—I catch it *midair!* But Cordy was too busy dealing with the asphyxiation and all to notice. So I hid it in a napkin, took it home, then wrapped it up and gave it to her as a birthday present later that night. We laughed so hard, the neighbors complained."

The Juniors laughed too. "Classic," said Kloo, wiping tears from her eyes. "Classic."

"Yeah. She almost died." Lex grabbed a near-empty ketchup bottle and shook it vigorously over the onion rings that had been given to her. When nothing came out, she ran to the door of the diner and stuck her head in. "Dora!" she yelled across the restaurant. "Would it kill you to replace these ketchups once in a while? I know you treasure your relics from the Stone Age, but it might be time to let go!"

The elderly proprietor hobbled over. "What a mouth on this one," she grumbled to herself, practically throwing a new bottle at Lex. "Whatever happened to respecting your elders?"

"Isn't that what paleontologists are for?"

Pandora scowled, her wrinkles like crags. "Young lady, you are the rudest, most despicable hellion ever to disgrace the grounds of this establishment." Her frown transformed into a hideous gaping grin. "You remind me of me."

Lex smiled. "Thanks, Dora. Oh, this morning's weirdest was a guy choking on a hamster."

"Sweet sassy molassy," Pandora said in awe.

A couple of weeks before, Lex had naïvely bragged to Dora that she had already witnessed every single way a human being could possibly bite the big one. Dora, a former Killer herself, promptly smacked Lex upside the head and informed her of her error. "I once Killed a gentleman who had fallen into a swimming pool full of porcupines," she said. "Some deaths defy all reason. There'll always be a few humdingers, mark my word."

The endless cavalcade of inconceivable deaths soon forced Lex to concede. There was the woman who tried to use a hair dryer in the shower. The airport runway attendant overrun by a rogue luggage cart. And the kid who fired a nail gun into his chest in order to kill the mosquito that had been sitting there.

The list was endless. The more bizarre deaths Lex observed, the more she was forced to admit that a lot of people were just plain imbeciles.

But by far the strangest fatalities were the white-eyed ones, which were growing both in number and peculiarity at an alarming rate. None of the bodies had yet to exhibit any clear-cut signs of death — in fact, more often than not, the targets were dying in the most harmless settings or situations imaginable. Clearly, something unusual was being done to extinguish these perfectly healthy people in such an instantaneous manner — the glassy, icelike eyes were proof enough of that — but none of the Juniors had come any closer to figuring out what it was. Or who was doing it.

So on they plodded to the end of July, every day brainstorming new ideas but never coming to any solid conclusions. Discussion abounded among the Juniors after every shift, but all they had to show for their work was a handful of empty leads and a byzantine list of suspects.

But all that was about to change. "Uh, guys?" Ferbus said in a strange voice, paging through that day's copy of *The Obituary*. "You might want to take a look at this."

Lex returned to the fountain and squeezed in around the paper. "'Unusual Deaths Crop Up in Necropolis,'" she read out loud. "'Last night, seven Senior Grim teams returned from their overnight shifts with reports of abnormal target activity across the Midwest region. While details of the irregularities have not yet been released, authorities have publicly stated that there is no cause for concern. However, they ask Field Grims who observe anything out of the ordinary during their shifts to please contact their local mayor as soon as possible.'"

"Whoa," said Ayjay.

"Abnormal targets?" said Kloo. "That must be the same thing we've been seeing, right?"

Ferbus flipped through the rest of the pages. "Seems like it."

"But we've only gotten one a day here. Seven in one night seems like a lot."

"Not if you think like a serial killer," Driggs said. "We're assuming this person is a Croaker, right? So —"

"Why are we assuming that?" asked Zara.

"This is the first mention in *The Obituary* of any strange deaths elsewhere in the country. So unless there's another Grim town with a society of plucky youngsters determined to solve the Mystery of the Arctic-Eyed Stiffs on their own without alerting any Seniors, I think we've got a monopoly on this one."

"That's true," said Zara, nodding. "Continue."

"Okay. So far, this person has only been able to Crash to locations within Croak's jurisdiction, staying primarily in the eastern region. But now they're spreading their wings a little, finding that they can scythe farther and farther out, halfway across the country, until — bam! All-night crime binge."

"Wow," said Lex. "Nice work, Nancy Drew."

"This is impossible," Elysia huffed. "Everyone in Croak works either all day long or all night long, with no time to break for homicidal sprees. They'd have to be in two places at once. It doesn't make a lick of sense."

"Yeah," Lex said, thinking. "I mean, are we supposed to be finding some sort of meaning in all this, or maybe a pattern? What's this crackpot's objective?"

"Maybe there isn't one," said Kloo.

"You think they're killing all these people just for fun? Is that what Grotton did?"

Elysia took a deep breath, the way she always did before talking for several minutes. "No, he — "

"SHHH!" everyone but Lex hissed.

Lex looked around. "What?"

"Uh — nothing." Driggs was a terrible liar. It was one of his many faults.

"Come on, guys," Elysia said. "She'll find out sooner or later."

"It's always sooner, in your case," said Ferbus. Elysia showed him a choice finger. He returned the sentiment.

"Okay, there might be a teensy bit more to the Grotton legend that we didn't tell you," Driggs told Lex guiltily, his voice lowering. "But people never talk about it — "

"That's because no one knows for sure what it is!" Elysia interrupted.

Driggs glared at her. "I'm sorry, Elysia, do you want to tell the story?"

"Yes, I do." She swept an anxious glance around the street, then spoke in a whisper. "Grotton learned how to Crash with direction and murder people while time was frozen, but he didn't stop there. One day, the messy slaughter stopped. No more stabbings, no more crossbows."

"What do you mean?" Lex asked. "He gave up?"

"No," Elysia said. "Grotton was doing something even worse than murdering his victims. But the stories were so horrid, only a few of them got passed on — only crazy rumors of bodies piled up in the woods, corpses that had been incinerated."

"He set people on fire?"

"From the inside out," Ayjay said.

"Ew." Lex frowned. "How'd he do that?"

"No one knows," said Elysia. "And get this — their souls *disappeared*. Or at least they didn't end up in the Afterlife, that much is for sure."

Lex let out a long breath. "So what happened to them?"

"No one knows that either," said Kloo. "But if this person is even remotely hoping to achieve the same end . . ."

They were quiet for a moment.

"Guys, we gotta tell Uncle Mort," Lex finally said. "No matter how much trouble it gets us in."

"Finally," said Zara triumphantly. "At least *some*one doesn't want us all to get killed."

"But who would want to kill us?" Ferbus countered. "Can you honestly think of anyone in Croak who could do this?"

They shrugged, defeated. "No," Driggs said simply. "I can't. At all."

"Great. It's utterly hopeless," Ferbus said, throwing up his hands. "Shall we grab a Yorick and call it a day?"

"And why might we be doing something like that?" a shrill voice sounded from above. A raptorlike Heloise stood over them.

"Feed it something," Lex said loudly, "before it gets cranky and devours an unsuspecting passerby."

Heloise sneered down at them as if they were something she had just picked out from beneath her pointy shoe. "Hilarious." She looked at her watch. "Is there any particular reason why you're not back at work yet?"

"We're sunbathing," said Driggs. "Tell me, how has a vampire such as yourself managed not to disintegrate into a pile of ashes by now?"

Heloise was less than delighted. "I was under the impression that you *children* have a job to do." Her thin eyebrows sharpened. "I hardly think that even a prominent dignitary such as Mort's beloved niece should be exempted from her duties."

"Hey, did you read the paper today?" asked Ferbus, oblivious to her scolding. "Should we be keeping our eyes open for anything weird?"

Heloise pursed her lips. "Nosy little weasel, aren't you?" She glanced at the newspaper. "Not that it's any of your business, but *our* office hasn't noticed anything out of the ordinary. I suspect this whole thing is just the same old capital nonsense. Necropolis has always been plagued with its share of problems, just as Croak has been perpetually cursed with slothful adolescents."

"LEXINGTON!"

Lex was so startled, she dropped what was left of her hot dog into the fountain. She turned around to meet the furious, reptilian face of Norwood. "Hiya, Woody," she said, frowning as she batted at his tie. "This color doesn't suit you."

He snatched the tie out of her hand and tucked it into his shirt. "Why have you been stalling at your target sites?"

Lex hesitated. True, she and Driggs had been lingering a lot longer around the abnormal targets. And yes, there was that one time (or two, or maybe seventeen) that her hand had brushed up against her partner's and they'd both been rendered hopelessly awkward and incompetent for a full minute or so before regaining their composure. But Norwood finding out about any of it — she hadn't prepared for that. "Hey, we're not breaking any rules," she said, trying to sound unconcerned. "We scythe out eventually. What does it matter when it happens?"

He made a face. "It matters because when you little cretins get in trouble — *when*, not *if* — it's going to be *me* who deals with it, *me* who has to send in reinforcements, *me* who bails out your sorry—"

"And *me* who has to suffer through all of your smelly tirades," she said, waving her hand in front of his mouth. "Seriously, Woody, a Tic Tac now and then wouldn't kill you."

This did not sit well. Norwood looked about ready to hurl every last Junior right into the fountain. "I know you kids all think this is a joke, a lark, a goddamned summer camp for gene pool bottom dwellers like yourselves. But if you don't quit screwing around out there, I've got one word for you: exile." With that, he smoothed his tie, ran a hand through his lifeless hair, and stalked off. Heloise followed, giving them a vindictive nod as she left.

"And I've got two words for you," Ayjay said quietly. "Anger management."

"Wow, he *really* hates you, Lex," Elysia said in awe. "More than Driggs, even! You see the distance on that spittle flying out of his mouth? Must have been about five feet."

Lex watched him go. "What a crapbag. Out of his mind."

"Well, not completely," Driggs said.

Lex's face was murderous.

"Sorry!" he said. "But he's right, isn't he?"

A glacial silence ensued.

"Um, we better get back to work," said Kloo. A murmur of agreement swept through the group as they hurriedly gathered their things and made their escape.

Ayjay patted Driggs on the shoulder. "Good luck, man."

Once they were alone, Lex grabbed Driggs by the ear and began yelling into it. "I am only helping you with your beloved investigations. You know full well that I'm the fastest Killer in this place and I could be in and out of the ether in less than a second. The only time I drag it out is whenever we get one of those white-eye deaths, so that I can look around and try to solve this little whodunit."

Driggs wrestled his head away from her grip. "I just mean that you've stalled on other ones, too," he said with a suspicious look. "What about — "

"Come on, Driggs. I'm just doing it to mess with Norwood."

He scratched his arm. "Okay," he said curtly, unconvinced. He began walking toward the Bank.

"Wait! You don't believe me?"

"Lex, I just — "

She folded her arms and glared at him, which, if anything, only irritated him further.

He narrowed his eyes. "You think I don't see what you're doing? Sniffing around like a bloodhound every time we reach a target, looking for someone who deserves punishment?"

Lex gritted her teeth as she walked past him. "You don't know what you're talking about."

"I think I do," he said quietly, following her. "And I think *that* pisses you off more than anything."

Lex, who didn't have an answer to this because of its disturbing degree of accuracy, kept walking.

||||||

"Driggs!" Kilda shouted as Lex and Driggs returned from their shift that afternoon. She waved him over to the information desk. "Oh, Driggs!"

Driggs let out a low groan. "Hi, Kilda," he said, attempting a polite smile. "What can I do for you?"

"I need more Amnesia! I'm almost out!"

"That's impossible, Kilda," he said in a patient tone. "I milked the spiders a month ago and took out enough to last through the end of the summer."

"Well, I don't know what to tell you! It's practically gone!"

He gave her a sideways look. "Kilda, are you sure haven't been dipping into a little bit of Amnesia yourself?"

"I take offense to that!"

"Okay, okay," Driggs yelled over her protests. "I'll get you some more."

He and Lex walked into the hallway and up the stairs to deposit the Vessels. They chatted with Ferbus for a bit, but as soon as the conversation veered to the computer and his new goblin-resistant armor, Lex slipped into the Afterlife.

"Hi," Elysia said, rubbing her eyes as Lex sat on her desk. "I'm so glad you're here, I'm about ready to kill myself — oh, sorry, Emily." She quickly apologized to a sobbing Emily Dickinson. "Why don't you go play with Dr. Seuss for a while? He usually cheers you up." Emily dabbed at her nose with a soiled handkerchief, then moped off. "She's such a downer."

Lex did not reply, as she had grown too distracted by the targets that were materializing in the atrium, including the white-eyed dentist she had Killed while he was performing a root canal. She shook her head, baffled. How the hell were these people dying?

"Hey," she said to Elysia, an idea occurring to her. "Can I go talk to that guy? Ask him if he remembers what happened?"

Elysia winced and fiddled with her necklace. "We're not really supposed to talk to the new arrivals. It sort of messes with their heads."

"But what if he can tell us something important?"

Elysia shook her head. "He won't remember. Targets usually have very little recollection of the circumstances surrounding their deaths. Especially these white-eye deaths — time is frozen, so they'll never even know what hit them."

Lex thought for a moment more. "I'm asking anyway," she said, getting up.

"Lex — wait!"

"Hey!" Lex shouted at the hapless dentist. He turned to her, dazed. "Hi, I'd just like a brief moment of your time. Can you tell me how you died?"

The dentist staggered. "I'm dead?"

"Oh. You didn't know that?"

He rubbed his head. "Last thing I remember, I was giving Mrs. Costello a root canal. Those gums of hers, my goodness, I've never seen such advanced periodontitis . . ."

Lex was shoved aside by an irritated Betsy Ross. "Scram, my dear." She took the befuddled man by the arm. "Right this way, Dr. Nolan," she said, escorting him toward the Void. "My, what a pretty white coat!"

"Let it go, Lex," Elysia said as Lex returned to the desk. "Leave it to the authorities. You're just a kid. Have fun. Go play in the fluff."

"Not over here, though," said a pale, miserable figure from behind a nearby pile. "I've constructed a Fortress of Solitude."

Lex watched the dentist for a moment more, then gave up. "What's wrong, Edgar?"

"Nothing." He pouted. "Okay, everything." He sighed dramatically as he approached, greasy black hair falling into his face. "I bit my tongue this morning, I dropped guacamole onto my favorite boots, Teddy Roosevelt made fun of my mustache, and — oh yeah — I'm dead." He crossed his arms with a small huff.

"Hey, Quoth," Lex said to the bird atop his shoulder, "go poop on Teddy Roosevelt." The raven gave a slight nod as he launched into the air and flew over to the tangle of presidents, where he stopped, aimed carefully, and dropped a plump white bomb directly onto the face of America's twenty-sixth.

Edgar stuck out his tongue. "Where's your big stick now, Teddy Bear?"

"Dammit, Poe!" Teddy roared, shaking his fist. "I'll get you for this!"

Edgar let out a screech not unlike that of a seven-year-old girl. He dove back into his fortress, sending clouds of the white fluff into the air. Lex watched them float around, her mind clicking onto something —

"Oh my God, that's it!" She jumped up from the desk. "Elysia, I'll catch you later. Edgar — you're a *genius.*"

"I am aware of that," a muffled voice replied.

15

"Where are we going?" Driggs asked as Lex dragged him down Dead End.

"Corpp's."

"The first step is admitting you have a problem, Lex."

Lex gave him a light smack on the head. "Not for drinking." She pulled him onto the sidewalk. "Whatever's killing the targets is doing it instantaneously, right? What's the one thing we know of that can do that — that Grims even *produce?*"

Driggs thought for a second, then smacked his own head. "Elixir."

"Right. And who's the only person in Croak with constant access to large quantities of it?"

Driggs looked at the tavern door. "You don't think — "

"No, I don't. But let's see what he knows."

Corpp's had a different feel to it so early in the evening — empty, cooler, and far too quiet. Lex and Driggs sat down at the bar as the elderly owner emerged from the house he and his wife shared out back — the "shag shack," as Pandora liked to put it, usually to a chorus of gagging.

"A bit early for you kids, don't you think?" Corpp said, cleaning out a mug. "There are other ways to have fun besides drinking, you know."

Driggs's mouth dropped open. "Corpp, let's not say things we can't take back."

"We're not here to drink," Lex said. "We just wanted to talk to you about something. Do you have a minute?"

He looked around the empty room. "Why yes, I believe I can squeeze you in," he said with a chuckle, handing them a bowl of nuts.

"Great. So I was just wondering, where do you store your Elixir?"

Corpp frowned. "Why do you ask?"

Lex cringed and glanced up at the THREE-DRINK MAXIMUM OR ELSE sign. "Um, I'm doing a report on it." Driggs coughed loudly. Lex kicked him in the shin.

"Juniors get homework nowadays?" Corpp asked, looking confused.

Lex thought quickly. If this lie was going to work, it had to be believable. "It's a punishment for mouthing off to Norwood. He said I need to learn how to respect my elders, so he's making me write a paper on the Croaker I admire most. And that . . . apparently . . . is you." She smiled sweetly.

An appreciative grin spread across the old man's face. "Well, I'll be a son of a gun."

"I know, it's quite an honor." Lex grabbed a handful of peanuts. "So tell me — how do you make those Yoricks so scrumptious? It all starts with the Elixir, I bet."

"Indeed it does," Corpp said, his eyes sparkling. "And I must say, it's better now than ever. See, back in my day, we had to import Elixir by the kegful and store it in the cellar. It never went bad, of course, but after a while it began to lose its zing. But about, oh, fifty years ago, me and some of the boys decided to run a pipe directly from the Afterlife right here to the bar." He reached over to the tap and lovingly patted its head. "Now every drop is as clean as a whistle!"

"So let me get this straight," Lex said. "There's absolutely no way to access Elixir, in all of Croak, other than through this tap right here."

"You got it. And me and the wifey are the only ones who know how to use it." He indicated Pandora's diner. "But what you really want to know about are the mixers! Well, I can't divulge my secret recipes, but I will tell you the one ingredient I can't live without is — "

"Thanks, Corpp!" Lex jumped off the barstool. "That was really interesting. Really. Thanks for your time. See you tonight, okay?"

"But — well, all right." He smiled bemusedly. "Take some nuts!"

Driggs, who eagerly accepted a handful, could barely keep his snickers in as they left. "And the Oscar goes to . . ."

"Bite me. We found out what we needed to know, didn't we? Elixir can't be stolen from the bar, which means — "

"That it's being taken from the Afterlife?" he said dubiously, chewing. "The place is on constant lockdown. There's no way to smuggle Elixir out of there without half a dozen people noticing."

"Then it's coming from somewhere else." She stopped walking. "Which means we need to ask more questions. And who knows more about Croak than anyone?"

Driggs looked reluctant. "Fine," he said after a moment. "But only on one condition: let me do the talking."

||||||

"Hi, Uncle Mort!" Lex blared as they walked into the kitchen.

"Unbelievable," Driggs muttered.

Uncle Mort sat at the kitchen table, scouring a copy of *The Obituary* and picking his teeth with his scythe. "Hey, kids. How was work?"

"Well," Driggs said, "it wasn't — "

"How was *your* day, Uncle Mort?" Lex butted in as charmingly as possible, sliding into the seat next to him and fixing an earnest look on her face. Driggs took the seat across from her and mouthed, "Subtle."

Unlike Corpp, however, Uncle Mort wasn't falling for it. "What do you want?" he said, eyes still on the paper.

Lex pretended to be offended. "I don't want anything!"

"If it's money you're after, I don't have any. And I thought we discussed my policy on dinner."

Lex took another breath, but this time Driggs was too quick for her. "Mort, there's something we've been meaning to ask you," he said.

Uncle Mort tossed the paper aside and began perusing a journal titled *Jellyfish Care and Maintenance: Getting the Most Out of Our Beloved Harbinger of Death.* "Yeah? What now?"

"We've been noticing something weird during our shifts," Driggs continued. "Now, it could just be a coincidence, and we might be wrong, and we're not even sure that it means anything at all, but — "

"Someone's murdering people who aren't supposed to die," Lex burst in.

Driggs looked furious. "Lex!"

"Oh, grow a pair." She clasped her hands together and leaned in. "Uncle Mort, we've been seeing these cases on almost a daily basis for about a month now — actually, we think it's the same sort of thing that was in the paper this morning. These are targets who have no injuries or diseases, except their eyes are completely white. We think that a Grim is Crashing with direction and then murdering them, but so far we haven't been able to figure out how they're doing it. Or why. But something's definitely up. And we figured that if anyone should know, or if anyone could explain, it would be you."

Uncle Mort, his face blank, sat very still. Silence filled the room. The screen door blew open, scattering a candy bar wrapper across the floor like a tumbleweed.

"Well," he said portentously, leaning in. "It's about damned time."

Jaws dropped. "What?"

Uncle Mort rubbed his stubbly cheek. "About a month ago I lost a bet to one of the graveyard shifters and had to take his shift — which was fine by me, I'll take any excuse to get out into the Field. But the last target of the night was a woman sitting by her pool, eating a grapefruit and watching the last of a meteor shower. It was dark, and I assumed she had gotten hit — until I saw her eyes."

Lex and Driggs nodded vigorously. "Yeah, that's a lot like what we've been seeing," Driggs said.

"I thought it odd," Uncle Mort went on, "because I've handled such deaths before, and I can tell you, with a meteorite attack, there's usually very little target left over to Kill. And the eye thing — I'd never seen anything like it. Ever since, I've been waiting for the Field teams to come to me with more anomalies

— can't ask around myself, don't want to start a panic — but I haven't heard a thing. Though this is due, I take it, to a Sofi-aided monopoly on your part?"

Driggs looked nervous. "The Juniors — we thought we could — "

"No surprises there." Uncle Mort cracked a smile. "From you kids, I'd expect nothing less."

Lex stuck a triumphant tongue out at Driggs.

"It's gotta be a Crasher," Driggs pressed on, ignoring her. "Who do you think it is?"

"Beats me." Uncle Mort got up from the table, ducked into the living room, and began digging through a pile of papers. "The techniques involved in directed Crashing are thought to be so advanced that not even the oldest Grim on earth would have enough experience to pull it off." He returned to the kitchen and dropped a stack of printed pages onto the table. Lex glanced at the top sheet, a news article under the headline MYSTERIOUS DEATH AT FENWAY PARK, along with a picture of the man she had Killed at the baseball game.

She turned to her uncle, stunned. "You've been following this?"

"Yep." Uncle Mort sat down again. "One of my many jobs is to keep an eye on the mainstream media for any abnormal deaths. So when these drop-dead-for-no-reason stories started popping up — a couple days after meteorite lady and strictly limited to the eastern region of the country — I figured the two were connected." He pointed to one of the pages. "Autopsies have turned up jack shit. And the victims' eyes are fine, so whatever's killing them must wear off pretty fast."

"Elixir!" said Driggs, desperate to be of some use.

"Hey!" Lex yelled. "*I* thought of that!"

Uncle Mort nodded slowly, deaf to their bickering. "Don't know where they'd get it from, but yeah, that would make sense. Doesn't leave a trace."

"But why should that matter?" Lex asked. "Why would a Grim go through the trouble of getting Elixir — which, you're right, who knows *how* they do that — when they could just as easily use arsenic or cyanide or, I don't know, a gun? Why bother keeping it clean? It's not like any of the authorities out there can catch them."

"They're sending us a message," Driggs said, thinking. "Using any old weapon is no big deal, but stealing Elixir? That takes some serious balls. Whoever is doing this wants Grims to know that they've outsmarted the system, that they can harness this power and are willing to do horrible things with it."

Uncle Mort nodded in agreement, then handed the paper to Lex. "And here's where it gets really crazy. Check out the target."

Lex scanned the article. "Arnold Scadden, thirty-two years old. No wife, no kids." Her eyes bulged. "Convicted sex offender?"

Driggs grabbed the next sheet off the top and skimmed through it. "Susan Karliak, forty-nine. Awaiting trial for third DWI."

"Dr. Dennis Nolan, fifty-six. Twice sued for malpractice," Lex said, showing Driggs the picture. "Look, the dentist!"

Uncle Mort sifted through the rest. "And thirty or so others charged with assault, extortion, child pornography, fraud, rape, drug trafficking, arson — you name it."

A fervor gripped Lex. Someone was really doing it. Someone

was going after the criminals who needed to be stopped! "Murderers too?" she said, looking up in excitement. Yet no sooner had the word left her mouth than she realized her mistake.

Uncle Mort was giving her a harsh look. "No, curiously enough," he replied in an even tone. "No murderers."

"Too bad," Lex said under her breath.

Uncle Mort exchanged a glance with Driggs. He leaned in to his niece. "You remember those Terms we went over, right, kiddo?"

"Yes."

"Good," Uncle Mort said. "I just want to make sure we're all on the same page here. These are *not* okay, Lex. I don't want you to start worshiping this nutjob. You of all people should steer clear of their plans, especially since — " He cut off abruptly, a hesitant and slightly surprised look on his face.

"Since what?"

"Well, since I've never seen anything like this until you arrived."

Lex gaped. "You think it has something to do with me?"

"No. Not directly, of course. Still," he said quietly, and more to himself, "it's a hell of a coincidence."

Lex looked up at Driggs, who was looking at her with a strange expression. She made a face back at him. "So where do we go from here?"

"I'll jump into the Field for the next few days, see for myself what's going on," Uncle Mort said, standing up. "Thank you for telling me about this. And keep the criminal pattern between us, will you?" He hurriedly left the kitchen for his lab, locking the basement door behind him.

Lex picked at a stain on the table and thought about the implications of what her uncle had just told her. All the evil that was loose in the world . . . a way to rein it in . . .

She looked at Driggs, who was still glaring at her. "May I help you?" she asked peevishly.

"Knock it off."

"Knock what off? I'm not doing anything."

"Yes, you are. You're scheming." He got up and walked toward his room. "Scheming leads to crazy ideas. Crazy ideas lead to trouble. I get dragged into your trouble, we both get kicked out of Croak, and the next thing you know, we're freezing to death in the waters of the North Atlantic."

"Dude, you are way too obsessed with *Titanic*."

Driggs looked indignant. "What is so wrong with having a healthy respect for heart-wrenching filmmaking of unequaled —" He shook his head. "Look, this isn't about me. Just quit it with the evil plots, all right? If you get exiled, I'm going to be pissed as hell." He slammed the door.

"Why?" she yelled.

He poked his head out. "I don't want to have to clean out your room again." He slammed the door once more and disappeared into a crash of drums.

Lex was not amused. Although secretly, she was.

16

After finding Corpp's devoid of Juniors later that evening, it didn't take Lex and Driggs long to guess that their crew had decided to hole up in the Crypt's common room for the night. Together they headed down Dead End and made their way through a darkened, narrow tunnel, eventually emerging into a small green courtyard surrounded by a block of rooms. As they approached the largest one, a heated argument between Sofi and Ayjay wafted through the window.

"I've got ten hotels on the Conservatory. Seriously, you owe me, like, eighty gatrillion dollars."

"Not until I get my triple-letter score for passing Go."

"No way! You couldn't remove the Charley Horse, remember?"

"So? I still found the Lead Pipe in Park Place!"

"Which you had to mortgage after Queen Frostine totally sank your battleship!"

Lex attempted to follow this conversation as she walked through the door, but she failed somewhere around the time Elysia almost toppled over on the Twister mat. "Jump in," Elysia said from the floor, wobbling way too close to the jellyfish tank. "There are a couple of tokens left in the box."

Driggs sat down on one of the many battered couches and dug through the box, removing a wrench, a top hat, a rook, a green gingerbread man, and a decapitated Rock'Em Sock'Em

Robot. Lex looked at the game board on the table, a mangled conglomeration of Monopoly, Clue, Candy Land, Scrabble, and chess.

"What the crap?" she asked the room.

"Don't touch the Candlestick or you'll automatically lose," Elysia warned from the mat, flicking the spinner with her free hand. "Right foot red. Okay, so one night last year we came home from Corpp's really late, but we were all still too drunk and giggly to go to sleep, so Ferbus took all of the board games that had been sitting in the closet since the dawn of time and mashed them up into one."

Lex held up a rogue Uno card. "What are the rules?"

"No one really knows," Kloo said, peering at her tray of Scrabble tiles. "We kind of just make them up as we go along."

"I see. And what do you call this game?"

"Doesn't have a name," Zara said, absently watching a *Simpsons* rerun playing on their ancient television.

"Lies!" yelled Ferbus, twisted into a pretzel underneath Elysia. "It's called Ferbusopoly, and you all know it!"

"Hey, Milton Bradley? Your railroads are flooding."

"What?" He crashed to the floor and ran over to the board. "Dammit. I should never have left Colonel Mustard in charge," he moaned, mopping up a soggy Short Line.

"Hey, you guys are never going to believe this," Driggs said to the room. "Mort already knew about the white eyes. He's been tracking them since they started."

"No way!" Sofi said. "That's so crazybread!"

"My thoughts exactly," Lex said dryly.

"Was he mad?" asked Kloo, handing them a couple of slices of pizza.

"Nope," said Driggs. "In fact, he seemed kind of proud of us."

"That's because Mort is infinitely cooler than Norwood," said Ferbus. "What else did he say? Any ideas on who? Or why?"

"No. And . . . no." Driggs shot a warning glance at Lex to keep her mouth shut about the pattern of criminals. "But we did figure out how."

"We?" Lex said.

"Okay, Lex figured out how."

She told them about the Elixir and Corpp's interrogation. "Duh!" Elysia cried, pulling at her hair. "I work with that frickin' stuff all day long, why didn't I think of that?"

"Still, if it's not coming from Corpp's or the Afterlife, where are they getting it?" asked Ferbus. "And how are they killing people with it? And why did we stop playing my game?"

The discussion continued as they battled into the night, devouring box after box of Pandora's delicious pizza. Lex herself built a Jenga tower on Boardwalk, sank Driggs's destroyer with a double word score, and captured a bishop in the Peppermint Forest with Mrs. Peacock, making it obvious that years of family board game nights had crafted her into a force to be reckoned with.

Perhaps it was too vivid a reminder — Lex's memory jumped back to her family with each roll of the dice. She gazed longingly at the Scrabble board, remembering the time Cordy had theatrically thrown a pile of useless consonants at her face.

Lex sighed. No matter how hard she tried to ignore it, the thought of home was always there, perched in the back of her mind like a lurking vulture. Her strategy of squashing any images of her family before they could fully surface just wasn't working anymore. As amazing as her time in Croak had been, the wound of separation from her family remained fresh and raw — and the further she slid into the Grimsphere, the worse it got. She had been gone just over a month, yet already she was being torn in two distinct, worrisome directions. Never in a million years had she expected to *enjoy* herself on this upstate summer banishment. But her immersion in Croak had been so swift, so complete. It felt as if she had lived there all her life. How was she expected to yearn for a home that now felt unbearably mundane by comparison?

A loud yell from Ferbus snapped her back. He drew a Candy Land color card, then placed the Revolver on Baltic Avenue. "What's Professor Plum doing here?"

"Protecting the queen," Driggs said.

"What? Duel!" The two boys jumped up and stalked to the middle of the room, eyeing each other like prowling tigers.

Lex felt a sharp jab in her ribs. "Come on," Zara said quietly, nodding in the direction of the kitchen.

"Wait, they're going to fight," Lex said. "I wanna see."

"Those morons, fight? They're just gonna play Hungry Hungry Hippos," Zara said, pulling her out of the room. "The winner gets to be Supreme Ruler of the Electric Company and the loser has to spend a turn trapped inside the secret passage between the Kitchen and the Library."

"Crap. My submarine is hidden in there."

Zara's eyes flashed as she dragged Lex to the stove, out of the others' view. "I want to ask you something."

Over the past few weeks, on the sporadic occasions when they were able to steal away from the group, Lex and Zara had established an unusual relationship. Zara wasn't exactly her new best friend, but upon her confession that she too felt an overwhelming shock while Culling, Lex thought it might not be such a bad idea to have some company on her descent into madness. Little by little they had begun to confide in each other, swapping stories of the jolts they experienced. And secretly, Lex was glad to have someone with whom she could entrust these allegedly shameful feelings. Every time she brought them up to Driggs, he gave her that same look, the one that made his blue eye appear extremely judgmental. Not so with Zara.

Yet the cutthroat rivalry between them remained palpable. Now that Lex had superseded Zara as Croak's best Junior, their exchanges had gotten a bit pricklier.

"How's work going?" Zara asked, stealing a glance at the doorway. "No changes to your . . . you know. Right?"

"No," said Lex. "They're getting stronger, I keep telling you that. Yours are too, right?"

"Of course they are!" Zara looked offended. "I'm just paranoid, I guess. That yours will stop and I'll be the only one left."

"Which is what you really want, isn't it?" Lex muttered under her breath.

Zara looked stung. "I'm going to ignore that."

"Anything else?" Lex said, growing impatient.

"Yes." Zara came closer and lowered her voice. "Is that really all Mort said? Or is there something else you're not telling us?"

Lex noted the flash of jealousy in Zara's eyes. Should she bring her in on this? There was no denying that her expertise had some worth, but Lex could easily imagine Zara taking all the credit, proudly declaring to Uncle Mort that she had figured out everything by herself. That simply couldn't happen.

Plus, Lex thought somewhere in the far reaches of her mind, *if someone really is going after criminals,* I *want to be the one to find them.*

"No, that's all," Lex said.

Zara's face morphed into the expression of someone who knows she's being lied to. "Come on, Lex. Maybe I can help. And admit it — you owe me."

Lex's shoulders slumped as she remembered the secrets Zara had kept, the knowledge of Lex's shocks and vengeful urges that she hadn't spilled to the other Juniors — or even to Norwood. Lex really did owe her.

So she caved.

"That's insane," Zara said, her eyes worried, after Lex had told her everything about the criminals.

Lex chewed on the inside of her mouth, images of the girl with the teddy bear flashing across her mind. "Is it?" she said quietly, an angry fever burning up her neck.

"What do you mean?" Zara gave Lex a look. "You're not still lunging at murderers out in the Field, are you?"

Lex narrowed her eyes and backed up against the stove, an empty pizza box digging into her back. She knew she shouldn't push things any further, but the words just spilled out, growing louder and louder. "Is going after these monsters unethical? Yes, absolutely. Is it wrong?" Her face was red, her hands burning hot. "I'm not so sure."

"We're not supposed — "

" — to interfere. I know. But maybe we should!"

"But that's against the Terms — "

"Screw the Terms!" Lex exploded, slamming her hand down. It happened faster than either of them realized. They froze in horror, unable to move, staring at the pizza box that had burst into flame.

After a beat, they sprang into action. Zara flung open the refrigerator and grabbed a pitcher of water while Lex reached for a nearby spatula and began to bat at the box, trying to push it into the sink. Eventually their combined efforts succeeded and the flames were extinguished, the smoking, charred shell of the box giving off an acrid smell.

Zara looked at Lex with giant, scared eyes. "What was that?"

"I don't know!" Lex cried, just as alarmed. She pointed at the stove. "I must have turned it on by accident!" They both looked at the burner knobs, all plainly in the off position. "And turned it off too, I guess?"

"Right. Yeah." Zara studied her. "Has this happened before?"

"Has *what* happened before?" Lex shot back, Zara's accusatory expression sparking her rage all over again. "A kitchen fire involving grease-soaked cardboard? Only about a billion times, probably!"

Zara gave her a dubious look and opened her mouth to say something more, but a loud cry from the other room made her stop. "We should go back — "

Lex didn't know what made her do it, but she grabbed Zara's arm. "Don't tell anyone."

Zara wrestled out of her grip. "Might want to get rid of that," she said icily, nodding at the soggy box as she exited the kitchen.

Lex swallowed, then busied herself with destroying the evidence. As she shoved the box into a trash bag and started waving the fumes out the window, her mind churned. It was an accident, obviously. There was no other explanation.

Except . . . she had brought her hand down on the box, not the knob. She was sure of it. And why were her hands still scalding hot, her temper still flaring?

Stop it, she told herself. *Accident. Nothing more.*

As she shoved her hands into her pockets and made her way back into the living room, Lex was relieved to discover that both her absence and the fiery incident had gone unnoticed. Ferbus held his fists over his head in triumph as the others cheered (including Zara, who was acting as if nothing had happened), while Driggs looked dejectedly at his losing hippo.

"He cheated," he complained to Lex as she sat down. "Distracted me with a Hershey bar."

Ferbus rolled the dice and moved his top hat token forward. "And that would be a Connect Four." He grinned. "I win."

The group heaved a collective groan of defeat. Lex looked around in disbelief. "What?" she said, still fuming. "He *won?*"

"Geez, Ferbus." Driggs sighed with a hint of admiration. "You ever gonna lose?"

"Of course not, he's making it all up!" Lex yelled.

The group gasped.

Ferbus clucked his tongue. "You just insulted the Almighty Conqueror of the Universe," he said, handing her a box. "Which means you have to clean up."

Twenty full minutes of repacking later, Lex and Driggs headed home.

Lex decried the rules (or lack thereof) the whole way, focusing her anger on something real, something that made an iota of sense. "Marvin Gardens is a no-fly zone, my ass."

"Only for thimbles," Driggs said, climbing up onto the roof. "Hey, what did Zara want with you?"

"Oh — um, she just wanted to trade for a Get Out of Jail Free card."

He frowned. "But she wasn't in jail."

"Would it have mattered?" she said peevishly.

Lex was, in a word, torn. She trusted Driggs, but the truth was just so damn tricky. The fire thing — well, she didn't know what to make of that, and neither would he. All of this Zara business, the shocks they shared — it was too hard to explain. And she didn't even want to think about what would happen if she told him that she'd gone and spilled the secret of the criminal pattern Uncle Mort had found. To Zara, of all people. He'd probably dropkick her off the roof.

So she said nothing.

"You sure know your way around a Jenga tower," Driggs said.

"What?" Lex replied, distracted. "Oh. Thanks."

"How'd you get so good at those games?"

"My family — we played them all the time. I could probably recite the Monopoly properties to you in my sleep." A small smile appeared on her face. "I don't know, I guess my parents thought they were educational."

Driggs watched her. "You really think they'll make you go back at the end of the summer?"

She sighed. "I don't think. I know."

"But you're an adult. You should be able to do whatever you want."

"Yeah, right." Lex snorted. "Not in the real world. You have no idea what it's like to have — "

"What? Devoted parents?" he said coldly, his eyes suddenly hard. "An endless supply of unconditional love? People who actually give a damn about where their kid is?"

Lex clenched her fists, the anger rising yet again. Seemed like it was on full blast tonight. And she was sick of backing down from the "woe is me, I'm an orphan" defense, anyway. It wasn't her fault her home wasn't broken.

"What happened to your parents, Driggs?" she said in a voice that was exceedingly frosty, even for her. But she was feeling reckless. "Why are you so secretive about them? Everyone else seems to love wallowing in their tales of misery and sorrow. Why not you?"

Driggs's nostrils flared. "I don't want to talk about it," he said in a low, distant voice. "Is that so hard to understand?" He leaned in. "Do you, *Lex,* find it so unfathomable that a person might want to keep a few secrets for himself?"

That hit a nerve. Lex returned his gaze, both of her black eyes drifting automatically to his sole blue one, which was reading her perfectly. "What is that supposed to mean?"

"You tell me."

"Oh, for shit's sake." She jumped to her feet. "Enough of this cagey, elusive crap that you people incessantly spout! Can't you ever say anything of substance?"

"Why?" he exploded, leaping up as well. "So you can come back with something witty and sardonic that'll make you seem all self-important and superior, even though it's clearly a half-assed attempt to hide your own insecurities?"

"Oh, nice work there, Freud. At least I don't have to boost my low self-esteem by inhaling fistfuls of Oreos, downing a keg of Yorick, and pretending to be a homicide detective."

"Do you honestly think I can't tell what sort of warped stuff you've been entertaining in that sick little mind of yours? You might be able to dupe the others, Lex, but not me." Breathing heavily, he tapped her forehead. "There are a lot of malicious impulses rattling around in there, and it's pretty clear that you're in no hurry to get rid of them."

She donned an expression of mock terror. "Oh, excuse me for not dropping dead with terror at the thought of breaching one of Croak's beloved Terms." She was inches from his face. "I wouldn't want to end up as a scaaaaary exile!"

"Maybe you deserve it!"

"And maybe you should just go back to your sanctuary of spider friends and cry yourself to sleep!"

"At least they're not abominations like you!"

"Coward!"

"Freak!"

It suddenly occurred to both Driggs and Lex, in that very same instant, that neither of them wanted anything more in the world than to tear off every single piece of each other's clothes and make wild, passionate, messy adolescent love under the radiant glow of the full moon.

Their chests rose and fell. A few seconds passed.

"I'm going to sleep," Driggs panted, clambering off the roof.

"Me too," Lex huffed, right behind him.

And without another word they fled to their rooms, slammed the doors, and threw themselves into bed, where they both spent the next five hours dazedly contemplating their respective ceilings.

The next morning, things were awkward.

To say the least.

Fleeing the bathroom they shared, Driggs mumbled a hasty apology after accidentally knocking Lex's toothbrush into the toilet. At the breakfast table, Lex poured orange juice into her cereal instead of milk.

"What's with you two today?" Uncle Mort asked on his way out the door.

" . . . not much sleep . . ." Driggs grumbled.

" . . . that time of the month . . ." muttered Lex.

Their silent walk into town was eclipsed in unease only by their check-in at the Bank, which vastly paled in comparison to their shift. By the time they arrived back at the Ghost Gum and headed to the Morgue for lunch, Lex sensed that she was only seconds away from spontaneously combusting into a cloud of mist and thorny resentment.

It didn't help that Kloo and Ayjay were the only ones there, and that they had decided to spend the majority of their lunch hour eating each other's faces rather than their burgers. Lex and Driggs sat on either side of them, silently lamenting the discomfort of the situation. Lex examined the salt shaker. Driggs picked at a piece of gum.

Eventually the mortification of it all became too much to bear. "Wanna go?" Lex honked in a weird voice.

"Uh, sure."

"Make up, you two," Pandora said as they slunk out the door. "At this rate, you'll never get into each other's pants."

||||||

At the Bank, Driggs handed Lex his scythe and bolted up the stairs. "You check in," he said, undoubtedly in a rush to escape her. "Back down soon."

"Wait — oh, fine," she said bitterly. "Say hi to your wife Ferbus."

Lex was majorly out of sorts. Not only had last night's fight left her and Driggs's already-muddled relationship in a full-blown state of emergency, but the whole fire thing was still really bugging her. So much so that she finally decided to simply stop thinking about it, to lock it in an abandoned part of her brain, far, far away from any important thoughts, in a space normally reserved for sports trivia and the preamble of the Constitution.

She scoured the hub. The only available Etcetera was Sofi. "Naturally," she muttered to herself, approaching the desk.

"Hi, Lex," said Sofi. "Checking in?"

Lex grimaced. Interacting with Sofi always made her want to jam a thumbtack into her eye. "Yeah." She plugged in the scythes and slid onto the desk, knocking over a snow globe in the process. "Sorry."

After it became clear to both of them that Lex wasn't going to pick it up, Sofi sighed and did it herself. "Why don't you like me, Lex?" she asked with a pout.

Lex decided to issue a denial. Sofi wasn't exactly a shrewd individual; she could easily be duped. "Of course I like you," she said, thinking up a way to change the subject. "In fact, I was wondering — what do *you* think the Loopholes are?"

Sofi looked pleased to be consulted, but she shrugged. "Like I'd know!" She leaned in. "Whatever they are, I bet they're, like, Crazy McCrazyface. Why else would they get destroyed in the process?"

"Wait a minute," Lex said, shocked that what she thought would be a ditzy filler conversation was actually going somewhere. "What do you mean?"

"That's the only known part of them — that whatever the procedure is, the Loopholes themselves are involved in it and get used up or something."

"So the number of Loopholes grows less and less each time one is found?"

"Yuppers. And because no one knows how many there were to begin with, no one knows how many are left. Since it's been so long since the last one was found — in the early eighteen hundreds — some people think none."

"Although judging by what's going on now, that's obviously not true," Lex snapped.

Sofi raised an eyebrow. "Chica, you need to relax." She reached into her desk and handed Lex a sparkly gel-filled stress ball. "Here."

Lex gave the ball a squeeze. "I'm just — and this Loophole — it can't have anything to do with the Smacks? There's no way to override the system?" she asked.

"Not unless you turn into a jellyfish," Sofi said. "They're the only ones who can pick up the Gamma signals. They send them to us, and we send them out to you via the scythes, which are synchronized perfectly. They'll always take you smack-dab to the middle of the death, at exactly the right time. You can't scythe any other way. It just won't work."

"And you guys never interfere?" Lex said, throwing a suspicious glance at Norwood and Heloise.

"No," Sofi loudly replied. She threw a fearful glance around the hub, then lowered her voice. "Only when you guys make special requests, which I'm *not* supposed to agree to. Or if, like, your grandma dies. No one expects you to Kill your own family."

"And there's no way for you to program Grims who aren't checked in?"

Sofi was starting to hesitate. She looked at the door. "Where's Driggs?"

"Upstairs. Why, do you need his permission?"

Sofi let out a high-pitched huff. "I don't take orders from Driggs."

Lex snorted. "Except that you do, all the time."

"It's complicated, okay?"

"Why? You guys hook up or something?" Lex blurted with all the subtlety of a rocket-propelled grenade.

A smug grin spread across Sofi's face. "I knew it!" she screeched. "That's *totally* why you don't like me. You think we got a thing going on."

Blood pounded through Lex's cheeks. She swore to herself that the next time her tongue started wagging without express written consent from her brain, she'd hack the damn thing right off.

"You're blushing!" Sofi said triumphantly. She grabbed a nail file and went to work on her tips. "Well, don't worry. I've never jumped aboard the big Drigg. Though it's seriously not for lack of trying."

Lex, her lip curling, throttled the stress ball.

Sofi widened her heavily mascaraed eyes. "Honestly, though? You're barking up the wrong tree with that kid. You know how he carries that photo around with him everywhere? I think he's got a girl, like, on the outside or something, because no one here has ever gotten so much as a peck on the cheek from him."

"That's not — "

"Seriously, he's a lost cause." She clicked her tongue. "Major issues."

Lex gave her head a violent shake, as if to expel all of the uninvited thoughts clanging around in there. "Whatever. I don't care, okay? This has nothing to do with anything, and you're wrong about everything anyway."

"Okeydokey, Grumpypants," Sofi said, that coy look still plastered across her face.

Flustered, Lex abandoned her line of questioning and jumped off the desk to leave. "Are we checked in?"

"Yep," Sofi replied, unplugging the scythes. "Say hi to loverboy for me."

A thick film of goo instantly blanketed the cubicle.

"Sorry," Lex said, tossing the exploded stress ball at a dumbfounded Sofi. "It slipped."

Over the next few days Lex decided to focus her nervous energy on something useful: the computer. She sneakily read article after article, extracting every bit of information about the unexplained deaths that had been reported all over the East Coast and the laundry list of offenses that each of the targets had racked up. And the more Lex read, the more she resolutely believed — no matter what her uncle or Driggs or Zara said — that every one of the victims got exactly what he or she deserved.

What Lex did not do, however, was write a single email. She ignored her brimming inbox, pretending not to notice that Cordy had emailed her at least once a day, sometimes twice. Lex just couldn't bring herself to respond. When it came to Cordy, silence was better than lies.

At least the awkwardness between her and Driggs had dissipated. This was no more evident than the afternoon Lex caught Driggs lying face-down on the ground of the Lair, allowing scores of black widow spiders to crawl over his body. "Again?" Lex said, exasperated. "Really?"

"You gotta try it," he said contentedly into the floor.

"No way. They don't like me the way they like you."

"Probably because you don't cry yourself to sleep in their presence," he said, quoting her taunt from their big fight. The whole thing had turned into something of a running joke between them. Often, when bored or uncomfortable, they repeated the insults they had hurled at each other that night, loudly guffawing at each reiteration. This is what is known as a defense mechanism.

Driggs had, however, started to spend a lot more time in his room, banging away at his drums. He was doing just that so loudly one evening as Uncle Mort got home from work that Lex, reading an article about a notorious arsonist, didn't even hear him come in.

"What are you doing?" Uncle Mort asked her.

She snapped off the screen. "Solitaire."

He rubbed his eyes and banged on Driggs's door. "Hey, Ringo, give it a rest!"

The drumming stopped. "How'd your shift go?" Lex asked as Uncle Mort sank, exhausted, onto the couch. He had been taking on as many shifts as he could over the past few days. "Did you see any more?"

"Yeah," he said. "Weird as hell."

"So now what? More shifts?"

"No," he said, thinking. "You guys keep doing what you're doing, and let me know if anything changes. I don't want it to look like I'm too involved. I don't have the time, anyway."

"Really?"

He let out a sigh. "Why do kids think adults lead such opulent lives of leisure?" He shook his head. "Believe me, I don't. I've got a town to run, reports to be sent to Necropolis — plus this anomaly, whatever it is, I've spent way too much time obsessing over it — not to mention the hunt for this year's rookies — "

"What do you mean?" Lex said. "I thought *I* was the rookie."

"Yeah, well, this was a bizarre year. The Junior training period usually starts at the beginning of what would be the eleventh grade — in September, not June. But last September's duo washed out right away, and then Rob took off for business school — "

"Loser!" Driggs yelled through the wall, apparently listening in.

"It was his choice," Uncle Mort shouted back. He looked at his niece. "There's always a choice."

Lex fidgeted.

"Anyway, that left us three short," he continued. "But once I

learned that you had turned delinquent, I decided you'd be a suit-
able replacement."

"But I'd been that way for two years already. Why didn't you
bring me here last September in the first place, for my junior
year?"

"I really shouldn't have brought you at all," Uncle Mort said
softly. "But the world, as it turns out, had different plans."

Lex said nothing for a moment. All this talk of September was
only serving as a reminder of her impending departure. She
looked at the jellyfish, then down at her hands. "Do I really have
to go back home at the end of the summer?" she asked in a quiet
voice.

Uncle Mort looked at her thoughtfully. "I'm sure your parents want you to finish your education." He removed a glass ball
from his pocket and distractedly rolled it through his hands.

"But who cares about senior year?" she half yelled. Driggs was
probably still listening, but she didn't care. "I already know more
than most of the teachers at that worthless school, and I'd just
come right back here after I graduate anyway. I'm training for a
career! It's the same as college!"

"All valid arguments. You be sure to present them during your
visit."

"What visit?"

He tossed the bauble into the air. "Your mother's birthday, I
believe?"

Lex clapped her hands over her mouth. It's fairly common for
children to forget a parent's birthday, of course, as most kids can't
conceive of a situation in which the world stops revolving around
themselves for twenty-four hours. But due to Lex's strategy of
suppressing all thoughts of her family, that particular date — to-

morrow, she realized with growing remorse — had completely slipped her mind.

Not only had Lex forgotten to send a card; she hadn't bothered to call in weeks. She couldn't begin to imagine how disastrous an actual visit would be. They'd hang her on the spot.

"You're taking the weekend off," Uncle Mort said.

"No, I'm not! There's no such thing as a weekend here! Death waits not for five-day workweeks!" she chanted in desperation, quoting the mantra Driggs had recited a month ago when she first asked why he was jumping on her bed so early on a Saturday morning.

"We'll somehow survive without you," Uncle Mort said. "Besides, I already got your bus tickets."

"Tickets?" Lex asked in apprehension. "With an *s?*"

A loud *ba-dum-CHING* crashed forth from Driggs's room. This triggered the panic. "Oh no no no . . ."

Uncle Mort grabbed a newspaper from the top of the pile. "This reporter at the *Post* seems to have taken a real interest in the mystery deaths, has written about a fair number of them. I got Driggs into a meeting with her tomorrow under the guise of an internship interview. He's going to find out how much she knows."

Lex was instantly jealous. "I could do that!"

"You sure could. If you didn't have to visit your family."

She let out an anguished grunt. "This is so unfair."

"I had a feeling you'd react like this," Uncle Mort said. "Which is why I booked you for only one night. I told your parents we need to get an early start on the cow inseminations this year."

Lex stared at him, open-mouthed.

"You can thank me later," he added. "Just remember to give the family my best. And obviously, not a word of Croak's business to anyone."

Lex slumped back, defeated. There was no weaseling out of this one. Her stomach gave a lurch at the thought of soon seeing her house, her parents, her relentlessly inquisitive sister, her bedroom with its photos and bookshelves and —

"Wait a minute." She pointed at the ball dancing through Uncle Mort's hands. "I've seen that thing before! You gave one to me and one to Cordy that time you visited!"

"Did I?" He tossed it to her with a sly smirk. "How imprudent of me, bringing my young nieces an unperfected invention."

Lex studied the sphere. Similar to a flickering light bulb, its surface was made from smooth, cold glass. Inside, dozens of small flecks of light whizzed and flung themselves about the space, crashing into the sides and each other, emitting small, bright flashes with every collision. It almost looked like a preserved Gamma.

"What is it?"

"This," Uncle Mort said proudly, "is a Spark. Measures the life force of any given being. In this case, mine."

Lex studied the little orb. "So how many years have you got left?"

Uncle Mort let out an offended huff. "Sparks measure quality, not quantity. Right now I'm alive, so my life sparks are in motion. When I die . . ." He trailed off and cleared his throat. "Well, I haven't died yet, so I don't know what happens. But I'm sure it indicates death somehow."

Lex gave him a dubious look.

Uncle Mort smiled at her. "Even *I* don't have the answers to everything."

Word of Lex's weekend plans traveled quickly. At Corpp's that evening, Kloo and Ayjay barely mumbled out a hello before running off to slobber all over each other in the corner. Zara and Sofi, engaged in a fierce game of Skulls, ignored her completely. And Ferbus kept glancing at her with a very weird expression.

Lex felt terrible. She had bent over backwards to avoid any reminders of her familial ties around her friends, yet now here she was, practically shoving it in their faces. She glanced at the bar, wishing Driggs would hurry up with the drinks. And where was Elysia?

"Hey," Ferbus said, taking a swig of his drink. "On this New York thing — you take care of Driggs, okay?"

"Why?"

Ferbus ran a hand through his moppy hair. "I'm pretty sure a jerk such as myself only gets one best friend in life," he grumbled, almost sincere for once. "Once he's gone, no free refills."

Lex was somewhat touched by this rare display of affection. So much so that she said, "Well then, I'll be sure to shove him in front of the first bus I see."

"See that you do." By now, Lex and Ferbus had tacitly come to understand each other better than any other pair in Croak. He was the best friend, and she was the threat. It was a healthy, demoralizing relationship.

A moment of awkwardness passed. "Now I must pee," Ferbus announced.

He stumbled off to the bathroom, passing Elysia as she returned. "Hi, Lex!" she said, friendly as always. "I heard about your trip. Are you excited?"

Lex hesitated.

"It's okay," Elysia said, sensing her reluctance. "I won't feel bad."

"Okay," Lex started unsurely. "I'm kinda dreading it, to be honest."

"Why?"

"Oh, tons of reasons. I'll be happy to see them, I guess, but you know how it is." She shot her a nervous grimace. "Or maybe you don't. Crap. Are you sure you don't mind me talking about this?"

"Lex, relax. What is wrong with you?"

Lex sighed. "Everyone hates me all over again."

Elysia looked around at the embittered Juniors. "They don't hate you," she said. "It's just all that baggage — it still hurts once in a while. They've had pretty rough lives, you know? Mine was tame by comparison."

Lex nodded, willing her mouth to stay absolutely closed.

Elysia nudged her. "You're insanely curious, aren't you?"

"Insanely," she let slip.

"I don't blame you. It must be weird, meeting all of us sad young ruffians without having a sob story of your own."

"Yeah," Lex said in a mournful, sarcastic voice. "It's been really hard."

Elysia laughed. "The others may get all defensive, but they'll come around. You're one of us now, no matter where you came from." She took another gulp of Yorick, then seemed to make a decision. "Okay. I was sixteen," she began, "and dating the captain of the football team. Which made total sense, since I was the captain of the cheerleading squad."

"I knew it," Lex said into her drink.

"First week of junior year, homecoming weekend. We win the game. After the dance, one thing leads to another, my underwear ends up in a ditch somewhere, and next thing you know, I'm pregnant."

She took another sip. "Two weeks later I tell my parents and they kick me out of the house. I'm shocked. I mean, I guess they were always kind of conservative, but I loved my parents and I thought that . . . well, apparently it wasn't mutual. So they grab a bunch of clothes from my closet, throw them out onto the front lawn, and lock the door.

"All my friends — they're disgusted. Which by the way is incredibly hypocritical, since they were all fairly raging sluts. But whatever. Every time I go to one of their houses, they get this snobby, superior look in their eyes, and I completely lose it. Like, scary. Throwing things around their houses, physically attacking them. None of their parents would allow me to stay. And who could blame them, really?

"So I go to the boyfriend's house. He wants nothing to do with me. Not surprising, he was always a dick. But I flip out. I break the guy's *arm*. How did I do that? I'm five feet tall, can barely lift my own backpack. How did I snap the bones of a two-hundred-fifty-pound quarterback?

"So what am I supposed to do now, drop out of school? You gotta understand — up until this, I was a perfect kid. Straight A's, president of the honor society, planning for college. I wanted to be a teacher. But now I'm just lost.

"Eventually I wind up at my neighbor's house. He's around my age, goes to a different school. He sneaks me into his basement. I stop going to school. I leave during the day while no one's home and shoplift stuff at the mall. Why? Out of boredom? I don't know what's making me do it, but I certainly don't need five pairs of earmuffs, that's for sure.

"Then one day I can't get off the couch. My insides feel like they're ripping apart, and there's blood everywhere. I wait until the family leaves, then run up to the bathroom and . . . well, that was the end of that. I cry for seven hours straight, the next day Mort shows up." She downed the remains of her Yorick and gave Lex a weak smile. "And here I am."

As Lex lay in bed that night, trying to fall asleep, a flood of emotions surged at the thought of seeing her unconditionally loving family.

And gratitude was now one of them.

18

"'Morning!" Driggs shouted at the surly bus driver. "Lovely weather we're having, isn't it?"

But he and Lex could barely hear his reply for all of the rain pounding down upon the pavement. Uncle Mort had piled them both into the cheddar-yellow '74 Gremlin that apparently lived in his garage and was to be used only for "field trips," then rocketed out of town — the **CROAK! POPULATION** sign automatically switching from 85 to 82 — and dropped them off with a disconcerting "Try not to die out there!" Twenty soggy minutes later, the bus finally rumbled up the street and pulled over to the muddy ditch in which they stood.

Neither the weather nor the bus's tardiness, however, had done anything to dampen Driggs's exuberant mood. Not only had he never been to New York City (or any large city, for that matter), but this particular form of transportation was also a first for him.

"I have a bus ticket!" he exclaimed upon boarding.

The driver did not share his enthusiasm. "Yes. You do."

"Where do we sit?"

"Right here," Lex said, shoving him into the nearest open seat. "Now shut up before we get stabbed."

"What do you mean?"

"I mean," she said through gritted teeth, "that probably half

the people on this bus are carrying weapons. So just sit down —
no, sit *down!*" He had gotten up to look inside the overhead storage compartment. She grabbed his shoulders and forcefully
pushed him onto the seat. "Sit down, look out the window, and
eat your candy."

Driggs took out a Snickers bar and happily munched away,
occasionally pausing to marvel at the appearance of roadkill.

"Flat as a pancake," he'd say to the window.

Lex closed her eyes and took a deep breath. If a plan existed,
she didn't know a thing about it. All Uncle Mort had said was
that Driggs was to escort her home, and that her family would
expect her at around one o'clock. Most likely they would not be
aware that she had an eighteen-year-old boy in tow. She wasn't
sure how she would explain his presence, let alone how she might
answer the questions that would inevitably surface regarding
what she had been doing with herself all summer. And on top of
all that loomed the Horrendous Atrocious Thing she had decided to tell them. She didn't know what she was more worried
about, saying it out loud or hearing their reactions . . .

She bit at her nails.

"Skunk," Driggs reported.

Upon their arrival at Port Authority, Lex sniffed the foul air with
disdain. Driggs, meanwhile, gaped at the bus terminal in sheer
delight, his excitement increasing as they entered the subway station and boarded a Queens-bound train. He hung on to a pole
for dear life as he read the various ads.

"This doctor sure hates zits," he said. "And this community college has got it all — education, affordability, and convenience!"

"Be quiet," said Lex. "Where are your Oreos?"

"I ate them."

"Already?"

"I was excited!"

Lex sighed and let her gaze drift to the floor. A newspaper lay crumpled into a corner, the word UNEXPLAINED the only part that she could see. She picked it up and read the headline.

"Look at this," she said, showing it to Driggs.

"Fifth mystery death this month," he said, skimming the article. "Authorities still baffled, Centers for Disease Control rumored to soon declare an epidemic — gimme that." He stuffed it into his bag. "Souvenir for Mort."

When at last they arrived, Lex dragged Driggs off the train and began walking the short distance to her house. "Okay. Okay." She was almost hyperventilating. "So when you get back from the interview — I still don't know how to explain who you are. Suspicions are going to rise. I can't necessarily guarantee that my father won't threaten you with a shotgun."

"He won't."

"Are you kidding? This is a man who wouldn't even allow our Barbies to play with Ken dolls."

"Then it's a good thing I'm not going to meet him." He grinned. "Mort said it would be cruel and unusual punishment to subject his brother's family to both of us at the same time. After the interview, I'm on my own until we meet up again tomorrow."

"I — huh? What are you going to do with yourself?"

Driggs unfolded a subway map with one graceful snap of his wrist. "I read somewhere that Hershey's and M&M's both have gigantic flagship stores in Times Square. I plan to clean them out."

She stifled a laugh. "But where will you sleep tonight?"

"Don't worry about me, Lex. I'm a fully functioning adult."

Lex seriously doubted this claim, but she couldn't deny the relief that was already flooding through her panicked system. One less thing to worry about. "This is it," she said, coming to a halt a few yards away from her front stoop.

He looked the house up and down, a wistful look on his face. "It's nice. Homey."

"No, it isn't. It's a crapshack." She was pacing back and forth now.

Driggs grabbed her arms and made her stop. "Relax, spaz." He gave her a sideways smile. "Why are you so nervous?"

"Because I miss them, and because they miss me probably more than anything in the world, and because — " Her shoulders drooped. "Because they're going to flip out."

"It's just four little words."

"I know." Lex pointed to the train. "Just go. They're inevitably going to look out the window, and you can't be here when they do."

"Okay. Meet you back here tomorrow?"

"Yeah. Wait," she said, reaching for his collar. "Your tie is crooked." The suit that Uncle Mort had lent him for the interview was a tad too big . . . but it was still a suit. Lex had caught herself staring more than she cared to admit.

"How do I look?" he asked.

Lex, who could have sworn she caught a whiff of cologne, grew very hot as her mouth tried to remember how to form words. "Fine," she eventually stammered, stepping back. "Grown up."

He snickered. "God forbid."

"Okay, go," she said, unable to keep it together for much longer. "Good luck with the reporter."

"Thanks. Good luck with the folks."

What happened next was an odd conglomeration of each of them moving in to give the other a hug, each thinking that the other was moving in to do something more, a subsequent dual retreat in the form of an awkward, octopus-like limb flailing, and a grand finale of something that could only be described as a clumsy, platonic chest bump.

It wasn't pretty.

After murmuring a humiliated goodbye, Driggs took off for the train and Lex headed back to her house. Her insides churned, all thoughts of Driggs and Croak and everything else evaporating as she remembered what she was here to do. She looked around in anxious bewilderment. How could her neighborhood look so familiar and so foreign at the same time?

"You can do this," she said to herself as she climbed the steps to the front door, took a deep breath, and rang the bell. "They'll despise you forever and possibly set fire to all of your earthly possessions, but you can do it."

"What's she ringing the doorbell for, she lives here, doesn't she?" Lex heard her mother rambling as she flung open the door. "OH MY SWEET BABY!"

"*Kugk*." Lex fought for air, her airway choked off by the force of the hug. "Happy birthday, Mom." Her father and Cordy came to the door a few seconds later, and by the time all of the embracing had concluded, Lex was already exhausted.

"What happened to your hair?" Cordy said, aghast.

"Look at her," said her mother to her father, as if Lex were not capable of hearing. "She looks different. She looks good!" she cried, surreptitiously stashing a handful of jump rope restraints behind her back.

"What are those for?" Lex asked warily.

"Just a precaution. Look at her eyes, dear! She doesn't hate us anymore!"

Lex shifted uncomfortably. "I never hated you."

"You haven't been getting into any trouble up there, have you?" her father asked in a stern voice. "I told Mort to call the second you became a nuisance."

"Thanks for the vote of confidence, Dad."

"You punch anyone?" Cordy asked.

"Only on the first day," Lex said. "But he deserved it."

Her mother flinched. "What?"

"I'm just kidding," Lex quickly lied. "So, how are *you* guys?"

A flurry of activity carried them all into the dining room, where they sat down to a meal of Lex's favorite foods, making her feel infinitely worse. Her parents talked at length about their summer so far, including a fifteen-minute tirade on the slovenly neighbors and the "illicit" trash that often flew in from their yard. Her father had also just gotten a raise, and her mother was staying busy teaching summer school classes.

"And how's your job?" Lex asked Cordy.

"Unfulfilling." Cordy irritably shoveled a forkful of corn into her mouth. "If I have to stare into the sticky face of one more spoiled brat as it asks for extra 'spwinkles,' I'm gonna drown my-self in a bucket of hot fudge."

Lex cringed. She loathed children.

"Tell her what else you're doing," their mother said.

"Oh yeah, I'm volunteering at the nursing home down the street."

"Ewww." Lex gagged. The only thing more repugnant to her than children were the elderly. "Gross."

Cordy shot her a deprecating glower. "They're not gross. Just old."

"Same difference." Lex thought of all the wrinkly geezers she had touched over the past few weeks and shuddered. "Well, more power to you," she said. "Someone's got to prevent them from operating kitchen appliances, right?"

Cordy rolled her eyes. "They're perfectly delightful people, Lex. Just because you aren't capable of—" She stopped and pointed accusingly. "What's wrong with your hands?"

Lex hid her pale, emaciated fingers beneath her napkin. "Nothing. Corn, Mom?"

The afternoon steadily progressed with more talk of the neighbors and their dreadful transgressions. By second helpings, Lex had become such a quivering blob of nerves she didn't know what to do with herself. Why weren't they asking about her sum-mer? How could they torture her like this? So much time had elapsed that she began to entertain the ridiculous notion that they hadn't cared about her absence at all.

This, of course, was laughably erroneous. She had just spooned a mountain of mashed potatoes into her mouth when her father cleared his throat. "So, Lexington. Were you planning on telling us about your summer, or are we just supposed to guess?"

Lex slowly worked the mush around her gums, its wet, smacking noises echoing conspicuously in the otherwise silent room. Her parents looked at her, then at each other, then back at her again. Eventually she swallowed.

"I . . . have been . . . working," she said, carefully choosing each word.

Cordy narrowed her eyes in suspicion. "With cows, right?"

"Yes," Lex said to her parents, ignoring Cordy. "With cows. I milk them. And stuff."

They exchanged confused glances. "And stuff?" her mother asked with a small frown. "Can you elaborate?"

"Um, I clean the pigpens," she said with forced enthusiasm. "The goats, also . . . I feed."

Her father looked perplexed. She was losing them. "Oh, and I collect the eggs from the chickens," she said with more confidence, shoving another dune of potatoes into her fraudulent mouth. "Yeah, there's this one rooster who's really awesome. He's always, like, strutting around and displaying his plumage."

"His plumage," her doubting father repeated.

"Yes." She slapped on the most innocent face she could muster. "His plumage."

Cordy crossed her arms. "What's his name?"

"Mr. Frizzle."

Her parents stared. Cordy coughed.

"Well," their mother said after a moment, "I think that's wonderful. You seem to be doing marvelously, you haven't gotten into any trouble, and you made friends with a chicken!" She beamed at her daughter. "What a wonderful opportunity you've had, Lex."

"She's like a different person!" her father said. "We're gonna get a brand-new daughter when she comes home."

"Um," Lex said, folding her napkin. "About that."

The smiles melted right off their faces. Except for Cordy, whose stone-cold expression of skepticism had not wavered even for a moment.

It was time. Lex sucked in a deep breath.

"I want to stay."

Looking at their stunned faces, Lex almost took it back. Yet she forced herself to go on. "I want to stay with Uncle Mort. I don't want to come back."

"But you have another year of school," her father said matter-of-factly, as if unable to comprehend any alternative.

"And then college!" her mother shrieked.

"I feel that my talents lie elsewhere."

The room plunged into silence once more. Cordy still stared, her mouth now hanging slightly open. The refrigerator let out a belch. An ice cream truck drove by.

And then, as if Lex had never even left, the Bartleby household exploded into its natural state of chaos.

||||||

"What did you think was going to happen?" Cordy asked, sprawled across her bed while their parents continued arguing downstairs.

"In all honesty?" Lex said from her own bed as "She takes after *your* mother!" wafted up from below. "This."

"I can't believe Dad threw his turkey leg."

"I can't believe Mom reloaded him with another one."

Cordy abruptly sat up to face her sister, her eyes fierce. "What the hell is the matter with you, Lex? You haven't written a single word back to me all summer, and now this? You want to *stay*?"

"I do."

"With the cows, right?"

"Yeah. The cows."

Cordy got up and crashed down on her sister's bed. "Lex, you better tell me what's going on *right now,* or so help me God, I'll drag you right down to the nursing home and introduce you to Mrs. Needlemeyer."

Lex recoiled. "You wouldn't."

"She has a goiter, Lex." Cordy smiled demonically. "A *goiter.*"

"All right!" Lex yelled in defeat, getting up to close the door. "I'll tell you. But keep your voice down. And you can't tell anyone."

"I won't."

Lex tried to silence the voices that were screaming at her not to do this. "No, Cordy, I mean it." She sat down on the bed and leaned in close. "You can't tell a single person on the entire planet."

Cordy, who was getting more than a little spooked by the strange behavior of her twin, let out an anxious laugh. "Because then I'd have to kill them?"

"No. That's my job."

||||||

Twenty minutes later Cordy lay flat on the bed, her face a blank slate. "I think I may require some heavy drugs."

"You wanted to know," Lex said, drained. What would happen now? Could she really get kicked out of Croak? What would they do to Cordy?

Cordy sat up. "But Lex, this is *insane*. Think of what you're doing! I can't believe our own uncle would put you up to this."

"He didn't put me up to anything! I love what I do!"

Cordy looked scared. "Yeah, I can see that."

Lex glanced around her room, across the towering mosaic of photos, until her eyes finally came to rest on the two animated Sparks perched on the shelf. Tiny flickers of light whirred and flew around the glass orbs.

"So what happens if you don't go back? Will no one be able to die?" Cordy said sarcastically. "Immortality for everyone, all because some random teenager had to leave to get her high school diploma?"

"Look, if you don't believe me, fine. I wouldn't believe it either if I hadn't — "

"If you hadn't what? Started killing innocent people with your own bare hands?"

"It is *not* like that."

"That's what it sounds like. Look, even your finger's all burned," Cordy said, grabbing her hand.

Lex yanked it away. "You just don't understand."

"No, I don't! How can this be something you enjoy? That you want to do for the rest of your life?"

"Because I was born to do it!" Lex yelled so loud that even her parents downstairs fell silent for a moment.

Cordy gaped at her sister. Then, slowly, she nodded. "Yeah," she said in a low voice. "Maybe you were."

Lex looked away. She ran her hand over the wooden rocking chair where her mother had sat and sung lullabies to her girls every single night, until the day they sheepishly informed her that they had become too old for such nonsense.

"So what happens now that you've told me?" Cordy asked. "Will the fiery demons of hell be arriving to claim your mortality?"

"No, the fiery hell demons have the weekend off."

"Answer my question! Is that why you wouldn't talk to me?" Cordy said, her voice rising. "Or is it because you have friends now and don't give a shit about your own sister anymore?" She was angry now, her face a mess of hurt. "All this time I stuck by you, Lex, I defended you — even at school when you did all those terrible things! How could you just forget about me like that?"

"*Forget* about you?" Lex pointed across the room at the computer. "Do you realize how many unsent emails I've got stored up, filled with every little detail of being a Grim, every person I've met, every inch of Croak, every single insecurity and thrill and fear I've felt since I got there? Do you have any *idea* how much I've wished I could tell you all that, how much I wished you were right there with me?"

Cordy looked as if she had been slapped across the face. Silence filled the room.

"I'm sorry I ignored you," said Lex in a quieter voice. "I thought it would be better than lying."

Cordy's expression softened. She leaned against the wall and hugged her stuffed octopus. "You really wrote all that?"

Lex nodded.

Cordy looked like she wanted to say something more, but didn't know what. Lex glanced out the window at her old tree house. Something shifted inside it. Apparently the raccoons had moved back in.

"Come on, Cordy," said Lex. "Don't fear the reaper."

Cordy snickered, despite her best efforts not to. "How long have you been waiting to say that?"

"Since I arrived."

Cordy finally broke into a smile. "I miss you, turdface."

"I miss you too," Lex said, relieved.

"Do you know how weird it was that first night, sleeping in this room without you?"

"It couldn't possibly have been weirder than mine," Lex said, recalling Kate Winslet's heaving bosom.

Cordy watched her for a moment. "Who was that boy?"

Lex froze. "What boy?"

"That boy I saw you with, before you came up to ring the bell. The windows of this house are fully functional, you know."

Lex didn't even bother with a lie this time. "His name is Driggs. He's my partner."

"Ah, partner. How very *Law and Order*."

"Shut up, that's just how it works."

"I see. And have you two had a romp in the hay yet, or would that upset Mr. Frizzle the rooster?"

"What?" Lex sputtered, searching for a viable retort. "What?" she eventually repeated.

Cordy gave her an incredulous look. "Come on, Lex. He's effin' gorgeous. Anyone with half a retina could see that."

Lex snorted. "Whatever. He's just my stupid partner."

"Yeah, okay. How come he didn't come in?"

"Why, you want me to hook you two up?"

Cordy eyed her, then let out a grunt. "Could you? Michael Thorley turned out to be an assclown, and the rest of this place is nothing but a barren wasteland of undateability. The only guy

who's shown the slightest amount of interest in me this summer
is Mr. Papadopoulos on the third floor of the nursing home. He
says I have the ass of a Russian call girl."

"Ah, senility."

Cordy laughed and shoved her twin's face into a pillow. "You
better come back, or I'll drive up to Crack or whatever it's called
and find you myself."

"Why don't I just send you there right now?" Lex said, grabbing the pillow and smacking it against her sister's head.

They continued to batter each other senseless until long after
their parents' screeching ceased, and only when their mother
cried, "You're almost *seventeen,* for heaven's sake!" did they finally let go of each other's hair.

||||||

"Goodbye, sweetie," Lex's mother cooed the next morning as
they all walked to the door. Lex rubbed her eyes, exhausted. De-
scribing every last detail of Croak to Cordy had taken all night.
"Are you sure you have to leave so soon?"

"Yeah, Mom. The cows — "

"Right, right, the cows. My little farmer!" She wrapped her
daughter in another suffocating hug. "You have fun up there.
And really, would it *kill* you to call once in a while?"

After the sisters embraced (and Cordy whispered, "Whack
Michael Thorley for me, would you?"), Mr. Bartleby finally took
his reluctant daughter into his arms.

"Enjoy the rest of the summer, honey. And we'll see you in a
few weeks."

"But, Dad — "

"The answer is no," he said gently. "But we still love you."

"Whatever," she muttered, descending the stairs to the sidewalk.

A disheveled Driggs stood waiting for her at the train station, elbow-deep in a novelty bucket of M&M's. He was wearing jeans and a T-shirt, both wrinkled and dirty, and the tie was still knotted messily around his neck. He looked like a homeless person.

"Hey, Lex. How was — "

"I told Cordy everything."

He stopped chewing for a second, then nodded. "I know."

"What? How?"

"Because you're Lex. There's a law against telling people, so of course you shattered it into a thousand pieces."

She bit her lip. "You won't rat me out, will you?"

"No. But thanks all the same for making me an accomplice."

"You could take it as a compliment, you know. That I trust you."

"I'm deeply touched." He downed another handful of candy. "What did they say about staying?"

Lex scowled. "They said no."

Driggs's face fell. "Oh. What about after next year?"

"They said we'll talk about it," she said as they boarded the train. "But I know them. If I don't agree to college, they'll disown me." She sighed and ran a hand through her hair. "But whatever, I'll figure something out. What about you? How'd it go with the reporter?"

His face lit up. "Awesome. She told me everything — I think because she was so psyched I believed her. No one else will listen to her crazy crackpot theories." He reached back into the bucket. "She's been reading the autopsy reports of all the mystery deaths, trying to find something that links them together. Granted, she's had a harder time than we've had in figuring out who the victims are, since the white-eye thing wears off out here. But of the bodies she's managed to track down, it turns out that each one has had a very tiny puncture wound, like from a syringe or something. But since no trace of drugs has been found in their systems, medical examiners haven't been able to explain it."

"That's it!" Lex said. "They're being injected! With Elixir!"

"Well, yeah, I figured that, but I couldn't exactly come out and tell her." He grinned. "Mort's head is gonna explode."

"To put it mildly," she said. "Any other shockers?"

"Yeah. Did you know you can buy M&M's in any color you want?"

She cracked a smile. "So I've heard."

"And I ate a Reese's Peanut Butter Cup that was bigger than my head."

"Congratulations." An earthy scent had begun to waft through Lex's nostrils. Puzzled, she sniffed at Driggs's shirt. "Um . . . where did you stay last night?"

He scratched his head. "I found a place. Drafty and a little cramped, but not bad."

They rode the train back to the bus station and the bus all the way back to Croak, and not until Lex was in bed, staring at Leonardo DiCaprio's eyelashes and thinking about the supposed raccoons in her tree house, did she finally realize where Driggs had slept.

19

After her disheartening visit, Lex hoped to devote whatever leisure time she could find to figuring out a way to stay in Croak, especially since she seemed to have gotten away with squealing to Cordy. But as August rolled on, work got busier and busier.

"It's the heat," Kloo explained one day after a particularly brutal morning shift. "The geezers can't take it."

"I wish they'd sack up a little," Lex said. "It's getting repetitive."

"What about that Jet Ski guy?" said Driggs. "He was cool."

"That's true. Head just popped off like a cork, huh?"

"And we got a really gnarly fireworks accident the other day," Ayjay said. Kloo shot him a disapproving look. "I mean, shame about his kid's fingers. But they'll grow back, right?"

At lunch Pandora flew past their booth with barely a hello. "Whaddaya want?" she barked, balancing a tower of boxes atop her arms. "Oh, I don't have time for orders," she said before anyone could answer. "We're swamped as it is, trying to get rid of all these blasted stargazers. Professor Elbow Patches over there can't seem to take the hint." She gestured toward a tweedy-looking man and his wife poring confusedly over the multitude of brochures Kilda had thrust into their hands. "Just eat this." Dora hurled a plate of hot dogs and several glasses of Poisonberry Juice onto the table, then hurried back to the kitchen.

"What's with her?" Lex asked as they dug in.

Her fellow Juniors stared.

"Hi," she said. "I'm Lex. We may have met before, perhaps in one of the hundreds of other times you've had to explain something to me."

"Ohhh," said Ferbus in his best condescending voice. "I don't think she knows."

"Tonight's the Luminous Twelfth!" Elysia said as Lex kicked Ferbus under the table. "It's like a big block party for the whole town. Tons of food and Yoricks and music and dancing, and then we stay up all night to watch the meteor shower!"

"Cool," said Lex. "This happens every year?"

"Every August twelfth," Sofi said. "It's like our Fourth of July."

"And do we have to do anything?"

Driggs shook his head as a loud crash issued from the kitchen. "Nope, Dora's got it under control," he shouted over the resulting torrent of profanities. "All we have to do is show up and do our best to scare away the tourists."

"I think there's a Band-Aid in my burger," the professor whispered to his wife.

Ferbus menacingly shook his fist.

"Our compliments to the chef," the woman shakily replied, grabbing her husband's hand and fleeing to the street.

That night, after work, the party began.

Lex and Driggs made their way out onto Dead End, which had been whimsically transformed into a festive, colorful street fair. Food and drink tents lined the street, vibrant lanterns and streamers cheerfully adorned the buildings, and the cobblestones of Slain Lane boasted dozens of drunken dancers all laughing and screaming to the beat of lively music. Corpp passed out Yoricks to the eager revelers gathered around him, stopping to plant kisses on Dora whenever she dropped by to deliver a fresh batch of onion rings. A large disco ball hung over the square, its luster rivaled only by the twinkling stars streaking across the sky above.

As Driggs ran off to grab some Yoricks, Lex wandered over to one of the open-air booths and marveled at the impressive array of meats sizzling on the grill before her. "Um — " She pointed. "That one, I guess?"

"You got it, little lady," said the butcher, stabbing what appeared to be a T-bone steak with legs.

"I wouldn't eat that," Zara told Lex as she lugged over a large cooler, sweat plastering a clump of silver hair to her forehead. "It's one of his own concoctions."

"Ew." Lex glanced at the butcher, a short, piggish man with beady eyes. She could see why he might not be the most enjoyable employer.

"You're better off planting yourself at Corpp's tent," Zara said. "That's where everyone else is."

Lex scrutinized Zara. Ever since the fire incident their relationship had been fairly strained. Zara had even stopped pestering her about the shocks — not a good thing, in Lex's mind. It probably meant she was planning on tattling about Lex's subversive leanings any minute now in order to reclaim the Junior throne of awesomeness for herself.

"Will you be joining us?" Lex asked in the friendliest voice she could muster.

"Maybe later. I have to work until all the food is gone. Save me a Yorick or two. Or ten."

Lex honked out a nervous laugh. She slumped back to the Juniors, whose inebriation levels had begun to surge at an impressive rate.

"No, YOU'RE a platypus!" Ferbus screamed at Elysia.

"That doesn't make any sense!" she yelled back.

"YOU'RE a sense!"

Driggs sidled up to Lex and handed her a Yorick. "Having fun?"

"I'm trying not to nod off."

Driggs laughed. "That's the spirit."

"You just missed it, you just mizzit," Elysia told her. "Ferbus swallowed a button."

"It fell off my shirt!" he yelled, as if this explained something.

Lex looked around. "Kloo and Ayjay still aren't here?"

"Guess not," Driggs said. "They might have traded with some of the graveyard shifters." He pointed at an eccentric-looking gaggle of Senior Grims who were paler than everyone else. "It's traditional to split up shifts on the Luminous Twelfth so that everyone's able to come for at least some of it. Juniors aren't required to work, but maybe they volunteered."

"So this shindig is really going to rage all night long?"

"Yep. Or until everyone passes out, whichever comes first."

She looked up just in time to catch a brilliant flash of white arcing across the sky.

"This is so cool," she whispered, mostly to herself.

Uncle Mort, Yorick in hand, tottered to the fountain in the center of the square. "Hey everybody, listen up!"

"Hang on!" Pandora knocked him out of the way and scuttled onto the ledge of the fountain. "Smush in, smush in," she barked.

Everyone instinctively crowded together, as if they had done this many times before. Dora held up a large camera and took their photo, a bright flash briefly illuminating the street.

"Thanks, Dora," Uncle Mort said.

"Bite me!"

As the photo subjects disbanded, he climbed onto the fountain and cleared his throat. "Happy Luminous Twelfth, Croak! A hearty welcome to you all, and an even heartier welcome to the Skorski family, who can't remember where they parked their car!" A cluster of travelers, huddled under the watchful gaze of Kilda, gave a small, terrified wave.

"So, you all know what comes next," he continued. "The annual snoozefest known as the State of Croak Address." A polite round of applause swept through the crowd. "I've gotten a number of requests to take up as little drinking time as possible this year, so here's the abridged version: numbers are up, expenditures are down, and our educational efforts continue to provide troubled youth with the moral integrity they so desperately crave." The Juniors let out a whoop and clashed their skull mugs together, spraying the crowd. "Long story short, Croakers are the best damn Grims this side of the Afterlife!"

The throng erupted into raucous cheers, taking this as a cue to continue the festivities.

Uncle Mort, however, remained atop the fountain. "And as such," he shouted above their merriment, a note of apprehension creeping into his voice, "you deserve the truth."

The noise and cheers abruptly died down, until the only sound left was that of Ferbus belching.

"As many of you have read by now," he continued in a stern voice, "troubling incidents are being reported out of Necropolis.

The powers that be have publicly declared these to be isolated occurrences, and nothing more." He took a deep breath. "But the powers that be are lying."

The Juniors shot worried glances at one another.

"The truth is, the same abnormal deaths have been witnessed by Grim teams right here in Croak. In fact, they originated here." Several panicked cries rang out, but Uncle Mort raised his hands to quiet them. "Hysteria will only make things worse. You guys know better than that. I expect nothing but the utmost level-headedness and composure from every inhabitant of this town. And in return, I will report to you what little I know about the situation."

Absolute silence settled over the streets, with the exception of the Skorski family, anxiously peeling out of town in their hurriedly found car.

"We don't know who is doing this," he continued, "or why. But it seems that a Grim has gained the ability to — "

A bloodcurdling scream cut the crisp night air. All eyes flew to the end of the street, where Kloo staggered out of the Crypt's tunnel dragging something heavy. As she came into the light, her burden was revealed to be Ayjay, blood-soaked and seemingly unconscious — or worse.

Uncle Mort jumped down from the fountain. "Bring him up here!" A pair of Senior Grims took Ayjay from Kloo's arms and laid out his lifeless body across the fountain's edge, careful not to touch the gaping wound across his forehead. Yet they jumped back within seconds.

"What's wrong with his eye?" Kilda screeched.

Uncle Mort took one look at Ayjay's vacant, milky eye and immediately felt for a pulse.

His face fell. No one spoke.

Uncle Mort grabbed Kloo by the shoulders. "What happened?"

"I don't remember!"

"Try!"

A loud, wet cough tore through the silence. Ayjay sputtered and thrashed about wildly, then sat up with a tremendous jolt, as if wrestling himself awake from a nightmare. He rubbed at his chest, blinked several times, and looked around, confused.

"Ayjay!" Kloo wrapped him in her arms. The crowd breathed a collective sigh of relief, but the peace didn't keep for long.

"How did this happen?" someone yelled.

"Mort! What's going on?"

"His eye!"

"Who did this?"

Uncle Mort ignored their questions and grasped Kloo's and Ayjay's arms. "I need to know what happened."

Kloo's face was colorless, but true to form, her tone remained composed. "I don't know. We were — " She cut herself off and looked embarrassed. "Alone. It was still light out at that point. And then — it happened so fast — someone appeared in my room. Out of nowhere!"

The concern of the crowd slowly ebbed. Glances of skepticism were exchanged.

Ferbus snorted. "Come on, Kloo."

"It's true! At least — " She looked at Uncle Mort. "At least I think it is. I can't remember anything after that."

"What about you, Ayjay?" Uncle Mort asked.

Ayjay, clearly still in a great deal of pain, shook his head.

Lex grunted in frustration. "How could they just *forget*?" she whispered to Driggs.

"And then I woke up a few minutes ago and he was just lying there," Kloo continued. "No breathing, no pulse, scalp laceration, small injection site on his chest, and . . ."

Ayjay was still blinking heavily. He rubbed at his bad eye until it was red and teary. He looked up at her. "I can't see out of it," he said quietly.

Kloo squeezed his hand. "You'll be okay. I'll stitch up your head, and the eye — " She swallowed, unsure. "I can fix it."

"I don't know about that, Kloo," said Uncle Mort, deep in thought. He gestured to a pair of Senior Grims. "He's not out of the woods yet. Take them to the doc."

As Kloo and Ayjay were escorted away, Uncle Mort climbed the fountain once more. "Don't panic," he said evenly, his face morose, "but this is almost identical to the murderer's typical plan of attack. They Crash to a certain location, then inject the victim with a few drops of pure Elixir while time is frozen, causing instant death and leaving no trace."

"Crash?" Heloise yelled. "You mean someone found a Loophole? And can Crash with *direction*?"

"It looks that way. But — "

"Wait just a damn minute, Mort," yelled an irate Norwood. "You can't just pick up Elixir from the grocery store!"

"That's true," Uncle Mort said. "I'm not sure how the Elixir is being accessed. But — "

"Who has been seeing these deaths?" Heloise interrupted. "And why hasn't anyone else witnessed anything unusual? Don't we have a right to know?"

"These particular individuals told me about the abnormalities in confidence," Uncle Mort answered sharply. "As long as they wish to remain anonymous, they will. As for the question of why they're the only ones who have seen them — well, they enlisted the help of an Etcetera, so maybe I should be asking *you* that question, codirector."

Heloise bristled and shot him a hateful look, but said nothing.

"But how did Ayjay survive?" Corpp asked.

Uncle Mort scratched his head. "He was assaulted in real time, rather than during a time freeze. Probably another type of experimentation with the process, just like when victims were chosen from Necropolis's jurisdiction instead of ours. My best guess is that Kloo instinctively batted the needle away, preventing him from getting the full dosage. The Crasher panicked, knocked them out, and ran."

Silence filled the air. "What are we going to do?" Elysia asked in a small voice.

"Right now, my advice is to be on constant alert. If you see anything unusual, let me know as soon as possible. But — " Uncle Mort exhaled and looked out sadly over the crowd. "But in all honesty, we're pretty defenseless here. There's no way I can think of to prevent a Crasher who can come at any time, anywhere, after anyone. Up until now, all of the victims have been out in the real world — but realistically speaking, it was only a matter of time before Grims were targeted as well. We aren't exempt. If anything, we're even more vulnerable. What we do here . . . well, someone has a problem with it, and they're willing to take lives in order to make that clear."

No one spoke.

"Which means that we need to carry on as normally as possible," he finished. "If we can't drunkenly dance the macarena until the sun comes up, the terrorists have already won. Or something." He hopped off the fountain. "I'm going home to report all this to Necropolis, and I'll get back to you as soon as I have more information. Try to have some fun, all right? Look, it's not even midnight yet and Ferbus is already wearing a lampshade."

With one last glimpse at his town's troubled faces, Uncle Mort turned around and began walking down the street. Lex started after him, but Driggs briefly caught the mayor's eye and pulled her back.

"He doesn't want us to come," he whispered to her.

"But we can help!"

"I don't think Mort wants the rest of the town to know that his most trusted advisors are in fact the troublemaking teenagers currently residing under his roof."

"Why?" She shook him off. "Just because we're Juniors doesn't mean we're not — "

"It's not because we're Juniors."

"What is it, then? Me?"

She took his silence as a resounding yes.

20

The party — if it could still be called that — persisted through the night, though the mood had shifted considerably; most of the revelers just ended up lying down in the street and watching the falling stars in silence. Around sunrise, they shuffled like zombies into the Morgue, where a seemingly indefatigable Pandora grabbed a pan and began tossing batch after batch of flapjacks high into the air.

"We don't even get a nap?" Lex yawned as the Juniors collapsed into their booth, exhausted more by worry than lack of sleep.

"Not really," a bleary-eyed Elysia said. "I might try later, but only if Alexander Graham Bell makes good on his promise to stop experimenting with ringtones."

"I *hate* that guy," Ferbus said. "I don't wanna go to work."

"Oh, please," Lex said crankily. "You just get to sit around and jerk off all day. We actually have stuff to do."

"Shut your hole," he countered weakly.

Lex looked around the table. Sofi was nodding off into her English muffin. Zara had bitten her nails to nubs. And Driggs had a Lucky Charm stuck to his forehead.

"You've got a — " Lex gestured.

"Bwa?" he answered sleepily.

"Purple horseshoe," she said, flicking it off.

"Oh," he said, his mind elsewhere. "I was saving it for later."

None of them knew where Kloo and Ayjay had been taken, or if Ayjay had even survived the night. So on they plodded through the meal, robotically shoving the utensils into their mouths and flinching at every random noise that dared to pervade the restaurant. By the time they left for their shifts, anxiety was at an all-time high — so much so that Lex practically tackled Uncle Mort as she caught sight of him on the way to the Bank.

"Where are Kloo and Ayjay?" she demanded.

"Recuperating," he said, walking briskly.

"What did you tell Necropolis? What did they say?"

"Words. Hey, pick up some sausages on your way home today, will you? I have to feed the jellyfish."

Lex frowned. "Jellyfish don't eat sausage."

"Look, I don't tell you how to do your job."

"Yes, you do, every day."

"Gotta go. We'll talk later, okay?"

And so Lex was left with nothing but more questions and now a shopping errand. Making matters worse was Kilda, who chanted, as they slumped past her desk, "A splendid night's sleep, and success you will reap!"

"She's gonna reap a beating if she doesn't shut the hell up," Lex said under her breath.

When they finished work that afternoon, Lex and Driggs rounded onto the cobblestones of Slain Lane and headed for the shop labeled Dead Meat. A small bell tinkled when they pushed open the door, though the rest of the store — cold, dark, and pervaded with an overwhelming stench — did not seem nearly as welcoming. Lex felt as if she had just entered a tomb.

Driggs stepped up to the counter. "Anyone here?"

"Be right out!" a voice rang from the back. Seconds later a harried-looking Zara emerged wearing a bloody apron. "Oh. It's you guys."

"How's the meat business?" Driggs asked.

Zara scowled. "I can't *wait* until this internship is over. I had to swipe into the foulest, most disgusting meatpacking plants on earth for that stupid party last night, and every single day I come home stinking of blood and guts and pig remains. I hate it!" she shrieked, a small globule of goo quivering in her silver hair.

"Wow, sorry," said Lex, who couldn't help but take a small amount of pleasure in Zara's distress. "That really sucks."

Zara glared at her. "Yeah, it does. And the nerves from last night aren't helping." She wiped her forehead. "Anyway, what can I get you guys?"

While Driggs placed the order, Lex glanced out the window. A pair of Senior Grims were walking down the street and looking around apprehensively, as if expecting an attack from behind or above. They were met by another pair of Grims who spoke with them in low tones. Before the group disbanded, they hugged.

Lex grimaced as she tried to imagine what it must be like for Grims who had been here for decades. A whole career of scything to strangers, examining and poking at bodies as if they had never even belonged to live humans, completely isolated within their little town. No wonder they had become blind to the real terrors lurking in the world. Death was old hat to Grims, a punch line to a joke told at lunch over the Morgue's greasy hamburgers. But gnarly fireworks accidents and missing fingers didn't seem so funny anymore. Now the threat was here, seemingly dropping in from the sky, and no amount of professionalism could stop Lex or anyone else from incessantly glancing over their shoulders in fear.

"I don't know," Driggs was saying to Zara. "Mort's not telling us much, but I think they're both okay."

"I hope so," Zara said, placing the sausages on the scale.

As she moved her arm away, however, the sleeve of her butcher's jacket got caught and rode up to her elbow. Lex took one look at Zara's exposed arm and gasped. "Oh my God," she said. "What happened to you?"

Several large clusters of red blotches ran the length of Zara's pale arm. The skin underneath was crumpled, scarred beyond recognition, while deep gashes crisscrossed like train tracks.

Zara's mortified eyes flew to her sleeve. "None of your business!" she snapped, yanking it down.

Lex was stunned into silence. Like everyone else in Croak, Zara wore the long-sleeved black hoodie most of the time, even in the heat of the summer; Lex realized she'd never seen Zara's bare arms until today. "I—sorry," she sputtered, now vastly confused.

"Just forget it," Zara said, giving Driggs a significant look.

His returned glance was one of apology. "Thanks, Zara," he said gently, taking the package and handing it to Lex. "Have a good afternoon, okay?"

Zara was shaking as they left. "Yeah, okay."

Driggs said nothing the whole way home.

As they neared the driveway, Lex couldn't take it anymore. "Okay, are you gonna tell me or not?"

"Tell you what?"

"What the hell was that all about? Why did Zara look about ready to claw my heart right out of my chest and wrap it up along with the rest of our order?"

Driggs remained silent. He jammed his hands into his pockets and headed for the porch.

"Hey," she said, following him. "I asked you a — "

"Lex, stop."

The edge of fury in his voice made her flinch. "What's wrong?"

Slowly, hesitantly, he rolled up the bottom of his hoodie until his chest was exposed. "You don't know what these are, do you?" he said in a low voice, looking away.

Lex examined his skin, which was mottled with about twenty dark, pill-size dots. "No," she said, squinting in the fading light. "I don't."

"Yeah, you wouldn't." He glanced at the setting sun. "They're cigarette burns. My father got a real kick out of using his only son as an ashtray."

Lex recoiled, a short breath escaping her lips.

Driggs's gaze was lost, foreign. "These aren't even the worst of it. But the point is, Zara and I aren't the only ones. Everyone here — except for you — came from their own personal hells, and most have the literal scars to prove it." He stuffed his shirt back down and glared at her. "So if you could manage to remember that every once in a while, we'd all greatly appreciate it."

Lex took a breath to say something, but nothing came out. Just then, the door sprang open to reveal a jubilant Uncle Mort.

"Grab your top hats and monocles, kids," he said, waving a wad of money. "I'm taking you out to dinner."

||||||

Fifteen minutes later the three of them sat at a table in a darkened corner of the fanciest and "most zoologically eclectic" restaurant in Croak, according to its sign. "The kangaroo is good here," Uncle Mort said while perusing the drink specials. Lex glanced at Driggs from behind her menu, but he was apparently too engrossed in the appetizer offerings to look her way.

"Wellllcommme to Asssshhes." A lofty voice floated over their heads as a tall, pale woman materialized at their table. Her long dark hair reached past her waist, while the train of her black dress trailed at least five feet behind her.

"Thank you," Uncle Mort said in a saucy tone. "A terrifying pleasure, as always."

"May I brrrrring you anythinnnng to drrrrink?" she asked, running a slender hand through his hair.

"I — mmm . . ." He moaned blissfully, closing his eyes. "I'll have an Essence of Newt. Straight up, no ice, with extra pulp . . . pulpy . . ." Lex kicked him under the table. His eyes sprang open. "What?"

"Annnnd for you twooooo?"

"Water," they quickly said in unison.

"Cominnnng right uuuup," she replied, drifting away.

Uncle Mort stood. "I need to, um, use the facilities," he said, wandering off.

Driggs watched him leave, then distractedly ran his fingers over the candle flame.

Lex mentally prepared herself. She had never been any good at apologies, and she doubted this one would be the break-through she had been waiting for. "Hey," she said. "I'm sorry about before."

"It's okay." His lips barely moved as he watched the yellow flickers. "You didn't know."

Lex nodded for a moment. "Do you want to talk about —"

"Nope."

"Okay. Um, if you ever want to, I'm always —"

"Yeah. Got it."

Lex nodded her head yet again, certain that it would soon de-tach. She opened her mouth, then closed it. She picked up the menu and looked at it. She put it down.

"Okay, clearly, I am terrible at this," she confessed. "What do you want me to say?"

He scratched at his neck. "It's not really something I like to talk about. It was a long time ago." He gave her a weak smile. "I ran away to Croak for very good reasons, just like everyone else."

Lex shrank. "Except for me."

"Oh, I'm sure you've got a reason," he said, indicating her blistered finger. "A better one than the rest of us, I'll bet, since you were plucked from such obscurity."

"Obscurity?" She grinned. "You mean a warm, loving home?"

Driggs finally cracked a smile and laughed. "Yeah. That's the official definition."

The waitress brought a basket of muffins as Uncle Mort re-turned to the table and picked up a menu. "I could really go for some badger gizzards," he said excitedly.

"Why are you in such a good mood?" Lex asked. "And what are we doing here? Why the sudden splurge?"

He chuckled guiltily. "Ah, I may have fined a nice Canadian couple for jaywalking."

Driggs gave him a wry look. "Was that before or after Kilda destroyed their camera?"

"After. But they were leaving anyway, due to the impending gas explosion —"

"Boys," Lex interrupted, "let's curb the A.D.D. for a little while, shall we? Are Kloo and Ayjay okay?"

"Shaken up, but otherwise fine," Uncle Mort said. "Afraid the eye is busted for good, though."

Driggs sank. "That sucks."

Uncle Mort thoughtfully stroked his own scar. "He'll get used to it."

"What did Necropolis say about last night?" Lex asked.

Uncle Mort lit up. "They're furious!" he said with glee. "Practically ready to string me up because I gave out so many details."

"To the town, you mean?" Driggs asked.

"Yeah. And to *The Obituary.*"

Lex inhaled sharply. "You told the press?"

"Yep. Cat's out of the bag," he said proudly. "Trust me, media coverage will help. One Senior team has already reported an Elixir death today, and more will follow. This bastard can't stay hidden for long with the entire Grimsphere on the lookout."

Lex picked at a muffin. "I liked it better when it was just us."

"Speaking of which," Uncle Mort said, shooting her a cryptic look, "let's not tell anyone about that, okay? If people find out that you were the first one to see them —"

"What?" Lex asked, determined to get to the bottom of this. "Are you embarrassed by me or something?"

His face clouded over. "Lex, I swear on the working cold fusion device in the basement that I couldn't be prouder of you. But not everyone..." He trailed off, searching for the right words. "You just have to realize that some people don't approve of you. That doesn't mean you don't deserve to be here," he added as she began to argue. "Because you absolutely do. But not everyone sees it that way."

"Like Norwood and Heloise."

"Yes."

"Why, though?" she asked. "Because I'm your niece?"

"Something like that," he murmured. "Listen, don't worry about it. As long as I've got your back, you don't need to give a rat's ass what anyone else thinks."

Lex, irritated, smeared a blueberry across the table.

He smirked. "Not that you ever do."

21

The next day, DeMyse's director of Ether Traffic Control dropped dead in the middle of his shift. The day after that, a Culler in Necropolis slumped headfirst into her bowl of breakfast cereal. By the end of the week, every team in Croak had witnessed at least one Elixir murder firsthand during their shifts. And morale was at an all-time low.

Everything had changed. The citizens of Croak were shuffling through their lives like soulless wraiths. Their nerves were fried from constantly flinching at the smallest rustle, cowering each time a cloud passed in front of the sun, fearing sudden death at every turn. There had not been any more attacks on Croak, but everyone knew it was only a matter of time. And since the source of the stolen Elixir was still unknown, Corpp's had been closed until further notice, leaving the populace with no way to ease the crushing dread.

So Uncle Mort called a meeting one stormy evening to discuss the sightings, address the Grimsphere attacks, and allow the populace to vent. Lex and Driggs agreed to meet Ferbus and Elysia after work and head over together.

Lex stood in the office, examining the vault door. "You know," she said to Ferbus, "I've been thinking."

"Well, there's a first time for everything."

Not in the mood for his antics, Lex grabbed a pair of scissors and brandished them in his face. "I really suggest you rid your workspace of sharp objects, Carrot Top. We wouldn't want any unfortunate castrations, now would we?"

"Driggs!" Ferbus yelled into the spidery Lair, where Driggs had wandered to get away from their constant squabbling. "Your partner is threatening to neuter me!"

"Yeah, she does that," Driggs said from within.

"You know, intimidating people with knifelike implements isn't really the best way to clear your name," Ferbus said as Lex lowered the scissors.

"Clear my what now?"

He leaned in. "I've heard what the Seniors are saying. They think you're connected to these murders."

Lex gaped at him. "What? Why me?"

"Think about it. None of this even started until you showed up, and now you're terrorizing poor innocent townsfolk with pointy weapons." He shrugged and went back to his wizard battle. "Just doesn't look that great, is all."

"Well, neither does your face."

Now troubled, she hopped off the desk and let herself in through the vault to the Afterlife, where Elysia stood over a pile of wood, plastic, and Wright brothers.

"Clean that up," Elysia scolded them as she returned to her desk. "They think they can make anything fly," she told Lex. "A table, a microwave, a subway car. It doesn't matter. If it doesn't have wings, it's an experiment waiting to happen."

Lex barely heard her. She looked back at the vault door and scowled.

"What's wrong?" Elysia asked, concerned. "Is it the fact that the very foundation of our world is crumbling all around us and we're barreling forth into a hellish vision of uncertainty and terror the likes of which have never been seen?"

"Sounds wonderful to me," Edgar said, drifting by.

Lex turned to Elysia. "Did you know that people think I'm connected to all this?"

Elysia's eyes fluttered guiltily. "Um . . . yes. I've heard some talk. But it's probably only because you're new." A sad look passed over her face. "No one wants to believe that someone we've known and loved for years could do something like this."

Lex scowled. "Well, they can all suck it once I go home and it keeps happening."

But the thought of leaving made her feel even worse. The summer was nearing a close, and she still hadn't been able to think of a way to stay in Croak. Meanwhile, Cordy had redoubled her emailing efforts, and though this time around Lex had actually replied to a few of them, she always made sure to conveniently leave out the part about a crazed murderer on the loose.

Elysia frowned. "You still think your parents won't let you stay?"

"You don't know my parents. If I don't go back of my own volition, I bet you anything they'll drive up here themselves and snatch me right out of the ether."

"Maybe home will be better. It's gotta be cheerier than it is here," Elysia said gloomily, watching the newest group of dazed-looking souls entering through the tunnel. "Even those guys are better off. Ignorance is bliss, right?"

Lex froze. "Wait a minute," she said, keeping her eyes on the distraught newcomers. "Why *can't* the souls remember their deaths?"

"The tunnel. It automatically represses that specific memory until they're able to deal with it."

"So it's not because of the Elixir in the fluff here?"

"Nope. Elixir doesn't cause amnesia. If it did, we wouldn't have to milk the spiders."

"Spiders . . ." Lex jumped to her feet and took Elysia's shoulders. "Elysia, listen to me. Think back to the beginning of the summer, before I got here. Can you remember anyone coming in here and removing Elixir?"

Elysia smiled confusedly. "No."

"Are you sure?"

"Yeah, that's all kinds of illegal. I'd scream my head off. That's the whole point of my job, other than wrangling the presidents."

A loud shout sounded from inside the office. Lex paused, then turned back to Elysia.

"Think hard," she continued, breathing heavily. "Are there any days that you can't remember? Like, maybe you lost track of a few hours?"

"No."

"Yes," Edgar said.

Both girls turned to him. "What?"

"One day, someone came in here and took a bunch of these silly clouds," he said. "You *did* scream your head off, but then you sat at your desk for a while without saying anything. I remember specifically because it was the day Eleanor Roosevelt threw a teapot at me —"

"What are you talking about, Edgar?" Elysia turned to Lex. "I do *not* remember that."

"Lex!" Driggs shouted from the other room. He sounded panicked.

Lex lunged for the vault door, then turned back to Elysia. "Ask around. Find out if anyone in here saw who it was." She flew through the door and into the office, where Driggs stood holding a broken test tube, an equally stunned look upon his face.

"Amnesia," they said at the same time.

"*That's* why Kloo and Ayjay couldn't remember anything!" Lex said.

"I thought Kilda was just being Kilda," Driggs said. "But she was right, it's practically all gone. The murderer must have taken it from the Lair — "

"Then stolen Elixir from the Afterlife — "

"Then drugged Ferbus and Elysia to make them forget the whole thing!"

Ferbus let out a shout. "I've never been drugged!"

"You wouldn't remember if you *have*," Lex shot back. "That's the point!"

"But — but — "

Lex and Driggs stared at each other for a moment more, then tore down the stairs (prompting a "What the hell?" from Norwood), out of the Bank, and into the pounding rain.

They burst through the door of the library just as the meeting was starting. Uncle Mort and everyone else in the room turned to look at them.

"Took Amnesia — stole Elixir — Afterlife — " they wheezed.

"Slow down," said Uncle Mort. "What happened?"

Norwood and Heloise appeared at the door behind them, followed by Ferbus and Elysia. Driggs took a deep breath and began to describe what they had figured out, all to a chorus of surprised rumblings from the townspeople.

"I asked around in the Afterlife," a sopping wet Elysia piped up. "But only a couple of souls saw it happen, and they couldn't see who was under the hoodie."

"Okay," said Uncle Mort. "Thanks, Elysia."

"You're *thanking* her?" Norwood burst in. He and Heloise were so furious, steam was nearly rising from their wet heads. "These kids are to blame for the whole thing!"

"How could you let this happen, you little ingrates?" Heloise spat at the visibly shaken pair of Ferbus and Elysia. "You have *one* job to do!"

"Heloise," Uncle Mort interrupted. "They haven't been here as long, so their immunity against Amnesia isn't as strong as that of the Seniors. That's probably why they were targeted. It's not their fault."

"Oh, bullshit." Norwood sneered. "Don't you get it, Mort? This is what comes of hiring all these useless amateurs! I've been saying it for years, and now look at the mess they've gotten us into!"

"Can it, you pompous gasbag!" Pandora screeched. "I don't see anyone else trying to figure out what's going on here. These kids are the only ones out of all of you who give a damn!"

"But they saw the deaths from the start and didn't tell anyone!" a new voice shouted.

All eyes flocked to Zara, who had jumped to her feet.

"Sorry guys," she said, looking at Lex and Driggs, "but enough is enough." She pointed at them and addressed the crowd. "Those two were the first, then the other Juniors joined in. You should have found out about this weeks ago, but they wanted to figure everything out by themselves. And Mort helped them, he's been scheming along with them the whole time. And you know what else he's not telling you? The victims aren't random at all — they're being specifically targeted because they're criminals!"

Driggs cursed under his breath. "You *told* her?"

Lex gave him a guilty look.

"Sofi!" Heloise's shrill voice rang out. "Have you been helping them?"

Sofi, quivering in her seat, could barely speak. "I — I didn't know — "

"Oh, of course you didn't!" Norwood spat. "None of these brats know a goddamn thing! These two can't even watch a door," he said, gesturing at Ferbus and Elysia. He pointed to Kloo and an eye-patched Ayjay. "These two can't stop sucking each other's faces long enough to realize they're being attacked." He then stuck a finger into Lex's face and turned to Uncle Mort. "And if you think for one second that this niece of yours is even remotely — "

"*Enough!*" Uncle Mort thundered. The room went silent.

When he spoke again, his voice was calm but firm. "Yes, Lex and Driggs were the first to see the abnormalities. Yes, they were assisted by Sofi and the other Juniors. They came to me — admittedly, later than I would have preferred — and described what they had seen. I allowed them to continue because I thought it was best to contain the situation and involve as few people as possible. I stand by that decision."

Norwood swore.

Uncle Mort ignored him. "As for the victims, Zara's right — it would seem that the majority of them are criminals. But as you've all read in the paper over the past couple of days, Grims are now being targeted as well, which is why it's more important than ever for us to come together like this. I called this meeting to discuss what everyone's been seeing, to gather our information together, and to try to make some constructive headway — not to point fingers. We don't have time for this petty, melodramatic bullshit. So we're going to continue with the meeting as planned, and if you don't like it, you're free to leave."

Norwood and Heloise did just that, slamming the door on their way out. Everyone else remained, though a distinct air of unease settled through the room as the discussion began.

Lex, meanwhile, was so mad at Zara that she could have strangled her with her own stupid silver hair. She scanned the seats and spotted Zara glaring at her — an activity that Driggs also seemed to be enjoying.

"What?" Lex quietly snapped at him. "What did I do?"

"I can't believe you told her."

"Oh my God," she said, rolling her eyes. "This is so high school. I'm gonna go cry into my locker."

"Forget it. We'll talk later."

"Good idea. That'll give me time to consult my cootie catcher."

The meeting continued into the night, and although there were no more outbursts, it was clear that Norwood's words had struck a chord with the townspeople. Their hostility became so apparent that by the end, Pandora had to sneak the Juniors out the back door so they could slink away to the Crypt in peace. All except for Zara, of course — who happily stayed behind to field any questions the Seniors had for her, the Most Responsible Junior in Croak.

Lex couldn't bear to face Uncle Mort, not after betraying his trust like that. So she ducked out of the meeting as soon as it was over, ran straight to her bedroom, and didn't come out until the next morning. Unfortunately, since Driggs stayed in his own room, pounding at his drums with a renewed ferocity, she ended up all alone with her uncle at the breakfast table, the awkwardness sitting between them like an ugly homemade centerpiece. She eyed him carefully, waiting for him to rip her a new one, but the scolding never came. He didn't even look mad.

"Here's a fun question," she said, hoping to preemptively distract him. "Why are Norwood and Heloise allowed to treat us like crap?"

"Because they'd probably firebomb the Bank if they couldn't," Uncle Mort said, flipping through the newspaper. "They're just set in their ways. Never been fans of the Junior program."

"Can't you fire them?"

"Lex, if everyone with a bad attitude got fired, the postal service would cease to exist," he said. "Norwood and Heloise are the best at what they do, and have undeniably earned their places here. Eventually, so will you."

Lex was indignant. "I've already earned my place here!"

"See," he said, looking up, "that's exactly the kind of arrogant thinking they loathe."

She grimaced and gazed into her cereal. Yet Uncle Mort kept staring at her, as if the solution to some overly complicated puzzle lay in the contours of her troubled young face. "Lex," he said at last, slowly running his finger along his scar. "How'd you like to help me catch this bastard?"

Her mouth fell open. "What? How?"

He got up and paced across the room, coming to a stop at the sink. "I have an idea. It's dangerous and comes with a high probability of failure. I assume you're in."

"Obviously!"

He walked into the living room, beckoning her to follow him. He waded through the accumulated junk on the floor to a small, dusty closet and opened the door. Lex squinted down at the familiar boxy object within.

She looked at him, stupefied. "Is that what I think it is?"

He nodded.

They headed back to the kitchen table, where Uncle Mort spent the next several minutes carefully outlining his plan. He made Lex repeat the details back to him three times, then instructed her not to proceed until he gave her the go-ahead.

"And lastly," he said, "the million-dollar question. Can I trust you with all of this?"

"Of course! How can you even ask me that?" She shrank slightly. "I mean — look, I'm really sorry about Zara. But she was the only one I told, I swear."

"*You swear?*" Uncle Mort's entire demeanor changed so quickly, Lex actually recoiled. "Don't play games with me, Lex," he growled. "You think I don't know about your little blabfest with Cordy?"

She went cold.

"You think all this surveillance equipment is just for decoration?" He gestured at the satellite dishes sticking out of the window, then leaned in and grabbed Lex by the elbow. "The only reason you are sitting at this table right now is because I've chosen to ignore a *very* large number of *very* serious Terms regarding Grimsphere disclosure. If you weren't my niece, you'd have gotten kicked out of here so fast you wouldn't even remember your own name, let alone where you've been all summer. What you did is inexcusable. You put Croak in danger, you put yourself in danger, and worst of all, you put Cordy in danger."

He let go of her arm, but his gaze did not soften. "So yes, I need to ask for your trust. I need your word that everything we've just talked about stays between us," he said, leaning back in his chair. "No more second chances, Lex. I can't protect you anymore. If you screw this one up, you're outta here. For good."

Lex stared back at him, floored. "Okay — " she stammered. "I mean, yes. Yes, you can trust me. I won't tell anyone."

He crossed his arms and watched her for a moment, then finally relaxed his gaze. "Except for Driggs, right?"

"No! I won't!"

"You should."

"What? But you just said — "

"He's your partner. It would be cruel to keep him in the dark. And isn't that what he's so pissed off about right now? Something you neglected to tell him?"

A furious series of cymbal crashes issued forth from Driggs's room, as if to confirm this.

Lex scowled. "I'll think about it. But he's going to freak out. He freaks out over everything I do."

"I can't imagine why."

She clapped her hands over her ears as the din got even louder. "Why did you ever let him get those in the first place?"

He winked. "Stress relief."

22

"Another geezer, huh?" Lex said to Driggs a few days later, over a man attempting to blow out each and every one of his eighty-eight birthday candles. "Nothing left to live for, you think? Bingo night get canceled?"

Driggs ignored her, much as he had since the meeting.

"Come on, Driggs, I said I was sorry," Lex said, Killing the man with the tip of her elbow. The shocks were getting to be too much for her poor hands to handle; she had begun shifting the duties to other parts of her body. "When are you going to start talking to me again?"

Driggs said nothing as he Culled.

Lex watched him, her stomach knotted. He'd been giving her the cold shoulder for almost a week now, and it didn't feel good. At all. The extra silence was giving her far too much time alone with her thoughts, all of which inevitably swirled right back to Zara and the fire incident, a once-shelved issue that, ever since the meeting, had festered and swelled until she could think of little else. Something had to give.

"I set a pizza box on fire," she blurted.

Driggs blinked. "What?"

As soon as they scythed back to the Ghost Gum, Lex told him everything — how she and Zara shared the same shocks, why she had told her about the criminal pattern, and, finally, what had happened in the kitchen. "I've been trying not to think about it, trying to tell myself that there's a perfectly logical explanation, which I'm ninety-nine percent sure there is — but what if there isn't?" She looked at him with worried eyes. "What if I really did it?"

Driggs, his irritation toward her evaporating more with every worried confession, sighed and gave her a smile. "Then I'd say it's time to crack open your uncle's head and feast on the sweet, sweet knowledge within."

||||||

That night Lex and Driggs microwaved some ramen noodles and entered the living room. The venerable mayor stood atop a ladder, looming over the jellyfish tank. Affixed to his head was some sort of binocular-goggle headpiece, the lenses of which were submerged beneath the water's surface. "Routine checkup," he told them as he inspected the tank. "What's up?"

Lex looked at Driggs. They'd agreed there was no way to go about this without being painfully blunt. "Uncle Mort," she said, "how did Grotton set people on fire?"

Uncle Mort's head snapped to attention, the binoculars splashing out of the tank and spraying the room with water, his eyes gigantic in the lenses. "Beg pardon?"

"Grotton," said Driggs, slurping up a noodle. "Fire."

Uncle Mort stared at them, then let out a short laugh. "I see you kids have been telling ghost stories again." He removed the binoculars, stepped down from the ladder, and sank into the couch.

Lex plopped down next to her uncle and put her face close to his. "Come on, Uncle Mort. Spill. We know you know, and in case it's unclear, we're going to be as irritating as possible until you tell us."

"Oh, it's quite clear." He rubbed his eyes, then sighed. "I'll tell you, but only because you sound so damned ignorant. You really think he set people on fire?" he said in a mocking tone.

"I hope not," she said, looking at Driggs.

Uncle Mort shook his head. "What I'm guessing you're referring to is something completely different. Something far more sinister, a power so disturbing that even the most comprehensive Grimsphere history books don't mention it, and so rare that Grotton is the only person we know of who's ever been born with it."

Lex swallowed. "What is it?" she asked, almost in a whisper.

"The power to Damn souls." Uncle Mort looked at his hands. "With a single touch, Grotton was able to destroy people instantly, without releasing the Gamma. It was different from being trapped or ghosted — instead of souls being confined to the body or lost into the world, they became infected. They withered and rotted, but never died. No Afterlife, no everlasting peace — only a grand prize of inconceivable pain and torment for all eternity."

His words hung in the air as Lex and Driggs tried to make sense of them. "That's . . . the scariest thing I've ever heard," said Driggs.

"Which is why we don't exactly make it part of the curriculum," said Uncle Mort. "Damning is a very archaic, malevolent ability, and the number of Grims on earth who know about it can probably be counted on no more than two hands. Plus, details are extremely scarce. No one knows how it worked or what it looked like. Burned bodies were found, and that's about the only hard evidence we've got."

"And no one other than Grotton has done it?" Lex asked.

"Well, they've *tried*. You think our little Elixir murderer here is the first to play God?" Uncle Mort said with a snicker. "I hate to break it to you kids, but when humans are entrusted with the power of death, there are bound to be a few crackpots thrown in along the way who think they can thwart the system and mess around with the framework of the universe. It's happened before, and it'll happen again. Why else do you think some Grims waste half their lives trying to find those goddamned Loopholes?"

Something about the way he said that — almost with a hint of frustration — made Lex think of the maps she had seen in his lab. She glanced at the basement door.

Uncle Mort caught her. "Don't worry," he said with a slight smirk. "If I ever find one, you'll be the first to know."

"But why was Grotton the only one who could Damn?" Driggs asked.

Uncle Mort shrugged. "Well, I suppose it's possible that there were others before him, but the history books only go back so far. In any case, there hasn't been anyone since. Like I said, the ability to Damn is something you have to be born with. And as if those odds weren't bad enough, anyone trying to emulate Grotton would also have to find the Loophole. *And* learn how to Crash with direction. Trust me, the guy was a perfect storm, and he knew it — that's why he was able to exploit his abilities in ways that no one ever had before."

"Maybe he couldn't help it," Lex said quietly. She looked down at her blistered hands, remembering that the last time she'd heard Uncle Mort mention innate talent and raw power, he'd been talking about *her*.

Uncle Mort studied his niece, seeming almost to read her

mind. "You're missing the point," he said. "Grotton wasn't forced to use his power. He chose to. His victims could have gone on to live perfectly fulfilling lives if he hadn't taken it upon himself to mutilate their souls." He stopped and gave them both a suspicious look, as if realizing he'd said too much. "Out of curiosity, why do you ask?"

Driggs looked at Lex. "Tell him," he said.

When she finished, Uncle Mort looked more amused than he had in quite some time. "But it was on a stove, right?"

"Yeah," said Lex. "So I guess I could have turned it on accidentally, and I just didn't notice in all the confusion."

"You think?" Uncle Mort gave her a sympathetic smile. "Lex, history is full of Grims who thought they developed special powers, that they were going to be the next Grotton. But *has* there ever been another Grotton? No. No one's been able to Damn since him. And if you're seriously entertaining the thought that you can, then I'm sorry to inform you that you've lost your impressionable young mind."

Lex and Driggs had nothing to say to that.

"Satisfied?" Uncle Mort said, standing up. "Good. We've got more pressing issues to deal with at the moment." He grabbed a printout from the computer. "Look."

Driggs skimmed it. "The birthday cake geezer was a senator?"

"And beloved grandfather of twelve," Uncle Mort added. "*And* under investigation for corruption. The FBI's all over this thing now, not to mention the media. Mystery deaths are the new black."

"But they couldn't possibly know what's really going on, right?" Lex asked.

"No. And they never will, if we can stop it in time." He gave her a conspiratorial nod, then strapped the binoculars on and got back to the jellyfish. Not wanting to tip Driggs off, Lex quickly arose and headed toward the kitchen.

"Hey, Lex?" Uncle Mort called after her.

"What?" she said sharply, dipping her head into the living room.

He held up a beaker of tank water and jiggled it excitedly. "We're a go for Friday."

"Great." She ducked back out again, desperately trying to get back to the kitchen before Driggs caught wind of anything. She wasn't ready to tell him yet.

"What happens on Friday?" he asked as she crossed to the sink.

"Nothing. Drop it."

"You know very well I wouldn't dream of dropping it."

Twenty minutes later Driggs had wrestled Lex into his bedroom, padlocked the door, and vigorously launched into a nonstop drum solo. Lex was curled up in a fetal position on the floor, jamming a pillow into her ears.

"STOP!"

His frenetic hands halted. "What happens on Friday?" he asked, spinning the sticks.

"I undergo surgery to regain my hearing!"

Driggs resumed banging. Lex screamed into the pillow.

An hour after that, they ended up on the roof. Lex had distracted Driggs just long enough to escape through his window, but he followed so swiftly that she panicked and scaled the ladder.

"Really? The roof is your getaway plan?" he said teasingly, balancing on the shingles. "Don't you watch horror movies?" He turned around and kicked the ladder away. It fell to the ground with a soft *thwump*.

Lex watched it fall. "Have you taken leave of your senses?"

"Tell me what happens on Friday."

Lex threw up her hands. "Okay, fine. But I am not responsible for the cerebral aneurysm you're about to have." She picked at her lip. "Uncle Mort has a plan. I'm going to try to track the murderer."

Driggs stared at her in silence. For all of two seconds.

"WHAT?"

"See, this is why I didn't want to tell you. I knew you'd flip out and do something lame like try to protect me."

Driggs gave her a serious look, his lopsided blue gaze popping in the moonlight. "Lex, in the space of two months, you've punched me in the face, kicked me in the nuts, and permanently demolished my kidneys. You really think I believe you need protection?"

Lex shifted. "No."

Driggs lay down and put his hands over his eyes. She sat beside him.

"How dangerous is this?" he asked.

"Dangerous is such a relative term . . ."

"Lex. On a scale of one to ten."

She winced. "Twelve?"

"TWELVE?" he shouted, bolting upright.

"Listen, Uncle Mort has it all figured out. As long as we do our jobs, we'll be fine," she said, placing her hand on his knee.

He stared at it. She removed it.

"I can't help but notice the change in pronoun there," he said.

"Well, yeah, you'd have to help too," she admitted. "I assume you're okay with that."

"Lex, the things you wrongly assume could fill a silo." He looked up, then exhaled. "What's the plan?"

"Okay," she began excitedly. "You know how the Croak population sign changes whenever a Grim exits or enters? That's because all of Croak is on a grid that Uncle Mort monitors, which means that he can tell if someone leaves town."

"I know that," said Driggs. "But Grims disappear and reappear all the time during their shifts. How's he going to zero in on only one person?"

"Precisely *because* it's only one person. All other Grims work in teams. If he can detect that a single Grim has vanished from Croak, he'll know that's our murderer."

"But the grid system only crunches numbers. It can't identify specific people."

"Right. Which is why Uncle Mort is going to use his own personal Smack to hack into the Etceteras' system while we're out on our shift. Using the advance knowledge that a single Grim has left Croak and that the next death will likely be an Elixir death, he'll hijack our trajectory and program our scythes to take us to that location faster than the Etceteras would be able to. So if we're quick enough, we can catch the murderer before they can scythe back out again."

"And then what?"

"We'd scythe back to Croak and tell Uncle Mort who it is."

"If they don't kill us first."

" . . . Right."

Driggs lay back down again. "This is pure lunacy."

"But it really could work! Plus, it's Uncle Mort's plan, not mine."

"Then why can't he be the one to do it?"

"Because I — " She paused.

He eyed her. "You what?"

She picked at a shingle. "He said I can scythe even faster than he can."

Driggs finally hesitated. "Mort said that?"

"Yes."

Driggs thought about this for a moment, then shook his head. "Lex, have you ever stopped to think that you might be playing right into the Crasher's hands?"

"What do you mean?"

"We already know this prick has a flair for the dramatic, right? Taking down Croak's youngest and most talented Killer in the line of duty — doesn't get more tragic than that."

She let out a bitter laugh. "Oh, I'm sure the town would love it." She stood up and watched the lights below. "They'd throw a ticker tape parade."

"What is that supposed to mean?"

"Ferbus said a lot of people think I'm in on all this." She spun around. "Were you ever going to tell me that? Or do you just plan to grab a pitchfork along with everyone else once the angry mob begins to form?"

"You don't get it, do you, Lex?" He got up. "This is a town that has operated flawlessly for hundreds of years. And then you show up and everything goes haywire. I mean, what are people supposed to think? You became the best Killer here in less than a week, you strut around like you own the place, and you haven't exactly made it a secret that you despise the Terms of Execution. So no, I'm sorry, but I really don't blame them for suspecting you."

"Then you're an idiot," she said. "And so are they, for thinking a rookie could pull off something that ambitious."

He let out a short, harsh laugh. "Ambitious, huh? That's not the word Mort used."

"So?"

"You admire this psycho, don't you?"

Lex's nostrils flared. "I have a certain appreciation for the amount of skill and ingenuity that such a rampage has required, yes," she said through gritted teeth.

"Appreciation? Come on, Lex. Don't tell me that the thought of systematically eliminating criminals doesn't send you into a fit of joy."

She balled her hands into fists. "I have been working on this just as hard as you have, if not more! I want to catch this — "

"Why, so you can join him?"

"SHUT UP!"

Her shout was so loud, they both stopped to listen as it echoed through the valley.

"I'm sorry," Driggs said. "I didn't mean that."

Lex tried to breathe evenly. "Look, I know I've given you very few reasons to trust me," she said. "And I agree that this whole thing sounds like a terrible idea, but it's Mort's terrible idea. You trust *him* at least, right?"

"I trust both of you," he muttered. His shoulders slumped as he looked out over the town. "Okay. If this is what you really want, then I'm in."

"Thank you," said Lex, relieved. "And if I'm wrong . . ." She trailed off. "I don't know. You're welcome to find a new partner once this is all over, I guess."

"I do *not* want a new partner," Driggs said, unable to hide the edge of panic in his voice. He took a step forward, his frame drawing dangerously close to hers. "But I don't want a dead one, either."

They looked at each other for a moment.

"Why do you care so much?" she asked.

Driggs sighed. "Don't you know?"

Then something happened in the next two seconds, but neither Lex nor Driggs would be able to recall exactly what. All they knew was that after it was over, their eyes met once again, this time in horror.

"Why did you just kiss my ear?" Lex asked nervously.

Driggs winced. "Because you turned your head."

"I thought that tree . . . moved."

"Oh."

Another moment of silence.

Driggs bit his lip. "Do you mind if I try again?"

She swallowed. "Okay."

Then something else happened, and this time both Lex and Driggs would remember exactly what it was.

23

The next morning, as Driggs and Lex came into the kitchen for breakfast, Uncle Mort took one look at them and began snickering.

"What?" demanded Lex. This only made him chuckle harder. "What??"

When they checked in with Norwood, he looked back and forth between them and grunted, "Oh, for shit's sake."

And at lunch Pandora studied them for all of two seconds before declaring to the entire restaurant, "It's about damned time!"

"Are we broadcasting some sort of signal?" Lex quietly asked Driggs at the lunch booth as the rest of the Juniors unabashedly smiled at them.

"I think they know," Driggs whispered to her.

"Of course we know," Elysia loudly affirmed. "It was just a question of when." She glanced triumphantly around the table. "Pay up, you guys."

A chorus of grumbling arose as the rest of the Juniors dug into their pockets and threw a mountain of cash onto the table. Elysia greedily swept it into her lap.

"I was off by three weeks," Ayjay said. "Thanks a lot, jerks."

|||||

The last few days of summer were a blur. By the time Friday arrived, Driggs's attempts to change Lex's mind had gotten desperate.

"I'll give you a hundred bucks," he told her at breakfast. "Come on, that's a whole week's pay."

"Oh, boy! Maybe I can get myself another *Titanic* poster!"

He groaned. "Mort, help me out here."

"Lex is a big girl," Uncle Mort said. "She knows the risks. But she's the best shot we've got at this."

Driggs heaved a frustrated sigh and stormed out of the house.

Lex watched him go, swallowing the sickening dismay that she'd been trying to ignore all week: whether the plan worked or not, she was leaving the next day. There was no getting out of it.

Uncle Mort, seeing her anguished face, revealed a parcel from underneath the table. "Going-away present," he said. "Little something of my own invention."

Lex untied the twine and loosened the wrapping, which, upon closer inspection, was actually an old T-shirt. From it she removed a glass structure about ten inches high, held in place by a metal frame with three rods. Small spheres on the bottom served as its feet, and a metallic spider welded from old nuts and bolts perched on top, its ruby eyes shining.

"An hourglass?"

"Wrong," Uncle Mort said. "A Lifeglass."

Lex rotated the shape in her hand. It was filled not with sand, but with a viscous ooze that shimmered faintly, all the colors of the spectrum swirling together into one iridescent blob. But the most remarkable thing was that the majority of the substance stubbornly remained in the lower half of the device, and no matter how many times Lex tried to turn it over, not a drop budged.

"It's broken."

"Broken, my ass." Uncle Mort took it from her hands and placed it on the table. "See, most hourglasses drip time away, bit by bit, until nothing remains but an empty bulb. But that, my friend, is no way to measure a life." He tapped at the glass. "This'll save and remember the elements of your life that are most important to you. It's not a countdown; it's a countup. That's why it goes backwards."

"Backwards?" No sooner had the word left her mouth than a small glob emerged from the sludge, rose to the narrow aperture, and wriggled its way through, finally settling quite happily in the valley of the upper bulb.

"There's one!" he said. "I started on this the moment your father decided you could come to Croak. Every important memory, thought, or emotion you've had since then is right here." He pointed at the upper bulb. Lex peered into the goo, and for a moment she could have sworn she caught a glimpse of herself, gawking for the first time in amazement at her brand-new scythe.

"But what happens when it runs out? I die?"

"It won't run out. There's more than enough space in there for an entire lifetime. Cram in as much nostalgia as you can."

"That's so cool," she said, inspecting it from every angle. "Does everyone have one of these? Do you?"

Uncle Mort's eyes clouded over as he stared into the glass. "I used to," he said in an odd voice. "But I broke it."

"On purpose?"

He didn't answer. His face was hard, lost in a memory he had apparently destroyed. Almost at once, Lex realized how little she really knew about him — who he'd been, what he'd done, or how he even became mayor. For the briefest of moments, this man was a stranger.

Lex studied his stony countenance. "Uncle Mort," she said, taking a shallow breath, "where'd you get that scar?"

He turned to her with a new, strange expression — a crooked smirk mixed with a fleeting, almost angry sneer.

"You ask too many questions, kiddo."

Lex didn't know what to say to this. So she broke the stare, took the Lifeglass into her hands, and got up to leave. "Well, I love it. Thanks."

"You're welcome. Just — " He seemed to want to say something more, but thought better of it. "Just use it well."

|||||||

Five hours later Lex sat in the Junior booth at the Morgue with a large WE'LL MISS YOU, LEX! banner over her head and a frown on her face.

Pandora plunked down a platter of deep-fried items at their table and squirted ketchup into Lex's drink. "Good riddance to bad rubbish, I say!" she cackled, determined to torture Lex with as much payback as she could cram into their remaining time together.

Driggs fired a cheese stick at Dora's head as she hobbled back to the kitchen. Elysia, meanwhile, heaved a wrapped package onto the table next to the Lifeglass, which Lex had brought to show off. "This is for you, Lex," she said. "We all chipped in."

"Chipped in, meaning you used the winnings from your little pool?" Lex asked wryly.

"Correct."

Lex tore off the paper to reveal a sizable wooden picture frame ornately carved with images of Croak. She recognized the homey façade of the Bank, the rickety Dead End signpost, several skulls of Yorick, a cluster of spiders, and a smack of jellyfish, among a host of other things that made the corners of her mouth involuntarily twitch. And centered proudly behind the glass of the frame was the group photo Pandora had taken at the Luminous Twelfth celebration.

Elysia gave Lex a small, sad smile. "Now when you go home, you can take a piece of us with you."

"Wow," Lex said softly. She skimmed across the faces in the picture, then raised her head to look at the real ones shining before her. She felt sick all over again. "I love it. Thanks, guys."

The festivities were broken up by Pandora, who lobbed a scoop of ice cream at Lex that landed on the table with a sticky *sploosh*.

"Don't let the door hit ya where the good Lord split ya!" she screeched, jigging back into the kitchen.

||||||

After storing the presents in Ferbus's desk for safekeeping, Lex and Driggs headed downstairs to the hub to check in for their afternoon shift. Sofi, who had not attended the party, glanced up at them with a look of disdain. "Hi," she said in a flat voice.

"Hey," Lex answered airily. She thought there *might* be a

chance that Sofi's recent coolness had something to do with the fact that she had gotten into major trouble with Norwood and Heloise . . .

. . . but knowing Sofi, she was probably just jealous as hell.

"She is, like, not a fan of us," Lex mocked as she and Driggs left the Bank.

"Hurry up," Driggs said, walking more briskly. "The sooner we start our shift, the sooner this dumbass plan will be over with."

"Would you stop it?" She stalked past him onto the Field, where the Ghost Gum waited, stretching its limbs in an apparent gesture of excitement. She rolled up her sleeve and mumbled "Leaving now" into her Cuff, then turned to her partner. "We're going to be fine."

"Your cockeyed optimism has only served to heighten my concern."

"Driggs, this is my last shift." Lex pulled her hood up and readied her scythe. "Make it a tolerable one, or you and I are so done."

He smirked. "Promises, promises."

||||||

Five hours, several geezers, three drownings, zero Elixir deaths, and a circus stampede later, the day drew to a close.

"One more to go," Driggs said, stuffing a Vessel into his pocket and glancing warily at a rogue elephant. "You ready?"

"You mean now that I know what an ostrich mauling looks like?" Lex said, beyond cranky. "Yeah, I'm good."

Driggs looked at her sullen face. With every scythe to a new location, she had been on her guard, ready to leap at the murderer with the rabid tenacity of a bounty hunter — but nothing had turned up. "I'm sorry the plan didn't work," he said sincerely. "I really am. I wanted to catch them too."

Lex scowled as they jumped into the ether, allowing the churning current to swirl around her — the wind pounding in her ears, her stomach flopping around like a wobbly water balloon, her heart sick at how much she would miss it all. The only way to achieve this kind of effect back at home was via psychotropic substances, and she was fairly certain her parents would prohibit those. Even if she asked nicely, without any punching.

Before long, solid ground materialized beneath her feet. She and Driggs stood on either side of a bed. An old woman with a swollen, bulging neck was sprawled out atop it, her eyes closed.

Lex glanced down at her, then at Driggs's puzzled face. "What's wrong?"

"She isn't dead. She's not the target," he said in an odd voice, looking up at Lex. "Who — "

The blood drained out of his face so quickly that Lex nearly looked at the floor, expecting it to be pooling there.

"Lex," he said very slowly, staring at something behind her. "Listen to me. Do not turn around."

She swallowed. "Why?"

Fear had crept into Driggs's voice. "Just don't," he said shakily. "Please. Take my hand. I'm scything home."

Lex extended her arm and stretched it toward his waiting fingertips. Inside, her mind was spinning. What was behind her? Could it really be that bad?

Her curiosity grew exponentially, gnawing harder at her insides with every second that passed. She had to know. Her hand froze an inch away from Driggs's. She took a breath, held it . . .

And turned.

"NO!" Driggs yelled.

But Lex could barely hear him. She could no longer feel. She could no longer think. All she perceived was coldness, a dark shadow settling over her raised skin.

The target, standing directly in front of her, was Cordy.

||||||

Amid the darkness, from somewhere deep within the abyss, a lone point of light broke through to the surface of Lex's consciousness. Rendered incapable of lucid thought, she registered it faintly and watched with something akin to heartsick amusement as it swam across her mind's eye.

She was sitting in her backyard, plopped askew in the green plastic turtle sandbox. A six-year-old Cordy sat across from her, legs splayed to make room for the elaborate contraption over which the two of them had been laboring for the past hour or so: a Rube Goldbergian sand dispersal device. Cordy examined and adjusted one of the wheel-and-pulley systems. Her tongue stuck out of her mouth, as it did whenever she was inventing. The entire mechanism was of Cordy's own design, of course, but Lex had contributed an equal amount of work in terms of construction, layout, and overall aesthetic appeal. They made a good team.

Lex watched her sister for a moment. Then, for no good reason at all, she picked up a handful of sand and hurled it at her face. Cordy looked up in shock, large clumps of dirt clinging to her scraggly bangs.

"Why did you do that?" she asked, her eyes wide.

"I don't know."

"Well, stop. This work is Very Important."

They continued what they were doing—Cordy fussing over the pulleys, Lex spreading out the blades of a windmill-shaped rotor—until Lex again dug her hand into the sand and inexplicably threw another gritty ball of dirt.

This time, however, her aim was off. It hit the windmill and exploded in midair, grimy grains of sand ricocheting back onto her dress, her hair, and directly into her right eye.

"Owww!" Lex howled in pain as she jumped to her feet, causing a part of the contraption's foundation to snap and break. The entire frame lurched perilously.

But Cordy took no notice of her ruined creation. "Are you okay?" She ran to her sister and hugged her around the shoulders. "Are you okay?"

Lex wailed. "It hurts!"

"Don't be scared," Cordy said in an attempt at a soothing voice. But her tone, too, was panicked. "Let's go inside. Mommy will know what to do."

Arms gripped over the shaking shoulders of her twin, Cordy led Lex inside. And as their mother held her head under the sink, aiming the faucet directly at her daughter's cornea, Lex's other, uninjured eye beheld a sight that she would completely forget until this moment: that of her sister standing a few feet away and watching the disastrous scene unfold, sick with worry, her previously Very Important construction project long forgotten.

||||||

Lex blinked heavily — once, twice. Vaguely aware that the shouting in the background had stopped, she locked on to her sister's frozen eyes and did not look away.

The longer she stalled, the longer the Elixir would rage through Cordy's body. Lex was allowed to scythe out and call an emergency Killer to finish the job, but too much time had passed already. She thought back to Ayjay and the pain the Elixir had caused him. She couldn't let Cordy suffer like that, even if it was only for a fraction of a second.

She swallowed, choking back the fear in her throat. She had to. She had to be the one to do it. Cordy would want it to be her.

From the dark sleeve of her hoodie, Lex shakily extended a bony finger and passed it over her sister's face, gently touching her on the forehead. A burst of light flooded the room. The usual shock tore through Lex's body, but this time she didn't care. It felt good, almost, for her body to be in as much pain as her heart was.

"Lex."

She turned around abruptly, as if surprised to find Driggs still there. His jaw was slack with shock, his eyes enormous. "You Killed her yourself?"

"I had to," she said, her voice cracking. "Didn't I?"

He remained speechless for another moment, then swallowed hard. "We have to go back."

"Wait, you have to Cull her."

"No," he said, watching Cordy's soul drift through the air. "Something is seriously wrong here. We'll find Mort, he can send emergency crews — "

"*Please?*" Her eyes were frantic.

He regarded her for a moment more, then nodded. He made

his way to her side and reluctantly raised his hand, his own eyes trained toward the floor. Lex walked over to where he had been standing and watched him work, until a noise sounded against her back.

She turned around.

And as her sister's hooded murderer stepped out from behind the window curtain, Lex staggered backwards, every emotion swirling within her suddenly replaced by a single new one — that of unbridled fury. Her past encounters with innocent victims, with the little girl and her bloody teddy bear — all felt like childish tantrums compared to this. Violent, irregular heartbeats thumped inside her chest, and without thinking — without listening to Driggs's futile cries for her to stop, without pausing for even a single yoctosecond to consider the consequences — Lex sprang at the looming figure.

As soon as they touched, a shock more powerful than anything Lex had ever felt before jolted through her hands. It rippled up her arms and into her body, colliding and fusing with the ferocious rage within. At the same time, a strong sucking racked her bones, as if it were extracting something very deeply rooted. The two opposing forces roared, each as strong as the other, until Lex could withstand no more and fell to the ground.

Driggs, who had been watching all of this in uncomprehending terror, began yelling again. But his words were soon washed away in the din of the ether, as Lex was dragged into it with nothing more than a fleeting glimpse of a metallic shimmer.

24

Lex crashed onto a dusty wooden floor.

She was in a cellar. A dim light bulb hung in the center of the room, scattering shadows across the barren cement walls as it swung back and forth. A window near the ceiling revealed an ominous gray sky. Large raindrops fell to the ground outside.

She tried to get to her feet, but she found she was too weak to stand. Whatever just happened had zapped her energy — and besides, her hands were being tied behind her back. A muffled groan came from the corner. Lex squinted through the darkness and saw a lumpy figure — a man, tied up and gagged. His eyes were terrified.

Lex's captor tightened a final knot, straightened up, and stood before her. The silvery glint flashed once more.

"Hi, Lex," Zara said wearily, her face pale.

Lex's mouth went dry. She tried to focus, but her vision kept blurring. Her hands, scorched from the shock, seared with pain.

"Zara?" she choked out. "What are you doing?"

"It worked," Zara whispered to herself, looking at her own hands. "Holy shit, it worked."

"What worked? Why —" She almost couldn't say it. "Why did you kill my sister?" she cried, groping her bound hands around the floor.

Zara held up Lex's scythe. "Looking for this?"

Lex sank, defeated. "And all those other people. All those Grims. There must have been — "

"Ninety-six. Well, ninety-seven, including Cordy. Ninety-seven and a half, if you want to count Ayjay."

Lex was too consumed with rage to respond.

"You wouldn't believe how easy it was, Lex." Zara stuffed the scythes into her pocket, leaned against the wall, and sank down to the floor. She looked just as shaken as Lex felt. "Swiping syringes from hospitals and scything off the radar, all alone in the back room of that filthy butcher's shop. And all I needed were a few stings from our friendly neighborhood jellyfish."

Lex's mouth fell open. "The Loophole?"

A small, tired smile found its way onto Zara's face. "The Loophole."

"What is it? How did you find one?"

"I have my sources. Hell, I started researching my second week in Croak. Dig long and hard enough, and you can find anything — especially if you know where to look."

"But — what *is* it?"

Zara gave her a wary look. "You're lucky. Under most circumstances, you couldn't torture that out of me — but it just so happens that I got the very last one." She smiled again. "A Loophole is a special ether-infused scroll woven from spider silk — just like the Vessels — with pictures that serve as the instructions. You drop it into jellyfish-inhabited water, wait for it to dissolve, and then sweep your arm through the tentacles. The solution becomes inactive after a few minutes, so you have to be fast. But after that, you can scythe to any location on the planet." She rubbed her arm. "Not that those jellyfish stings aren't painful.

They hurt like a bitch, in fact. And scar like you wouldn't believe."

Lex's memory swam back to that day at the butcher's, to Zara's mutilated arms. Her head began to pound.

Zara closed her eyes and leaned her head against the wall, but kept talking. "But the key to *directed* Crashing, is prolonged, heavy concentration. That was the really hard part. With practice — and practice, and practice — I learned how to scythe not only to specific places, but also to specific people. The scum that we've been letting go free for too long, the dregs of society who feed off the innocent and leave nothing but pain and misery in their wake."

Lex glanced warily at the man in the corner. She broke into a sweat. "Who is that?"

Zara ignored her. "Child molesters who were let off the hook, white-collar criminals who stole people's life savings, drunks who were maybe just one missed stop sign away from killing a mess of people — the world is a better place without them." She opened her eyes and looked at Lex. "And you know it."

Lex stared back. "But how did you find them?"

Zara let out a short laugh. "You aren't the only one with an Internet connection, Lex. Headlines, police blotters, sex offender registries — these lowlifes were practically begging for me to chase them down. And as for Ayjay and the other Grims — well, examples needed to be set. If you're part of the corrupt system, you're part of the problem."

"But what about Cordy? She's never done anything wrong in her life!"

"I know." Zara's face turned remorseful. "I'm really sorry, Lex.

You have to believe me. I didn't want to kill her, but I had no other choice. I needed you."

Lex furiously tugged at her ropes. "*Me?* For what?"

Zara stood up and began to slowly circle her captive. "You're different, Lex. I knew it from the moment we first met, the day you wanted to throttle that woman who had shot her husband. You feel the same way I do, that there's no earthly reason to turn a blind eye to the rapists and murderers, not when we can do something about it. Remember how excited you got when Uncle Sherlock finally cracked the criminal pattern? You said it yourself: bad people should be punished, no matter what the Terms say. And you know what? You're absolutely right."

"But you never even went after the murderers!" Lex protested. "Why bother with petty thieves and drunks when you could be going after the worst of the worst?"

"Exactly!" Zara's eyes lit up. "That's the question, isn't it? What to do with the *real* monsters? If only there were a way to know for certain that such criminals weren't let off the hook in the Afterlife, free to romp around in whatever carefree bliss they choose for themselves. If only there were a way to ensure that their souls suffered through absolute hell!"

Lex's heart bumped along at a nauseating pace. The walls of the room seemed to be closing in. Her hands throbbed.

Zara looked down at her. "You have no idea how special you are, do you?" she asked, a hint of envy creeping into her voice. "Tell me, has your dear uncle ever told you about the only other Grim with an overflow of Killing power so strong that it caused shocks?"

"You mean, besides us?"

"There is no 'us,' Lex," Zara said bitterly. "I've never felt a shock in my life."

"But — your hand — "

Zara held up her blistered finger. "What, this? I stuck it into the deep fryer at the Morgue."

Lex went cold. She felt as if she had been punched in the stomach.

Zara squatted down and grabbed her chin. "Grotton. Just you and Grotton. He dabbled in the same little Crashing deaths that I've been doing, but he abandoned all that once he realized his real talent — the one ability that I've coveted for years."

Lex squeezed her eyes shut. "Damning."

"You got it. A punishment far worse than death." She let go of Lex's chin. Lex opened her eyes and watched as Zara walked over to the restrained man. "You hear that?" she yelled. "Sounds like fun, huh?"

Lex swallowed, choking back the nausea. "You're lying," she said, though her gut told her otherwise. "I can't Damn."

"You can if you get mad enough. Just take that shock surplus and mix it with a healthy dose of rage," Zara said from the corner. "How do you think that pizza box caught on fire? And before, when you touched me — look at your hands!"

Lex didn't need to. She could feel the blisters puckering already. "But you're not Damned. You're not even dead!"

"Don't you get it, Lex?" Zara rushed back and sat in front of her. "Come on, you've been such a good little detective up till now. I raided the Amnesia supply, drugged up Ferbus and Elysia, stole Elixir from the Afterlife, injected it into those people — you got all of that! So think. Think hard."

She poked Lex in the chest. "You're special. I'm not. But what

I lack in born talent I make up for in intelligence. I figured out how to clone your powers for myself. That's why I had to kill your sister." She took a syringe out of her hoodie pocket — presumably the one she had used on Cordy — and dropped it in front of Lex. "Because you reacted exactly the way I needed you to: you tried to Damn me. And as soon as we touched, I Culled your power."

Lex's heart sank. It had been a trap. Cordy was dead because of her.

She stared at the syringe, unfeeling. "How did you know that would work?"

"Like I said, I have my sources."

Silence filled the room. Zara stood up and began pacing. Lex desperately clawed at the ropes binding her hands. They were beginning to slip, but just barely; it was difficult to work around the burns.

"Why are you doing this?" she asked. "Any of this?"

Zara's eyes darkened. She looked down at Lex from beneath a stiffened brow.

"Do you know where we are?" she said in a disturbingly blank voice. "My stepfather's basement. This is where he took me after dinner every night. I used to cower in that corner," she said, pointing at the man, "and this unimaginable bastard would hit me with whatever he deemed necessary for that day's crimes. Sometimes belts, sometimes his own fists, every so often a broken whiskey bottle. Always had plenty of those on hand."

Lex looked away. The rain pounded outside.

"The world is revolting," Zara snarled. "How could it allow things like that to happen to a defenseless little girl?" She was yelling now, angry flecks of spit flying out of her mouth, her hands balled up into fists. "How can so many despicable people be permitted to go on without punishment?" She took a deep breath. "They can't. They simply can't."

Zara stopped in front of her stepfather. She looked at him for a long time. Her breathing grew heavier. He let out another strangled groan and lolled around the ground, feebly attempting to free himself. His expression was one of pure terror.

Lex tried not to watch, but she couldn't help it.

With an abrupt, unearthly cry, Zara kicked him, hard. A cracking sound came from his ribs. His chilling wails echoed off the basement walls.

Zara stood over him, triumphant, as she extended her finger and touched him on the forehead.

But no flashes of light emerged.

No sound.

And no soul.

Instead, a thick, palpable darkness exploded through the air, shattering the light bulb. It engulfed the room so swiftly that Lex was knocked onto her back and could feel it whooshing across her skin.

After a second or two, light from the window began to creep back in. Lex, stunned, sat up and squinted across the room. A sinister black shadow now surrounded the motionless body. Wisps of darkness seemed to be seeping in from the walls, materializing out of thin air. They swirled over the man in an incomprehensible dance, churning and roiling, until at last the whole mass sank under its own weight and dissolved into his remains.

For a moment, nothing happened.

Then the man bolted upright, his eyes bulging in pure agony.

Some unknown torture took hold as he thrashed about the ground in a series of brutal convulsions, his fingernails leaving scrapes in the floor where he clawed at it. Smoke emerged from his nose, then his mouth, as if a fire had ignited inside his body. Soon, small licks of flame started to burst from his skin one by one, like popcorn. Before long, the entirety of his frame was engulfed, the fiery blaze throwing dramatic shadows onto the wall as inhuman howls of pain escaped his throat.

And then, with a sudden *whoosh,* the flames went out. The man crumpled into a heap, his body half ash, half melted flesh.

All was still. After a moment Zara rose from where she had been knocked to the floor and spit on her stepfather's corpse.

"I've been waiting to do that for ten years."

She sat back down against the wall, pulled her knees to her chest, and buried her head in her arms. A density settled over the room, a quiet stillness broken only by pings of rain, distant thunder, and the occasional sob from beneath Zara's hood.

Lex tore more furiously at the ropes binding her hands, but her fingers were getting too swollen. Her Cuff was emitting a slight hum, its surface vibrating against her skin, but she couldn't reach it to call for help. It wouldn't have mattered anyway — no one else could Crash to her location, not even if they knew where she was. Not even *she* knew where she was.

Zara got up, sniffed hard, and wiped her face with her sleeve. She turned to Lex with an eerily calm expression. "So where should we start?" she rasped, removing both of their scythes from her pocket. "I'm thinking death row. I know they're condemned anyway, but that can take years. We can help speed the process along."

"We?"

Zara gave Lex a startled look. "You're coming with me," she said, as if this were obvious.

"Why the hell would I want to do that?"

"Because you can!" Zara exploded, her face furious. "This is what you've been fighting for ever since you arrived, the ability to punish people who deserve it! What you just saw is nothing — *nothing* — compared to what that bastard's soul will be going through for the rest of eternity. So don't you dare sit there and tell me that you don't want to do this, that you don't believe this is the right thing to do. Think of the difference we can make! We have complete power over anyone with a pulse! And I mean *real* power, not just the puny little witchcraft that comes with being a Grim. You can't just throw it away!" She blew a sweaty clump of silver hair out of her face. "This is the side you belong on, Lex. And you know it."

Lex took a breath and held it. For any normal person, the choice would have been a no-brainer. Always choose good over evil. Anyone who's ever studied history, read a comic book, or seen *The Princess Bride* would know that. But Lex was not a normal person. And so, despite everything, she hesitated.

She knew that the depraved feelings inside of her would never lie dormant; the steadily intensifying shocks were proof enough of that. There was no way to quash them, no way to drive them from her mind and body, no way to prevent them from rearing their hideous heads and alienating the people she held so dear. It had become clear to her that impulses like that wouldn't ever go away, and they couldn't be destroyed. And now that she had touched her own sister's corpse, she wasn't even sure that she wanted them to. The world was a hideous place. It deserved the destruction she could create.

And Zara was right: it would be foolish to squander such a valuable gift. If Lex really could stop anyone she wanted to, why *not* go after the world's cruelest monsters? She'd be violating the Terms of Execution, and she'd have to abandon Croak forever, but maybe if it were all for the greater good . . .

But everyone back in Croak who had loved her and accepted her for the freak that she was would be devastated. They'd never forgive her; she'd never be able to return. She had made a true home there, somehow managing to cobble together a handful of real relationships that meant more to her than almost anything ever had before. Was all that worth throwing away? And the greater good — Lex didn't even know what that meant anymore. Was Uncle Mort on the side of good? Or was Zara?

Was anyone?

Lex swallowed. It wasn't worth it. The noxious, ever-wakeful rage would continue to surface, there was no doubt about that. And maybe one day she would succumb to it, but not yet. Not alongside Zara. If that meant death or Damnation, then so be it. The alternative, the thought of teaming up with the person who had murdered her sister in cold blood — it made Lex feel dirty, infected, diseased.

She could never live with herself.

Lex looked defiantly into Zara's wild eyes. "I'm not going anywhere with you."

"What?" Zara desperately pointed both scythes at her. "But to be born with a talent like yours — you're only the second person in history!"

"I don't care."

"You'd better care." Zara's lip curled. "Because you're either with me or you're Damned. I can't let you go. You must know that."

Lex scanned the stepfather's body, still smoldering. Where was his soul now? What was happening to it?

For the first time, Zara began to look uneasy. "Come on, Lex. Don't make me do this."

"Go to hell."

Zara angrily stalked off to the corner, where she stood in silence for a moment before letting out a small laugh. "Do you want to hear something funny, Lex?" She turned around to display a grotesque smile. "I sought out the ability to Damn because my life was a horrific, unbearable mess. My mother walked out on us—just left me alone with that sick pervert when I was nine and never came back. No wonder I turned out the way I have. But you . . ." she said with a glint in her eye, "you can Damn despite the utopian upbringing, despite the loving family. Why, Lex? Where is all of that malevolence coming from?"

Lex stared back blankly, as one does when faced with a question that has no answer.

Zara saw that she had struck a nerve. But Lex remained silent, and before long a flash of rage shot across Zara's face. "Suit yourself," she growled, shaking her head as she drew closer, extending her hand. "It's a shame, though. You could have been really, really good at this."

Lex cowered into the floor and prepared herself for the pain. But then she thought of Cordy, and how she hadn't gotten the slightest chance to defend herself. She never even knew what was coming.

And so with one final, desperate tug, Lex jumped to her feet, tossed the unknotted ropes to the ground, and grabbed both scythes out of Zara's hands.

"Sorry," Lex said. "But I'm really, really good at escaping, too."

And with a quick upward swipe of her scythe, Lex jumped into the ether, Zara's screams of surprise and fury echoing softly in the deafening wind.

25

Lex lay very still on the ground of the Field and looked up at the purpling sky. Cheerful pink clouds drifted lazily past the branches of the Ghost Gum as a warm breeze swept across the plain, carrying with it the tart, earthy scent of grass. She exhaled and watched the dust specks dance through the air, all the while trying desperately not to think about the fact that her best friend in the universe was dead.

Driggs's spiky hair immediately poked into her view, right in front of an ostrich-shaped cloud. "Lex?" he said softly, crouching down. "Are you okay?"

She sat up and blinked at the group of Senior Grims who were surrounding her. She gave her head a shake to quiet her racing thoughts. Cordy was dead. Zara had escaped. Everyone was in trouble. Cordy was dead. Jellyfish. Scars. Dead —

"The Bank. I have to get to the Bank."

Without another word Lex jumped to her feet, pushed past the Senior Grims, and sprinted across the Field. Driggs took off after her as she pounded up the stairs to the porch and into the lobby, where Kilda sat nervously wringing her hands. Lex blew past her and ran straight up the staircase, bursting into the small office on the second floor.

Elysia was waiting for her. "She's okay," she whispered, her voice trembling. "We got her, she's okay."

Lex, wielding both scythes, panted heavily and gestured at the vault door. "I want to see her."

"Lex," Elysia said gently, "it would be better not to. She's confused, she'll need a few days to understand. Give her some time."

Something in Lex collapsed. She remembered the befuddled dentist she had bothered, his look of disorientation mixed with a panicky fear. Accosting Cordy now would only make things worse. She couldn't do that to her.

"She's with Edgar." Elysia took Lex into her arms. "He'll take care of her."

Lex choked out a sob into Elysia's hair, which smelled like strawberries. Time seemed to dissolve as she clung to her friend. Hauntings of the ordeal blazed through her head in scattered fragments, ultimately settling on Zara's final, lingering question: Why *was* Lex born with such evil inside her?

And worse still, how could it possibly be worth the life of her sister?

Driggs soon bounded up the stairs, followed closely by Uncle Mort. Lex parted from Elysia's arms and glanced at Driggs's tortured face. He avoided her gaze.

"Uncle Mort," Lex said, "it's so much worse than we thought — "

"I know," he replied in a detached voice, peeling the scythes out of her hands. She had been holding them so tightly, even with the burns, that her knuckles had turned white. "You need to tell me everything."

She nodded, wiping her red, blotchy face with her red, blotchy hands. Uncle Mort, unable to tear his eyes away from the silver scythe, eventually put it into his pocket and turned to Driggs.

"Gather everyone up at the fountain. Emergency meeting. Mandatory."

Driggs nodded and ducked out of the room. Uncle Mort threw an arm over his niece's shoulder and began to lead her down the stairs. "Wait!" she cried, running back to Ferbus's desk to retrieve her presents. The top of the Lifeglass now appeared considerably fuller. Catching a murky glimpse of Zara, Lex hurriedly tucked it under her arm.

Uncle Mort brought her to the library, where he bandaged her hands as she recounted everything: what had happened in the dusty basement, what her flashes of rage had really meant, what she had just unleashed upon the world —

"And then I scythed out," she finished bitterly, "without attacking her, without doing a thing to stop her from being able to Damn anyone she meets."

"Which means that if you hadn't stolen her scythe, we all would have been in a lot more trouble," Uncle Mort said with a hint of pride. "Without a scythe, she can't Crash. She's limited to regular modes of transportation just like the rest of us."

"But she's still out there. Can't we look for a Loophole of our own and chase her down? She said she found the last one, but that's gotta be a lie, right?"

He shook his head. "I don't think Zara would have told you what it was if she didn't absolutely, one hundred percent believe that there are none left to find."

"But how could she know that?"

"From what I've read, a found Loophole somehow displays the number of Loopholes that are left once it's opened." He sighed. "I have no doubt that Zara saw a big fat zero on that scroll."

"So we've got nothing."

"Right." He fidgeted apprehensively, biting his nails.

Lex looked at her hands, then closed her eyes. "I tried to Damn her, Uncle Mort. I didn't know that's what I was doing, but I did know I wanted her dead. I must have broken dozens of laws." She looked back up at him. "How much trouble am I in?"

"I don't know. Given the circumstances . . ." He scratched his chin. "I'll talk to Necropolis, see what they say. I probably would have done the same thing."

Lex looked at the heavy Terms of Execution book on the table. Its pages were filled with past Grims' transgressions and punishments, the worst of the worst. And now she was one of them.

"You said Grotton was the only one," she said quietly.

"I know. I was wrong." He swallowed. "I'm so sorry."

"It's not your —"

"It is. My fault. You showed all the signs, I just never thought —" He shook his head and let out a long breath.

Lex studied her uncle.

"Uncle Mort, do you know *why* I can Damn?"

He stared straight back at her, his eyes hard.

"No."

Lex looked away. Apparently she wasn't the only liar in the family.

They sat in silence. The sound of people gathering began to grow louder, morsels of gossip floating in from the square.

"What should I say to them?" Lex asked flatly.

"You're not going to say anything." He got up. "They'll have too many questions, and you're not exactly —" He started to say something, but changed his mind. "Better for you to stay out of the public eye. At least for tonight."

Lex stood up and made for the door. "But — "

He grabbed her shoulders, blocking the way. "Please, kiddo, just trust me on this and stay here. Mutual respect, remember?"

Lex thought for a moment more, then nodded. She trudged back to her seat and collapsed into it, her energy depleted.

Uncle Mort headed out the door, pausing only to glance back at his niece for a brief second. "Lex," he said sadly, his hand on the knob, "you're a good kid. You really are."

|||||||

Lex sat alone at the wooden table and listened to the muffled sounds of her uncle's announcements, as well as the ensuing laments from the crowd outside. She watched the fading sunlight crawl across the floor, then studied the numerous group photos of Grims on the walls, from the black-and-white olden days to a copy of the picture she had just received. For some reason, they calmed her down. She was one of them; she belonged here.

So there she sat in a daze, just as she had when she learned for the first time what the Terms were and why she couldn't just go around bumping off whoever she wanted to.

But the thing was, she could.

And if she had, maybe Cordy wouldn't be —

She squeezed her eyes shut tight. She couldn't think about that right now.

Restless, she walked over to a large shelf crammed with decaying books. Her bandaged fingers swept across their cracked spines, leaving a trail through the heavy dust, until a faint glimmer of gold caught her eye. She wiped off some more of the grime and read the gilded title: *The Legend of Grotton: Deluded Myth, or An Outright Cock-and-Bull Lie?*

Lex realized she had stumbled into the Grotton section of the library. Why hadn't she thought to look here before? Zara obviously had. Irritated, she took the book from the shelf and opened its cover.

Scribbled messily across the title page in thick, heavy ink were the words, WRONG BOOK.

Frowning, she placed it back on the shelf and picked up the next one — *The Criminal Mastermind Hell-Bent on Worldwide Destruction Who Once Came Close to Obliterating All That We Hold Dear: A Pop-Up Book* — and found the scrawl once again. But it didn't look like it could be Zara's. Who had written this?

Anxious now, she tore through the rest of the volumes on the shelf, only to find that each one contained the exact same phrase — wrong book, wrong book. Lex scowled. Which one was the *right* book?

The answer lay at the end of the row. A gaping, empty void loomed within the shelf, almost taunting her. Zara. Zara must have taken it.

Defeated, Lex absent-mindedly paged through the book in her hand, an academic-looking tome simply titled *Grotton: A Biography*. As she flipped to the back, however, she stopped. Her eyes grew wider as she read to the bottom of the last page. Handwritten in very small lettering was a note.

IF REDEMPTION IS THAT WHICH YOU PRIZE,

DO NOT BELIEVE ALL OF THESE LIES.

THE KEY TO THE DEAD AWAITS OVERHEAD —

ALL YOU NEED DO IS OPEN YOUR EYES.
— BONE, THE SICK SCYTHE BANDIT

Lex mouthed the signature. For reasons unclear even to her, the white figure from the woods popped into her mind.

She looked up at the ceiling but saw nothing more than a few cobwebs. Unfortunately, she had no time to contemplate this any further, for the door to the library had begun to creak open. She hastily tore the page out of the book, stuffed it into her pocket, and turned to face Driggs.

"How are you doing?" he asked.

She shrugged. Tears stung at her eyes, but she turned around and smeared them away.

He walked over to her. "Mort just told us what happened," he said, shaking his head. "I can't imagine —"

"Driggs," she choked out over the softball-size lump in her throat, "I don't want to talk about it. Really."

"When you disappeared, I scythed back here as fast as I could, I handed off her Vessel, I called for help —"

"It's over, okay?" Anger overtook sorrow. "My sister's dead, I'm not, and Zara is — I don't know — on the lam, or something."

Driggs exhaled in disbelief. "How can you joke about this? Don't you realize what this means for the town, for the whole Grimsphere? Zara's —"

" — going to be lying low for a while. She didn't exactly plan on me escaping and leaking her plan. Uncle Mort'll report it to *The Obituary,* and tomorrow every Grim in the country will get a good look at her face. We'll find her."

Driggs frowned, disheartened at the obvious front she was putting up. He tried to catch her gaze. "Lex — "

"I should have stopped her," she chanted in a manic tone. "This is all my fault. I had her. I had her, and I let her go."

He gave her a sideways glance. "Why are you doing this to yourself?"

"Driggs, stop it."

"What?"

"You're trying to get me to talk about my feelings."

"So?"

"So you're not Oprah. Leave me alone."

"Come on, talk to me. Cordy's gone, but I'm still — "

"But I left her first!" she finally exploded at the sound of her sister's name. She couldn't hold back the tears any longer. "We'd never been apart for more than a few hours, and I just *left*. Like it was nothing!" She was yelling now. "You want to know why I'm doing this to myself? Because half of my existence was just torn away and it was *my fault!* Because it feels like someone lopped off my arm or heart or guts or some other vital piece of me with a rusty hacksaw!"

"I know," he said, touching her shoulder.

"You *don't* know!" She batted his hand away. "You got a twin?"

"No, but — "

"Then you have no idea!"

The room sank into a pained stillness. Lex and Driggs stared at the floor, then at the ceiling, then at every other object in the room, until finally there was nothing left to look at but each other.

"I'm sorry," Driggs said. "I guess I'm no better at this consola-tion thing than you are."

Lex felt drained. "Guess not."

"I'm just glad you're alive." He wrapped his arms around her. "You really scared the shit out of me."

She sniffled into his shoulder. "What else is new?"

A forced smile came to his face, then faded. They stood in an awkward silence yet again. But this soon led to where most awk-ward silences lead, and their lips remained locked for several minutes until Lex finally pushed him away.

"I'm not so sure about this," she said reluctantly, wiping her mouth.

Driggs gave her a look. "Don't do that."

"What?"

"That lame thing that superheroes do, where you push me away because you think you're putting me in danger. I can make my own decisions, thanks."

"But she'll come after you first. Then Uncle Mort, then Ely-sia — I'm like a plague now."

"I'll try to suppress the bile," he said with a smirk.

"Yeah, but . . . what about your girlfriend?"

"My what?"

"That picture you're always carrying around. Who is she?"

He thought for a moment. Then his face broke out into a shy grin.

"What?" Lex asked. *"What?"*

Some secrets, owing to their potential for tremendous embar-rassment, should receive a great deal of consideration before they are divulged. Driggs at least had the good sense to stall. His strat-egy of choice was to rummage around in the pocket of his hoodie, as if Lex could possibly be duped into thinking that it hadn't slipped into his hand the moment he reached for it.

Finally, he sighed, pulled out the photo, and handed it over.

Lex stared. And stared.

And staring back at her were the two Bartleby sisters covered in finger paint, the very same photo proudly displayed in her bedroom at home, next to the Sparks.

"Um, I've kind of been in love with you since the day I got here," Driggs murmured, ruffling his hair. "Or your smile, at least. I was fourteen, and . . . uh, Mort always had pictures of you two all over the house, you know? And the minute I saw the one from your twelfth birthday, where you're throwing cake at each other, I thought you were really . . . yeah." He glanced, humiliated, at the picture in her hand. "I mean, I know that carrying around this *particular* photo makes me seem like a pedophile, but I guess it was just always my favorite. The grin on your face, your eyes, the paint — it looks like you're having so much fun." His eyes got dark. "My childhood wasn't very fun. And we definitely didn't have any photos of laughing people around the house."

"I guess this explains all the empty frames in the living room."

"Creepy, right? I know." His eyes darted nervously. "I know it sounds weird and stalkery. But it was just a crush, honestly. I had no idea you'd ever actually come here. I practically melted into the floor when Mort told me."

"But you'd never even met me, how could you — "

"I don't know, all right?" he snapped. "All I know is that I had never seen anyone like you, and your stupid smile was infectious, and I fell in love with it, and ever since you got here I've been falling in love with the rest of you, and now I'm so far gone there's not a damn thing I can do about it. Okay?" He yanked the photo out of her hands. "Happy now?"

Lex let out a throaty, rusty laugh. "Marginally."

Driggs shook his head in defeat, but his eyes were kind as he hooked his fingers into hers.

They were interrupted by a soft knock on the library door. "Lex?" Uncle Mort poked his head in. "You doing okay?"

"I guess."

"Then let's head home."

Driggs squeezed her elbow before they stepped out onto the street. "Hey, put your hood up."

"Why?"

He pulled it over her head. "Just do it."

And as the three of them made their way past the crowd, Lex began to understand. Though her face was barely visible, she could hear the whispers. She could feel the stares. And she knew that tomorrow — or whenever it was that she could finally go back out in public — they would have a lot of questions for her, the girl who started it all.

26

Funerals are depressing even under the best of circumstances, if such things exist, and Cordy's service was no different. Lex took solace in the fact that the casket remained closed, but otherwise she felt as if she had fallen into a giant blender full of salt and lemon juice.

The whole family had shown up, including aunts and uncles who Lex had forgotten existed, cousins she had never even met, and Captain Wiggles, Cordy's beloved octopus, who grimly surveyed the scene from atop a large flower arrangement. A sizable portion of her classmates were in attendance (including Michael Thorley), none of whom could seem to stop shooting quizzical glances at Lex. Many teachers also dropped by, as well as a handful of people who were only tangentially involved in the lives of the Bartleby family — the local grocer, the mailman, their plumber, and even the reviled next-door neighbors. Lex couldn't help but muse that if it had been her inside the coffin instead of her sister, the turnout wouldn't have been nearly as impressive.

Her parents, naturally, were inconsolable. Their relatives believed they needed kind words, and so dispensed an endless string of condolences throughout the day. Their friends thought that they needed some space, to be alone with their grief. And the rest of the community decided they needed casseroles, which were delivered to the house by the truckload.

But the Bartlebys didn't need any of those things. They

couldn't begin to comprehend why their daughter had been taken from them so unexpectedly, and there wasn't a single explanation to be had. The coroner was stumped. The police chief had watched and rewatched the security tapes of the nursing home where Cordy worked until he passed out into his nightly bowl of oatmeal, but he hadn't been able to figure it out. It was ultimately concluded that Cordy's demise had been yet another one of those unexplained deaths that had been sweeping the nation — the last one, in fact, for several days.

What Mr. and Mrs. Bartleby really needed was closure. Unfortunately, that was the one thing that neither their family nor friends nor neighbors could provide. And as Lex watched them stand next to their own daughter's casket, weeping silently and holding on to each other for dear life, she realized what she had to do.

||||||

Dinner that night was silent. The house grew dark as the sun set; no one could summon the effort to turn on a light. And despite the rather impressive spread of more than a dozen casseroles, the food just sat there, cold and mostly uneaten.

Uncle Mort sat in his dead niece's chair and poked at the grayish lump of goulash on his plate. Racked with guilt, he had not said much of anything since the day Cordy died. Lex, who hadn't left his house until it was time to drive to the city, had tried to reassure him that there wasn't a thing he could have done, that Zara's powers had grown so strong it wouldn't have mattered. For some reason, Lex gathered, this made him feel worse.

As the night wore on, the silence grew heavier and heavier,

until it threatened to collapse into itself and form a black hole right there on the dining room table. When eight o'clock rolled around, Uncle Mort slowly rose from his seat.

"I should get going," he muttered.

"Take some food," Mrs. Bartleby said flatly.

"Sure, sure. Just let me grab the car."

The screen door banged on his way out. Mr. Bartleby picked at his plate. And as the roar of the Gremlin's engine ripped through the walls of the house, Lex stood up.

Her parents looked at her in abject terror. "What are you doing?" her mother asked.

"I'm going back," she said softly.

"You absolutely are *not!*" Fresh tears sprang to her mother's eyes. "We just lost one child, if you think for a second we're going to let the only daughter we have left just . . . just leave . . ." She collapsed into a fit of sobbing.

Lex's father just stared.

But her mother fought on, gasping for air. "You selfish little—we already told you no! School starts in two days!" she choked, her face a hopeless mess of fury and grief. "And leaving your family at a time like this—how *dare* you?"

Lex looked away, unable to look into the eyes of the mother whose heart she was breaking all over again. "I know who did this," she said even more quietly. "And I have to go back." She looked up. "I have to go back and finish it."

Her mother, now too overcome to speak, wept. Yet her father was watching her with a strange expression on his face.

"You know who did this?" he repeated blankly, stealing a glance at her bandaged hands.

Lex nodded.

He stood up from his chair, walked over to his sobbing wife, knelt down beside her, and took her into his arms.

"Go," he told Lex.

"What?" Her mother wailed frantically, struggling against her husband. "No! She can't go! How could you let her — "

"Shhh . . ." Mr. Bartleby breathed, stroking her hair. Exhausted, Mrs. Bartleby finally crumpled into her husband's arms, emitting strangled moans of agony.

"Go," he rasped once again, gazing at Lex, his own eyes now filling with tears. "Go find the monster who murdered my baby girl, and you kill that son of a — "

He broke off as a sob choked his throat.

Lex left the table and noiselessly went upstairs. She grabbed Cordy's empty backpack and began stuffing various items into it, hurriedly stripping the contents of the room where she and Cordy had once built a spaceship out of a cardboard box and flown all the way to the Planet of Infinite Jungle Gyms. She took a few clothes out of her closet, a pair of heavy boots, several books, Captain Wiggles, a handful of photos, and —

She stopped. A sliver of light glimmered from the bookshelf. She moved aside a photo to reveal the girls' two Sparks, sitting there just as she had left them. Lex's was still glittery and flickering, the small glints of light whizzing around the globe and crashing into the glass, making them shine even brighter.

But Cordy's no longer contained any luminous embers. Instead, it shone white and clear, a brilliant beacon against the darkness of the room.

Like the flash of a soul, Lex thought.

She grabbed both Sparks, threw them into the bag, and zipped it up, shaking slightly. She had gotten what she wanted, she was returning to Croak — but for all the wrong reasons. This was not how it was supposed to happen. And even though Lex knew she was making the right choice, even though she wanted nothing more than to take up the fight that now rose before her, still she glanced back and took one last look at her room, wondering if she would ever see it again.

She went back downstairs. Her mother and father still clutched each other, now grieving the loss of not only one, but both of their children. Heaving the bag onto her shoulder, she made her way into the dining room and bent over her parents.

"Goodbye, Dad," Lex whispered, gently kissing him on his shiny head. She did the same to her mother, brushing a tuft of matted hair aside, distant memories of lullabies humming softly through her memory. "Goodbye, Mom."

That was how she left them as she walked out of the house, slammed the screen door, and sank into the seat of Uncle Mort's car.

And that was how she would remember them for the longest time thereafter, even in the bleakest of moments: her two loving parents, clinging to each other in the dark, crying long into the night.

Gina Damico grew up under four feet of snow in Syracuse, New York. She received a degree in theater and sociology from Boston College, where she was active with the Committee for Creative Enactments, a murder mystery improv comedy troupe that may or may not have sparked her interest in wildly improbable bloodshed. She has since worked as a tour guide, transcriptionist, theater house manager, scenic artist, movie extra, office troll, retail monkey, yarn hawker, and breadmonger. *Croak* is her first novel. She lives outside of Boston with her husband, two cats, and a closet full of black hoodies.

www.ginadami.co